I0692047

A VERY GRUMPY
LUMBERJACK CHRISTMAS

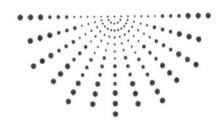

GWYN MCNAMEE

A VERY GRUMPY LUMBERJACK CHRISTMAS

© 2024 Gwyn McNamee

All rights reserved. Except as permitted by U.S. Copyright Act of 1976, no part of this publication may be reproduced, distributed, or transmitted in any form or by any means, or stored in a database or retrieval system, without prior permission of the author.

The scanning, uploading, and distribution of this book via the Internet or via other means without the permission of the publisher is illegal and punishable by law. Please purchase only authorized electronic editions and do not participate in or encourage electronic piracy of copyrighted materials.

This book is a work of fiction. Names, characters, establishments, or organizations, and incidents are either products of the author's imagination or are used fictitiously to give a sense of authenticity. Any resemblance to actual persons, living or dead, events, or locales is entirely coincidental.

To everyone who has ever found the heart in a grinch.

1
NOEL

Nothing feels better than driving into Mistletoe, Wisconsin, at Christmas.

The pure joy that rushes through my blood and lifts my spirits.

Simply knowing what I'll find in the quiet streets of the small town that's always been home can't be beat by *anything*.

Except maybe really good, hot, sweaty, mind-bending, make-your-legs-unusable-after-it sex.

But it's been so long since I've experienced *that*…I wouldn't really have any frame of reference anymore.

Just a flicker.

A lingering, distant memory of a man with evergreen eyes and a touch that set my skin and soul on fire.

I expected that inferno to rage on forever. The heat and passion to only grow the way my love for all things Christmas has every year that passes.

Instead, that flame burned out long ago.

Nothing but a wisp of smoke and charred ash now.

Not even a single ember left smoldering in the place where I once felt nothing but warmth.

But I'm not even going to *think* of him while I'm home.

Or dwell on the fact that he's merely a few miles down the road. Still living in the same cabin on his parents' land. Still helping them run the tree farm. Probably still looking sexy as fuck in his lumberjack plaid with that axe over his shoulder that always did me in every time I saw him.

Nope.

Not thinking about it.

I am one hundred percent concentrating on the road and singing along with "White Christmas."

Up here, you *have* to love all things Christmas—and pay attention behind the wheel—especially this time of year when the holiday smacks you full force in the face, and Mother Nature does, too.

The steadily falling snow currently covering the road and frozen tundra of Northern Wisconsin is *nothing* compared to the storm that's supposed to hit on Christmas Eve and carry into Christmas Day. More like a blustery taste of what could be a disastrous blizzard coming at the worst time possible.

Or the best...depending on how you look at it.

I, for one, *need* a white Christmas—like the song currently blasting through the speakers says.

Those bizarre years when the Midwest didn't have snow by the big day, things just felt *off*. Like some of the magic of the season was missing without the blanket of sparkling white and the frigid temps that always come with it.

But this year has been brutal for Mistletoe. Getting slammed by two major storms already, and—judging by the big, fat flakes drifting from the gray sky above now and the weather predictions splashed across every forecast I've checked—I won't have to worry about a snowless holiday.

What I *do* have to pay attention to is the slick roads.

The normal hour-and-a-half drive from Green Bay has taken over two today.

2

I tighten my hands on the wheel and keep my eyes straight ahead, practically bouncing in the seat and not bothering to fight my grin as I anticipate what I'll see as I make the turn around the approaching bend in the two-lane county highway.

Mistletoe…

As soon as the sign appears, my heart sings the same way I have been to my holiday playlist the entire drive up here from the airport.

Hand-painted vibrant red berries and the easily recognizable, softly rounded green leaves surround the town name—and Santa pops up over the top and waves, welcoming drivers.

Even if the town name didn't give it away, anyone seeing the sign would know what to expect entering Main Street. Christmas year-round—the sights, the sounds, the smells. There isn't anywhere to escape it.

And with the big day only two away, things are in full swing.

From half a mile away, the massive tree in the town square towers over the historic courthouse building—the tallest thing for a hundred miles, save for Jolly Mountain. I can picture what the fire trucks looked like a month ago when they used the baskets to lift town workers high enough to string the lights around the massive Norway spruce and to put the star on the top.

I laugh to myself like a total idiot, remembering the year Mayor Evans dropped it from seventy-five feet up and there was a mad scramble to find a new one before the lighting ceremony.

Dad almost lost his shit, but as head of the Mistletoe Decorative Committee, he took his job very seriously and reigned himself in enough to take control of the situation and fix the mayor's mistake before all the tourists flooded in.

For the first time since I started my drive home, my chest aches and tears I've managed to keep at bay start to blur my vision.

Not now, Noel...

If I let myself go down *that* mental road, I'll ruin my positive holiday vibes and make it impossible to enjoy my favorite time of the year.

Brushing away a stray trickle down my cheek, I finally make it to the spot where the paved highway changes to the bricked Main Street.

As always, the quaint shops lining either side of the road decked out in vibrant lights and decorations act like a warm hug to anyone visiting town for a dose of holiday spirit.

Red bows brighten up each antique lamppost.

Garland drapes between them all the way as far as the eye can see, with white twinkle lights wrapped around every strand.

Kids skate and play hockey on the two rinks set up in the town square on either side of the massive tree while their parents sip hot cocoa from Tami's food truck parked at the curb.

Smiling, I release a long, relieved breath.

I needed to come home.

No matter how hard it is to be here for the first Christmas since Dad died, I couldn't imagine *not* being in Mistletoe or allowing Mom to spend this time alone.

It wouldn't have been right.

And I'm going to do my best to concentrate on all the *good* things and *good* times rather than on what we so recently lost.

Though that won't be easy—

My thoughts and Mariah Carey belting out "Santa Clause is Coming to Town" are interrupted by my phone ringing through the car speakers.

"Crap…"

I should have called Mom to let her know the roads were making the drive slow.

Inching down Main Street through all the holiday traffic, I press the button on the steering wheel to accept the call. "Hi, Mom!"

"Noel, where are you?"

Betty Parsons waves at me from the corner as I pass, though I have no idea how she recognized me in this rental car.

I wave back and smile.

That old biddy is going to go running straight into the coffee shop to tell everyone I'm back in town.

Shit.

There are no secrets in Mistletoe. With five hundred residents, everyone knows everyone's business—and makes it their business, too.

Which means it's only a matter of time before it makes it through the rumor mill and to *him.*

But I've managed eight Christmases without seeing Luke Crisp in the flesh, and I will do my damnedest to avoid him this year, too.

It helps that he doesn't come into town around Christmas anymore, and I spend almost all my time when I'm home either at the rink skating or shopping and enjoying the bright holiday spirit he seems to hate so much.

Though it wasn't always that way, was it?

I push away thoughts of the Grinch of Mistletoe and concentrate on getting home—to the familiar scents, abundant decorations, and blaring music filled with cheesy lyrics I can't help but sing along with.

"I'm on Main Street, Mom." I pause to allow a family to cross, skates draped over their shoulders. "The roads aren't great, but I should be home soon."

Mom releases a relieved breath. "Oh, good. I was getting worried…"

"I know."

Regret instantly sits heavy on my chest for the concern in her voice. After losing Dad, the last thing I want to do is to allow that saint of a woman to worry about me or that something could have happened on the drive up.

"I'll be home soon. Love you."

"Love you, too. Drive safe. The mountain wasn't friendly when I was coming home this morning."

Her warning should make *me* concerned, but I've been driving up Jolly Mountain since before I should have even been behind the wheel, and this wintery weather doesn't scare me nearly as much as the fact that I'm going to have to travel right past Crisp Christmas Tree Farm on my way home.

It'll be okay.

Everything will be.

I keep telling myself that.

Have been every day for the last six months since Dad died, since I was last here for the funeral, but I'm still not sure I believe it.

First Christmas without Dad.

Born and bred in Mistletoe, Christmas was always *his* thing. *Our* thing that we shared. Mom always loved this town and the all-holiday-all-the-time vibes, but she never got as "into" it as we did. And without him here, it feels like finding my groove is going to be impossible.

I swallow back a little sob that threatens to come out and swipe away another round of tears as the snow starts to fall harder.

The one stop sign in downtown Mistletoe halts my slow trek down Main Street. I glance in my rearview mirror to ensure there's no one behind me, but the road is clear, at least of cars, if not accumulating snow.

It's my chance to pause for a moment and absorb all of it.

I crack my window and turn down my playlist to hear what they're pumping through town square. The moment "All I Want for Christmas is You" hits my ears, I cringe and roll it back up.

Of all the damn songs...

The *one* I never play—the *one* that inevitably makes me think of Luke and when he played it for me when we were sixteen. The night he kissed me for the first time and changed everything.

But nothing ever changes around *here*.

Wagner's bakery sits kitty-corner from me, its massive front window overflowing with pastries, cookies, and cakes. Nancy has undoubtedly already begun stockpiling Christmas treats for those who come in at the last minute—which always seems to be the case. Between locals and all the tourists who hit town for the Christmas Eve celebration at the big tree, she makes a killing every year.

As do most of the other shops—

A horn honks behind me, and I jerk and glance back at a massive pickup truck.

Shit.

I wave an apology, then hit the gas and cross the intersection, traveling past another half-block of shops before heading out of town and up toward the place I lived my entire life.

Until you didn't.

Until you left.

I try to push away the bad memories of those horrible few days, but it's nearly impossible as I approach the sharp right turn that will take me up what locals always call "the mountain."

Of course, there aren't really *mountains* in Wisconsin, but when the glaciers came through during the last ice age, they left the highest point in the state, which just happens to be where the Jollys—and eventually the Crisps—decided to settle three generations ago.

But before I can reach home, I'm going to have to pass the Grinch's abode.

Crisp Christmas Tree Farm...

Just drive past.

Don't look.

Get home.

It should be easy enough.

I've made this drive a thousand times in my life. Spent the last eight years forcing myself *not* to look at the farm or the beautifully decorated sales lot, only stopping *once* a year with Dad to get our annual tree. Knowing Luke never sets foot on the actual sales lot anymore and prefers to spend his time chopping trees and getting them ready for customers than actually *interacting* with people made the risk of running into him razor thin.

Though it didn't use to be like that, not when I knew him.

Not before he became the Grinch.

Skulking around the mountain with his axe and sneer.

Grumbling about how annoying the constant Christmas music is, despite the fact that leaning into those vibes brings the *only* real tourism to our small town.

Rarely leaving the family property or his cabin at all.

And when he does, it's apparently always with a permanent scowl on his handsome face.

I tighten my grip on the wheel as I approach the edge of the forest, where it opens up to Crisps' property.

Even Michael Bublé's smooth voice singing "It's Beginning to Look a Lot Like Christmas" can't distract me from what's coming.

Eyes straight ahead.
Eyes straight ahead.

I keep telling myself that, but as soon as the trees clear to my right, my gaze drifts that direction to the extravagant Christmas display and dozens and dozens of cut trees lining the lot next to a massive sleigh with eight fake reindeer attached to the front of it. Mr. Crisp's favorite spot to sit between customers and wave at passing cars, trying to encourage people to stop in for a wreath or garland or boughs even if they already have their tree.

He isn't there now, though.

The increasingly steady snowfall may have something to do with that.

Heavy, wet flakes splatter against the windshield, my wipers barely keeping up with them even though I'm barely going thirty miles per hour.

Hopefully, the weather doesn't keep the tourists away.

Not only does the town rely on the caravan of outsiders coming into Mistletoe over the next few days, but the Crisps do, too.

While early in the month between Thanksgiving and Christmas is always the busiest for their sales, I learned over my time with Luke that a shocking number of people drive up here to snag a tree immediately before Christmas Eve.

And this one looks to be blanketed in a massive snowstorm that could shut them down on one of their busiest nights.

I strain to see into the huge barn that houses their equipment and the sales office, but something darts across the road, catching my attention from the corner of my eye, and I jerk the wheel to avoid hitting it.

"Shit!"

The tires hit a patch of ice, and the back end slides out.

I death-grip the wheel and try to control the spin, but there's nothing I can do as the car careens into the ditch.

2

THE MISTLETOE GRINCH

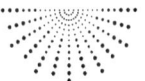

The axe blade cuts into the peeling white trunk exactly where I aimed it, easily biting into the wood and sending small fragments flying. I tug it free only to swing again, driving the sharp metal above my previous strike to help create the wedge.

Sweat trickles down my temple and back, despite the biting wind and the snow swirling around me, and I tighten my grip as I make the final cut and step back.

Seventy feet above me, the barren top branches sway then list slightly before the massive birch tree tumbles to the right, falling exactly in the direction I aimed it with the perfect notch.

It crashes into the clearing with a thud that shakes the ground beneath my steel-toed boots.

Thank fuck that's done.

I rest the axe head near my feet and lean against it, using my free hand to mop away the sweat from my forehead before it freezes to my exposed skin.

Against the glistening white, pristine snow, the peeling

bark of the dead tree almost disappears as it sinks into the several inches already on the ground.

Breaking it into manageable pieces can wait for another day.

I just needed to get it down.

After weeks of exhausting work keeping the sales lot stocked, today, I finally did what I should have done weeks ago, since it was damaged in the last blizzard.

It could have fallen on its own and landed anywhere, including on the cabin...

You're lucky it didn't.

The winds already whipping through the forest around me signal what's coming in the next few days.

One weatherman called it "the storm of the century"—but the blowhards up here are always saying that.

Every year, they stir everyone up, predicting several feet of snow, and we have yet to experience anything as extreme as the warnings. Still, at least it gets people to prepare ahead of time rather than getting stuck on the roads or in their homes without power, food, water, or heat.

I won't have that problem.

My holiday plans consist of trudging through the snow to the cabin and locking myself inside until after New Year's—regardless of what Mother Nature has in store for us.

Because it isn't this coming snowstorm that has my gut twisting.

There might be a dangerous blizzard bearing down on Mistletoe this Christmas, but Noel Jolly is the only storm that poses a real threat to me.

The mere thought of that woman and the fact that she's just a few miles up the road makes my body heat further, even as I try to fight the reaction. A combination of anger, scalding-hot memories, and regret that always hits me this time of year, knowing she's back and so close but so fucking far away.

Stop thinking about her, then.

I snort at the absurdity of that and force myself to scan the rest of the surrounding trees for any other widow-makers I might need to take down before the storm hits.

Feet crunching in the snow draws my attention away from the tree line and toward the narrow path I made from my cabin up to this part of the mountain.

Mom trudges through the already ankle-deep snow straight from the sales lot toward me rather than taking the packed down trail I created when I came up, likely because it's more direct and requires the least amount of time out in the elements. Bundled up in her parka, mittens and hat in place with her hood up and sealed tight around her wind-burned face, she offers me the look only a mother can.

"Don't give me that look, Ma."

She scowls. "You're out here again in that?"

I glance down at my cutoff shirt and jeans. "What?"

"It's *freezing!*" She waves a mittened hand around at the falling snow whipping through the trees. "Literally. And you're walking around like you're on summer vacation."

Snorting, I lift the axe to my shoulder as I wipe away more sweat. "I'm fine, Ma. You know how hot I get when I do this…"

Her thin lips twist down again. "When you catch a cold, don't come to me to make you soup and take care of you."

"You haven't done that since I was a child."

She points a finger at me, shivering. "Bullshit, son. What about last February?"

I cringe. "Okay. I was really sick, though…"

"Yeah." She nods, her brows rising. "And who made you chicken soup, brought you medicine, and checked on you every few hours?"

Honestly, I wish she wouldn't have.

I was fine wallowing in my misery in bed alone, and having her hovering only made me wish it was another woman who likely won't ever step foot in my cabin again.

"I could have done that all on my own. I'm a thirty-year-old man."

She snorts and shakes her head. "Don't act like it sometimes."

"Did you come out here to argue with me?"

Everyone calls *me* a grinch, but the spitfire who gave birth to me seems to be the one with the attitude today.

She shakes her head and motions behind her in the general direction of the lot. "Dad needs your help."

"With what?"

"Some guy drove all the way from Milwaukee to shop in Mistletoe and decided he wants a tree..." A grin plays at her lips. "And he wants that big eighteen-foot fir."

"Seriously?" I release a groan and drop my head back to stare into the gray sky, letting the icy-cold flakes sting my face. "What kind of car does he drive?"

Mom's laughter echoes across the snow. "Guess."

I return my focus to her and raise an eyebrow. "Passat."

She shakes her head, still chuckling. "Close."

"You're not going to tell me?"

"Come on." She reaches out and grabs the wrist of my free arm, tugging. "It'll be a surprise."

The woman knows I *loathe* surprises—about as much as I do this time of year, with the merry holiday music, string lights, baked goods, and all-around good cheer.

But I won't say no when she or Dad needs help.

And something tells me a battle with an out-of-towner trying to stick an eighteen-foot fir on a sedan will be one Dad needs backup for—the kind only *I* can provide.

Mom might be intimidating to some, but a six-five two-twenty-five lumberjack usually does the trick when the five-three petite blond can't talk or reason her way out of confrontation like the one that is probably brewing on the sales lot.

People get difficult this time of year.

Ironic, really, considering it's supposed to be "good will to men" and all that bullshit.

And it really *is* bullshit.

A charade.

An act everyone puts on to appear to be what they are not.

Which is exactly why I don't *do* people, especially at Christmas.

Mom knows that all too well, and what she's asking when she came all the way up here to get me. "Quickly now, we don't wanna leave the customer waiting."

It would've been so much easier for her to just text me.

But cells don't work up on Jolly Mountain.

Never have.

Our little speck of Wisconsin is so remote that the mobile companies don't give a shit what our coverage is like.

And *I* like it that way.

It's a lot harder for someone to bother me when they have to climb half the mountain to get to my cabin.

That means peace and fucking quiet—away from the constant noise and fake joy that permeates the air and space around Mistletoe.

Mom keeps peeking over her shoulder, ensuring I'm following and haven't made a break for my place.

Wouldn't be the first time I did...

The frosty flakes bite at my exposed arms, chest, and face, but unlike most people who cocoon themselves in the thickest, heaviest down jackets and knitted hats and mittens in this weather, I embrace the chill.

It matches the way my chest has felt for almost a decade. *Cold.*

Where once a heart beat, strong and fiery, now nothing remains but a broken shell. And the more time that passes, the harder it becomes to remember what it was ever like to feel true warmth.

A gust of wind swirls around us, and Mom shivers, but I just keep walking through the snow toward the barn and Dad down on the lot. He stands, talking to a man who gestures animatedly toward the massive tree leaning up against the weathered, red-painted boards.

"Bob, dear"—Mom hustles straight over to them—"I found Luke."

Dad glances over his shoulder and offers a relieved look as the guy in front of him eyes me suspiciously, his gaze darting from my exposed chest to the axe still draped over my shoulder.

The asshole crosses his arms over his thousand-dollar down jacket and motions toward his Audi e-tron GT. "Are you going to help get that onto my car?"

Despite my annoyance at having to come down here, I can't fight the smirk pulling at my lips. "*That* tree is *not* fitting on *that* car."

He gapes at me. "What are you talking about?"

"That's an eighteen-foot fir. It is not going to fit on your sports car and make the trip back to wherever the hell it is you came from."

His jaw drops even farther before he snaps it shut and grinds his teeth. A muscle there tics the longer he glares at me. "That's how you talk to a customer?"

I set my axe down and lean on it casually. "That's the reason I don't *do* customers."

Except when absolutely necessary.

Of course, the day will come—likely sooner rather than

later—when Mom and Dad can't run this place without my presence on the lot instead of tending to the trees and harvesting them. But I don't like to think about that time. I just pray it doesn't come before I've come up with a way to prepare myself mentally.

Then again, it's been eight years since the night everything changed, and I haven't figured it out yet.

The customer walks over to the tree and reaches in with his gloved hand to grasp the trunk and try to pull it from where it leans against the barn. "It isn't that big. I've seen these on cars like mine." He barely manages to move it a few inches before releasing it back to its original position. Coughing to try to cover his huffing at the wasted effort, he brushes off his glove with the other. "It will be fine."

In what universe, pal?

Dad gives me an incredulous look.

I offer a shrug. "If that's really what you want. But you're going to sign a waiver that releases us from any and all liability for any damage caused to your vehicle or for any potential accidents you may cause driving with that strapped on top."

He plants his hands on his hips, taking a defiant stance, even though he's half my size, even with his puffer jacket. "Like *hell*, I will."

Lifting the axe, I use the head to point at the tree. "Then I'm not putting *that* tree"—I swing the weapon in the other direction toward the parking area—"on *that* car."

The pompous jerk glances back where his blond trophy wife sits in the front seat, and a little girl presses her face against the back window, watching everything with wide eyes. "You're going to disappoint my daughter."

I lower the axe and shake my head. "I'm not doing anything but trying to make sure she stays safe in that vehicle, sir. *You* are being an asshole."

Mom smacks my arm. "Luke, you can't talk to customers like that."

"I don't think he's a customer anymore, Ma."

And with his attitude, there is no doubt in my mind that even if I had managed to secure that tree to his vehicle, he would have driven like a complete asshole and done something to endanger his family just to prove a point.

The guy fumes and storms back to his car, jerking his door open, slamming it, and then trying to tear out of the parking lot. His tires won't catch on the snow, and he slips and slides, almost slamming into one of the wooden fences.

He manages to right himself and eventually turns out onto the highway without killing anyone—but he still has a long drive back home.

I watch the car disappear into the edge of the forest and shake my head. "What a fucking d-bag…"

"Luke!" Mom glares at me. "Language!"

Dad gives me a reproachful look, too. "You didn't have to be that harsh."

I raise a brow at the old man. "Then you shouldn't have called me down here."

He presses his lips together, then immediately releases a cough and covers his mouth as he hacks.

"You okay?"

Raising a hand, he waves off my concern. "Just a little cough that started this morning."

It doesn't sound like nothing.

The older he gets, the more I worry about him—and Mom. And after seeing how quickly someone can be snatched away—here one instant and gone the next, the way Noel's father was—I'm not about to let him brush it off.

"Maybe you shouldn't be out here, Dad. With the storm coming, it's been slow today." I scan the empty lot and quiet road. "Why don't we just close?"

"Two days before Christmas?" Mom walks over to him and rubs his back as he continues to try to clear his throat. "You know, we can't do that, Luke. There might not be anyone here now, but at any minute, we could have ten cars show up."

She isn't wrong about that.

And they can't afford to miss any sales.

I can't believe I'm going to say this.

I squeeze my eyes closed, suck in a long, cool breath and release it. "I'll stay down here the rest of the day so you can take Dad home."

Not that it's far.

I can see their house twenty yards away, past the barn near the tree line.

Dad's eyes widen. "If you talk to customers like that, you being here won't be a benefit. Might as well just leave the place closed—"

He starts coughing again, and Mom pats his back.

"I'll get him set, and I'll come back and help you."

What she really means is *babysit* me and ensure I'm playing nice with anyone who might stop by.

Annoyed, I watch her lead Dad up the shoveled path to their house—cleared off because they actually *want* visitors.

I prefer to keep mine as uninviting as possible.

When people see the unmarked trek through the woods to my cabin, it might as well be a sign that reads, "Go Away!"

And that's the way I like it.

They disappear inside, and I release an annoyed groan and start to head into the office when a small blue sedan appears on the road at the edge of the forest, heading our way.

I don't recognize it, and I know *everyone* in town.

Which means it's likely a customer.

There isn't any other reason for anyone to be on Jolly Lane, since it only leads here and to Noel's house.

The car slows slightly, almost like it's going to turn in, but then it jerks wildly and spins out, sliding into the ditch before I can even react.

"Shit."

Tourists who have no fucking clue how to drive in this weather.

Lifting my axe in case I need it to extricate someone from inside, I break into a run across the snow-covered parking lot and down the gravel drive. With nothing more than a cursory glance in either direction, I cross the road and scramble down the ditch.

The car faces me, pointed slightly up toward the pavement, engine still running. Headlines stream right into my eyes, and I raise my free hand to block the blinding light and try to see the driver.

A blond head is dropped low, face pressed into the steering wheel. She doesn't move, the eerie stillness inside the car instantly stirring concern.

"Oh, hell…"

3
THE MISTLETOE GRINCH

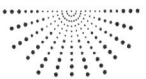

The driver keeps her head down against the steering wheel, unmoving, hands wrapped around the black fake leather in a death grip that makes her knuckles as white as the snow around us. But I can't tell if she's pinned there, passed out due to some medical issue, or just trying to get her bearings and gather herself after the crash.

Shit.

Each second that ticks by that she doesn't move or react to me approaching the car makes unease coil tighter around my spine.

Tightening my grip on the axe, I rush to the driver's side door and tug on the handle, but it doesn't budge.

Locked.

Dammit.

"Hey!" I pound on the window, trying to see through the glass that's starting to frost over now that the car isn't in motion and cold air is reacting with the moisture inside. "You okay?"

Muttered cursing barely reaches me through the barrier

between us, mingling with the familiar sounds of Mariah Carey belting out "Here Comes Santa Clause."

Fucking great.

Some tourist up here to experience Mistletoe just flew off the damn road in the one spot I can rescue them, but in order to do it, I have to be subjected to this audio trash I've managed to avoid so far this year.

She releases another couple of curses and shifts slightly in the seat, belt still pulled across her chest.

At least whoever is in there is conscious.

Even if she does have questionable taste in music.

The windows fog up even more, the crystals inching in from the corners of the glass with each breath she releases. She may appear okay right now, but if the tailpipe is blocked by the snow, the engine could be pumping poisonous fumes straight inside. "Hey, unlock the door!"

Blondie shakes her head, keeping her face low, but she peeks at me from between long, pale, wavy hair. Not enough for me to really see her. But she can definitely see *me.*

Christ.

It starts to click together in my head.

No wonder she's reluctant to open the door for me.

A complete stranger wielding an axe immediately after she runs off the road.

That would scare anyone.

Especially a visitor to town who doesn't know the area or me.

Hell, even some locals would be afraid of me these days.

I rest the axe head down in the snow and lean the handle against my thigh, holding up my hands to indicate I'm not a danger to her. "Ma'am, please open the door so I can help you. I just want to make sure you're all right."

"Shit, shit, shit!" The woman slams her palms against the

wheel, and the sharp blare of the horn makes both of us flinch. "Shit."

Well, she doesn't seem appeased by my statement.

I open my mouth to try to make another argument for her to act before I have to, but she slowly lifts her head and stares out the windshield.

She still doesn't look my way.

Maybe she's dazed.

Perhaps she struck her head against something during the spin-out.

I don't want to have to break into this fucking car…but I can't leave her in here like this much longer.

Fucking hell…

This is what I get for offering to work the lot.

I glance back toward the house, hoping to be rescued myself by someone far better equipped—at least mentally— to handle this situation and woman, but there isn't any sign of Mom and Dad.

They were probably inside before the crash happened and didn't see anything—which means I won't get any help from them. And the driver doesn't seem keen on accepting my assistance or responding to any of my requests.

I press my palm flat against the window, trying to control my voice so I don't further terrify this woman while still conveying the urgency. "Ma'am, I can't help you if you don't unlock the door."

Her head turns slowly toward mine, and through the partially frosted window, familiar bright-blue eyes I used to swim in meet mine.

My heart stops, my breath catching in my lungs.

Fuck.

I stagger back a step, then stand frozen in place as Noel turns off the engine, then hesitantly reaches over and presses a button on the door. The lock clicks, the sound somehow deafening in the quiet stillness of the falling snow.

Seconds tick by like hours.

Blood rushes in my ears, the *whoosh, whoosh, whoosh,* the only evidence that my heart has resumed beating even while I struggle to make my lungs function again.

Her door slowly swings open on the embankment, and she uses one hand to keep it propped wide while she reaches down and unbuckles her seatbelt with the other.

She climbs from the car on shaky legs. "Of all the places this could have happened—"

Noel staggers slightly, slipping on the snowy incline, her knees hitting the ground, and I reach forward and grasp her upper arm to steady her before she falls any farther.

Her eyes cut up to meet mine, a mixture of annoyance and something else even more unsettling flashing in her gaze, and she jerks herself from my hold. "I'm fine."

She isn't.

And neither am I.

The second I realized who was behind that wheel, my entire world became laser focused on one thing—ensuring she is all right and quelling the panic seizing me.

I grit my teeth to keep myself from tearing into her for being so reckless and running off the road. And from tugging her into my arms to hold her and smell her and feel her again. *And* to stop from saying the other things I've wanted to for so damn long.

Instead, I scan her from the tops of her fluffy UGG boots, which are barely visible in the deep snow of the ditch, up her skin-tight jeans, now covered in snow, and over the baggy sweater falling off one shoulder, exposing her pale, elegant collarbone to the elements.

She shivers, biting her plump, pink bottom lip in a way

that sends a zing of heat straight to a spot that should *not* be loving it so much.

"What the hell happened, Noel?" I search her face for any signs she might be injured or in pain—by anything other than my presence. "Are you all right?"

Releasing a huff visible in the chilly air, she reaches down and brushes the snow off her knees. "Fine, just a little…shaken…" Her eyes dart up to the road and narrow on the spot where she spun out. "Did I hit the rabbit?"

"What?"

"There was…" Her brow furrows, like she's having a hard time focusing. "A rabbit, I think. It darted out in the road in front of me."

I glance around at the snow falling around us, more rapidly than earlier today, for any signs of anything that might have been on the road. But all I find is the same barren stretch of desolate asphalt that has always been there, covered in several inches of slippery slush that was more likely the culprit than a stray bunny. "I didn't see anything, Noel. Are you sure you didn't just lose control?" Stepping back slightly, I scan the vehicle. "This isn't even four-wheel drive. What the hell are you doing coming up here with a blizzard on the way without a four-wheel-drive car or even snow tires?"

She crosses her arms over her chest defiantly, which only draws my attention to the luscious curves she hasn't lost over the last eight years. If anything, the time has filled her out in a way that makes me want to run my hands across every inch of her. "It's a rental, okay? It's all they had available."

I snort and look away from her, trying to contain my warring reactions to seeing this woman—and under these circumstances, that merely seem to enflame both my protective instincts and my ire. "And you couldn't rent a *jacket* with this piece of shit?"

It has to be near thirty degrees outside at the moment, and standing along the road that acts like a wind tunnel, there is no reprieve from the way it batters us.

And she's out here in nothing but a damn sweater.

Her eyes widen, and she motions back. "It's in the *car!*"

"You still got out without putting it on." I scan her up and down again, knowing how fucking cold she must be. She always used to snuggle up against me anytime we stepped foot outside, seeking my body heat, even when it *wasn't* the dead of winter. "You need to drive more carefully next time."

Those beautiful pink lips I spent so many hours devouring twist into a scowl. "First, look who is talking about being dressed appropriately for the weather. And second, I *was* driving carefully. I'm *telling* you"—she points toward some seemingly random spot near where she lost control—"there was a rabbit."

I glance at the road again, unable to see any signs that what she's saying is true, and my gaze drifts back over to the farm. "Are you sure you weren't looking at something *else?* Maybe distracted?"

By me...

Maybe it's stupid to think it.

To even consider that she might have been watching me rather than what was in front of her, especially with the roads already this bad...

But that tiny glimmer of hope lights in my chest, warming me from the inside out until I see her response.

She presses her mouth into a firm line, anger coloring her cheeks—or maybe it's the brutal wind and her lack of proper clothing. Either way, they flare the same way her eyes do. "There was a rabbit, Luke. And I'll prove it to you."

Good God...

Apparently, the passage of time hasn't dimmed Noel's fire in the slightest.

She storms past me, intentionally slamming her shoulder against my arm, and stalks over to the place in the road where she spun, the tire marks still visible in the fresh snow cover.

"What the hell are you doing?" I follow after her, scanning up and down the slushy pavement to ensure no cars are coming—since the lunatic is standing in the middle of the fucking street. "Noel, get out of the road!"

Bending over, she examines the tire marks. "Not until I find what I'm looking for."

"Which is what, your sanity?"

Those icy-blue eyes cut up to mine. "Funny, Luke." Noel returns her focus to the area around the edge of the ditch on the other side. "Aha! Right there!" She points, a smug smile crossing her lips, lighting up her already beautiful face even more. "Rabbit tracks."

I rest the axe head into the snow, squat down next to her, and examine where she's indicating. "Those could have been left days ago."

Gasping, she stands and crosses her arms over her chest again, defiant, tapping her foot. "Bullshit! They're fresh. Look at them and the snow around them."

Fuck.

When I do and see what she does, I can't argue with her anymore. At least, not about this. If she were some idiot from the city like Mr. Audi, I could expect cluelessness about the wildlife.

But not Noel.

She knows Mistletoe too well—the animals, the way the land works, the snow, and how to track things in it after years spent on the mountain with me.

And these are definitely *fresh* rabbit tracks that haven't even begun to fill in yet despite the rapid accumulation.

"Fine." I push up and rest my axe across my shoulder again.

27

"So, there was a rabbit...maybe next time you should worry about your own life instead of its." I motion toward the woods that it likely darted off into that eventually lead to my closest neighbor's property—aside from the Jolly's. "Mr. Niblitz is probably going to trap it and eat it for dinner, anyway."

Noel gasps, her mouth falling open. "Luke Crisp, you take that back!"

I reach back with my other hand and grasp the handle near the axe head, and her eyes immediately drift over my arms and down my open shirt. Almost as if—despite her earlier dig at my apparel—she is just now realizing how exposed I really am and is taking stock.

But I won't give her the satisfaction of retracting my comment that is likely true, given Old Man Niblitz's penchant for eating rabbit. "No."

"You know"—she takes a step toward me, pointing a trembling finger at me, so close she almost touches my bare chest—"Mom told me you turned into a real grinch, but I didn't realize how bad it's gotten."

"Did she now?"

Her words shouldn't bother me.

The name shouldn't.

Grinch.

It's hardly the first time I've been called that, nor will it be the last. But coming from those lips that used to beg me to do unspeakable, unholy things to her, it somehow stabs at my chest as if she'd driven my own axe straight into it.

"Well, my grinchy attitude isn't your problem anymore, is it?"

Noel flinches, visibly shaking now—from the cold or from proximity to me and the dig I just made remains unclear. "Well, apparently it *is*, since the rabbit decided it wanted to risk its life right in front of the farm."

This isn't getting us anywhere—except maybe her frost-bit, considering she isn't wearing a coat or any other protection.

Snow has already soaked her hair, darkening the long, blond strands that are now starting to mat around her face. She shivers again, wrapping her arms around herself, and glances back at the car—still lodged halfway down the embankment that she will never be able to drive back up.

I release a heavy sigh and run a hand through my own wet hair. "I'm going to go get my truck and pull you out of the ditch. Then, I'm going to follow you home to make sure you get there safely."

"Like fucking hell, you are!" She throws up her hands. "I don't need you to babysit me."

"Apparently...you do."

The Noel *I* knew all those years ago never would have done anything so reckless. She never would have ended up in that ditch or even considered getting out of her car without her coat on. But the Noel I *thought* I knew never would have broken my heart and walked away, either.

Lowering my axe, I stalk past her up the driveway before she can utter another objection and head straight for the barn where the Crisp Christmas Tree Farm truck sits, protected from the weather.

Unlike the woman who so badly wants to get under my skin today.

I'll need the winch system to get her out of that damn ditch. Though, getting her out of my head after today's run-in will be impossible.

I rest my axe against the wall, snag the keys off the hook, and fire up the truck. The roar of the diesel engine fills the space, and I pull out and down the driveway to find her leaning against the car, phone in hand, looking every bit as annoyed as she did when she first opened the door and we saw each other for the first time in eight years.

What does she *have to be annoyed about?*

All she's done is manage to fuck up my day and my head.

I maneuver the truck, so the front end faces her car, then climb out and grab the massive pulley from the winch. "You know damn well that thing doesn't work right there."

She glances up at me from her phone and frowns. "My mom's going to be worried." Her voice softens. "I should be home by now…"

That slight waver that hits her final words makes my chest tighten. I can only imagine what Maryann is thinking, sitting, waiting for Noel to arrive and having her be late so soon after losing Russell.

I attach the hook and move back to the front of the truck to run on the pulley. "You haven't been home yet?"

The sadness in her eyes when they meet mine is enough to make me regret my attitude this entire time—at least for a split second. "No, I just got into town."

Perfect fucking timing.

Not for me.

If Dad and Mom had only stayed on the lot a few more minutes…

Sighing, I motion for her to move away from the car. "Your mom will be happy to see you. I know this year has to be…"

I can't find the right word, so instead, I let myself trail off, watching the tears shimmer in her eyes the same way they did the night she broke my heart.

Fuck.

She stands frozen for a moment before I motion again, and she finally rushes to the other side of the road, giving me a wide berth to drag the car from the ditch without risking her getting caught if the wire were to snap somehow.

Once confident she's safely far enough away, I throw on the winch, climb into the truck, and slam the door as it starts slowly dragging the car up.

Eight years I've managed to avoid seeing Noel Jolly in a town small enough to bump into each other taking a piss.

And now, the woman literally crashes back into my life— at the worst possible moment.

What the hell did I ever do to deserve this?

4

NOEL

Why *is he so damn...grumpy?*

It's not as if I *intentionally* drove into a ditch in front of his place.

God knows, I would have rather hit a damn tree *anywhere* than end up stuck where I am now and have to deal with *him.*

The Mistletoe Grinch has certainly shown his true color today.

Green.

And not the beautiful evergreen I used to get lost in, like the woods surrounding us.

A sickly, putrid one filled with all the things his namesake is known for.

Luke drags the rental car from the embankment, pulling it out into the middle of the road, then tosses the massive truck into park and climbs down from the cab.

And despite not wanting to notice, he looks every bit as sexy as the day I left.

Lies.

He's even sexier than he was back then and just as crazy when it comes to waltzing around outside in almost nothing during the winter. The lunatic still walks around in an unbuttoned cutoff shirt with snow flying around us as if it isn't literally freezing outside.

Back then, he always claimed he got so hot working that he didn't even feel the cold. And it never seemed to bother him. Even after hours outside in this type of weather, he would come in and snuggle up with me—radiating that same scalding heat he had any other time of year while I was freezing even indoors.

Now, the chilliest thing is his attitude and the reception I've received.

He isn't the same twenty-two-year-old man he was when I left—emotionally or physically.

And despite being annoyed with his attitude, I can't help but notice how fluidly he moves. How confident he is in every step. The way his roped, thick muscles bulge with every movement.

His arms...

His shoulders...

His chest...

That perfect eight-pack of chiseled abs...

They all offer very real evidence of what he does day in and day out up here on the farm.

Even in the off-season, Luke never stopped.

He was always out on the mountain, tending to the trees and property. And not merely for Christmas, but *all* the types they farm and sell. Planting and moving things, felling trees, and preparing the firewood the Crisps offer year-round as part of their business. Doing anything and everything he can to keep the farm going.

And his body is a temple to that manual labor.

I can't tear my eyes from him as he bends to detach the hook. The way he moves...the way he works with his rough, calloused hands that I know the feel of against my skin so damn well.

Christ, that's not going to help the dreams I still have about the man...

That hard work has done him good.

At least physically.

Mentally, this Luke is every *bit* the grumpy, insufferable grinch everyone says he has become.

From the minute I climbed out of the car, he was *looking* for a fight. One I didn't want to have with him. Not when our last still lives in my head, as if it happened only yesterday instead of almost a decade ago.

That look on his face.

His words.

The pain slicing through my chest...

I reach up and rub at it, shivering as the blustery wind whips around me.

Luke allows the cable to roll back up into the winch without another word or glance in my direction. As if I'm not standing right here, wishing he would somehow morph and become the man I knew.

That would be a true Christmas miracle.

While I'm a firm believer in the magic of the season and what it's capable of, turning Luke Crisp, the Mistletoe Grinch, back into the sweet, kind, Christmas-loving man I once knew, seems out of grasp, even for the most potent woo.

Evidenced by the scowl on his lips as he finishes at the front of the truck, stalks back to the cab, and starts to climb in without even acknowledging me again.

I start to call out to him, to thank him for his help, despite the unpleasantness he's displayed, but before I can, he stops, standing halfway out of the door.

He finally looks over at me next to the spot where I went into the ditch. His green eyes hold none of the warmth they once did—only bitterness that instantly washes away any lingering pleasant memories of the man I once loved. "Be more careful."

That ass!

I open my mouth to argue again that I *was* being careful, and it was that dang rabbit that caused me to slide off the road, but before I can get a word out, Luke slams the truck door and tears off up the driveway toward the farm, leaving me shaking and trying to wrap my head around what just happened.

Apparently, his promise to follow me home was empty.

Like so many of the ones he made me.

Luke Crisp has changed.

It makes the fact that I've stayed away from him for so long seem far more justified than it felt before I ended up in that ditch. And now, I need to put as much distance between that man and me as possible.

I march over to the car, checking it for any damage, but thankfully, there wasn't anything to hit when I spun out.

Damn rabbit...

Damn Luke...

The entire incident has left me rattled, and I climb inside and fire up the engine, letting the warming air blow over me and ease some of the tension in my body created both by the frigid weather and the chilly reception Luke just gave me.

God knows I would've rather *walked* the two miles home and called a tow truck from there than ask for his help.

I don't want to be indebted to him.

I don't want to have any reason to think about him ever again.

All I want is to spend Christmas with Mom, to try to find a way to make it through and maybe find some joy even without Dad.

"Have Yourself a Merry Little Christmas" comes on my playlist, and I start to tear up again as I pull away from the farm and head up the mountain on tires not designed for this kind of weather.

This song always gets me right in the feels, but this year, it has a deeper meaning. One that hits at the very reason I needed to come home so badly.

After two agonizingly slow miles up the hill that definitely doesn't want me to make it to the top, our bright-red gingerbread house-shaped mailbox appears at the crest, and I grin.

At least some things haven't changed.

Except for the better.

Mom has repainted it since I was home this summer for Dad's funeral.

The reds look even brighter.

The greens more vibrant and not that grinchy green that seemed to have overtaken Luke's eyes.

Don't think about him anymore.

If I let myself dwell on what a twat he was, I won't be able to enjoy seeing Mom and being home. And I don't need to bring a sour mood through that door when things already feel so heavy.

I turn down the driveway and make my way up to the old farmhouse that's been in Dad's family for one hundred and fifty years. The front door flies open before I can even get the car in park, and Mom barrels out onto the wrap-around porch in her boots, clutching the phone in her hand.

The second I step out of the car, she's on me with wide, worried blue eyes that match mine. "Where were you? You should have been home an hour ago. I was so worried."

She throws her arms around me, and I return her hug, finally letting out the sob I've been struggling to hold back the closer and closer I got to home.

"I had a little run-in with a rabbit."

Pulling back, she furrows her brow. "What?"

I motion toward the house. "Let's get inside where it's warm. I'll tell you all about it."

Maybe leaving a few things out...

Like the fact that I was—possibly—not completely focused on the road in front of me when that rabbit darted out.

Not that it would have necessarily changed things if I hadn't been scanning the Crisps' property for something I shouldn't have been...but still.

Mom doesn't need all those gritty details.

I grab my single suitcase and parka from the backseat and nudge the door closed. A cold wind blasts biting flakes against my face, and Mom wraps her arm around me as we make our way up to the porch and in through the front door that still creaks the same way it did when I was a kid.

Dad always refused to fix it.

He said it helped him know when I was sneaking out to meet Luke—or coming back in from doing just that.

Of course, he knew I used my window trellis after he revealed his master plan with the front door, but he never said so or made any attempts to remove it from that side of the house.

Mostly because they loved Luke as much as I did back then.

The house still smells the same—like gingerbread and cinnamon and home—but something is missing. That "warm hug" feeling that always greeted me when I stepped inside these walls is somehow incomplete.

Something that can't be "fixed."

I drop my bag and inhale deeply, trying to brush away the uneasiness of being home this time of year without Dad. "Smells great in here, Mom."

She smiles and kicks off her boots, then makes her way

down the hallway toward the living room and kitchen. "I just made an apple pie and gingerbread cookies."

My mouth waters, but before I follow her, I scan the foyer and frown.

Instead of the glittery garland that typically wraps around the banister all the way to the top of the stairs, the wood stands starkly bare.

No bright-red bow on the newel post.

No family Christmas photos on the small table tucked against the staircase.

Nothing Mom and Dad usually do to decorate the space you first walk into.

I toe-off my UGGs and cautiously follow Mom through to the kitchen and attached living room, where our Christmas tree usually dominates the corner.

This year, nothing but a barren space greets me.

Not a single hint of the holiday in the house—save for the scents wafting from behind me.

My heart sinks.

I turn back toward where she stands at the stove. "Mom?"

"What, dear?"

"You didn't decorate or get a tree?"

Her shoulders stiffen, her entire body tensing as she pauses in moving the cookies off the cooling tray and into the jar that's always sat on the counter. She clears her throat. "I-I…I just couldn't do it without him."

The confession I understand all too well makes tears fill my eyes.

I approach her, grasp her shoulder, and turn her to face me to find wet streaks down her cheeks. "It's okay. We can do it together. Throw on *Mannheim Steamroller* like we always used to…"

The thought of having the house like this—so devoid of all the things Dad loved so much—doesn't feel right. As painful as it might be to have to go on without him, this is still Christmas.

Mistletoe's holiday.

His holiday.

He wouldn't want us to spend it depressed and without all the beautiful things that always make the house come alive.

Never.

Christmas is about joy.

Not this stagnant, empty feeling.

I pull out of her hold and squeeze her shoulders. "Where is Dad's box?"

She knows exactly what I'm asking about, and the corners of her lips twitch. "In his office. Everything else is in the basement."

But Dad would *never* put "his" box in the basement with the rest of the holiday décor. Not when it holds his most cherished items—the things he kept like trophies and displayed as such.

"I'll go get it."

Mom sighs, probably feeling the same heaviness I do. "If we're doing this, we're going to need some eggnog…"

Preferably spiked.

If Dad were here, it would be.

I move to the front of the house off the foyer, where Dad's office door stands closed, like I left it when I was here for his funeral.

Has Mom even been in here since then?

My hand shakes slightly as I twist the knob and nudge it open. The scent of his aftershave hits me so hard I have to cover my mouth to prevent Mom from hearing my sob. But I refuse to allow her to see me break down again.

He wouldn't want that.

I keep reminding myself of those words as I approach

"the box" placed carefully in the corner and lift it into my arms.

Growing up, it always felt so big, so heavy. Today, it somehow feels even heavier, like it carries all our Christmas happiness inside one small package.

Mom waits in the living room with two mugs in hand and raises them slightly. "I have the eggnog."

I raise a brow. "The good kind?"

She grins as I set down the box and take the mug from her. "Is there any *other* kind acceptable in this house?"

Dad's famous words each year when we got ready to decorate the house and tree make me grin and release a little of the sorrow that had threatened to drag me under in his office.

I take a sip of the boozy, creamy treat and moan. "That's delicious."

Mom nods and does the same. "It really is. He was right about it needing that little *extra* something, wasn't he?"

"He was right about most things…" I scan the living room, my gaze landing on the fireplace mantle. "And he would insist that we start the evening by putting out *the* nutcracker."

Giggling, Mom sets her mug on the end table. "He absolutely would." She kneels beside the box and pulls off the lid. "Nutsack was always his top priority."

I burst out laughing and set down my drink to join her as she moves the tissue paper to reveal the few precious items settled inside. "He did love Nutsack…"

And who wouldn't?

Affectionately named due to the large, red, Santa-style bag he carries to store your nuts in before breaking them open, the twenty-four-inch, hand-carved nutcracker has been the center of Dad's holiday decorating—and bad jokes —since Mom bought it for him nearly twenty years ago.

GWYN MCNAMEE

I lift him from the box and release a little sigh-laugh. "God, this thing is ugly."

Mom playfully slaps my shoulder. "Hey, don't disparage Nutsack."

Pushing to my feet, I maneuver the lever on the back to ensure his gaping mouth is still working properly. "I would *never* do that." Satisfied he is perfectly intact, I take him to his place of honor in the center of the mantle. "Don't forget to fill his sack tonight."

Her laughter draws me back toward where she squats beside the box. "I won't forget. So, weren't you going to tell me about a rabbit?"

"Oh..." I roll my eyes. "It darted across the road in front of me. Guess where?"

She raises her eyebrows. "I don't know. When we talked, you were in town already, so..." she trails off, her eyes widening. "No."

I nod. "Right in front of the farm, and guess who came to my rescue?"

"Oh, Noel." She presses her lips together and draws my hands into hers. "I'm so sorry. What happened?"

That should be easy to answer.

Just give her the facts.

But the whole thing felt so *wrong*.

It's left me more shaken than I want to admit.

"He proved that you were right about how much he's changed, Mom." I release a sigh, remembering that look in his eyes. So much disdain and anger there. "The Luke I knew never would've been that..."

I can't land on the right word for how he acted.

"That what?"

"That angry, that dismissive, that damn *grinchy*."

Mom sighs. "I did warn you..."

"You did. I just thought maybe…"—my chest tightens —"maybe he wouldn't be that way with me."

She squeezes my hands in hers. "I'm sorry, honey. When people change, it can be—"

"I really don't want to talk about it." I force a smile, trying to put what happened today to the back of my mind so I can concentrate on filling this house with as much Christmas spirit as it can handle without exploding. "Let's just get back to it."

"Okay…" Mom releases my hands and reaches into the box. "What do you want to do with this, then?"

Shit.

Somehow, I forgot that Dad not only put *his* most cherished Christmas treasures in here but also mine.

I swallow thickly as Mom lifts the green globe with the hand-painted red sleigh, Santa, and reindeer flying over a snowy landscape. The elegant scrawl around the bottom still looks perfect after all these years.

Merry Christmas to all, and to all, a good night…

I shouldn't love it so much—especially after today—but I still do.

My heart thunders against my chest, staring at it, remembering what it felt like when I opened it so many years ago.

All the love that surrounded the gift and the night I received it.

The pure, unadulterated joy that had overtaken me.

Now, my hands shake as I reach to take it from Mom…

But it slips from my trembling fingers and falls to the wood floor, shattering into a hundred pieces.

5

NOEL

S tepping out onto Main Street in downtown Mistletoe, my renewed holiday spirit goes into overdrive, fueled by the music, the people, and the entire vibe. After spending the evening and most of today decorating the exterior and interior of the house as best we could on our own with the bitter cold, driving snow, and high winds, there was only one thing left to do—

Well, two.

The fact that the corner of the living room still stands bare of the single most important piece of Christmas regalia doesn't sit well with me, but at the same time, the mere thought of having to step foot on the Crisps' property again prevented me from stopping to throw a tree on the top of the rental car.

Driving past it on the way into town, I *forced* my eyes to stay on the slippery road.

No rabbits or hunky, grumpy lumberjacks were going to distract me from my destination today—or my goal.

My gaze drifts down to the small box in my hands that holds the shattered remains of *the* ornament.

Let it go, Noel.

I could have thrown it away last night when I swept up the shards. I *should* have tossed it into the trash, along with the memory that came with it.

Could have.

Should have.

But couldn't.

In the end, as I stood over that open trash can, broken pieces of the beautiful gift mimicking the ones of my heart, my hand wouldn't brush them into the bin. It shook as I tried to. And eventually, I put them into this box—along with any hope of anything ever feeling the way it did *that night* again.

But that doesn't mean I won't allow Mistletoe and the sights, smells, and sounds of Christmas Eve day to envelop me and soothe away the pain that lingers from the losses I've suffered—both Dad *and* the man who gave me this ornament.

And it's already working wonders.

Tugging my beanie down farther over my ears to combat the wind, I scan downtown.

Mr. Monson stands on the corner across from me, dressed as Santa Claus, ringing the charity bell over his red bag for donations, greeting everyone as they pass by with a jolly, "Ho, ho, ho."

Members of the mayor's staff mill about the town square, still setting up for the ceremony tonight, despite the incoming major blizzard.

They won't cancel for *anything*.

Not even subzero temperatures have ever stopped a Mistletoe Christmas Eve celebration.

A "little" snow and wind won't, either.

Instead of heading for the square to watch everyone skating and the final preparations, the smell of Mrs. Wagner's sugar cookies draws me away from my car and toward the bakery.

I hadn't planned to make any stops other than to the Rose Boutique, but I can't resist that scent.

Which is precisely her intent.

The wise woman cracks the front door, even in the most frigid of temperatures, to ensure anyone passing by will get a noseful and be unable to resist stopping in.

My mouth waters, imagining the flaky goodness melting against my tongue.

Just a quick stop.

I tug open the already-cracked door, and the bell above jingles. Instantly, all eyes turn in my direction. A few people I don't know—likely tourists in town for the ceremony eye me before quickly returning to their conversations. But most of the faces and longer stares are far too familiar.

Nancy Wagner's eyes snap open wide. "Noel"—she rushes from around the corner, wiping her hands on her apron—"I heard you were back and that you got into a car accident. Are you all right?"

Word travels far too fast in this town.

"I'm fine, Nancy. Just swerved to avoid a rabbit and hit a little ice. Ended up in the ditch. No damage to the car or me, I promise."

I force a smile because she genuinely means well, and her concern isn't an act. As one of Mom's best friends, she practically helped raise me, so I shouldn't be dismissive of her—even if I have no desire to discuss what went down with Luke.

She wraps her arm around me and walks me over to a vacant table like I can't—or shouldn't—stand after my "ordeal." Squeezing me tightly, she leans in conspiratorially. "I bet you could use a sugar cookie"—she winks—"or two."

The woman knows me too well.

After thirty years of satisfying my sweet tooth, she should.

"And a cup of coffee, too." I slowly lower myself into one of the chairs at the small round table. "Please."

Her gray brows rise. "Would you like a latte or cappuccino instead?"

Latte?

Cappuccino?

Where the hell am I?

Last time I was here, the coffee came from the same old carafe it had for decades—with burned-on remnants of hundreds of pots before it permanently staining the bottom.

And it was the *only* option.

"When did you get an espresso machine?"

She grins as she motions toward it in the corner of the shop behind the counter. "It was a splurge. I probably shouldn't have bought it, but you know"—Nancy waves a hand toward the two tables of customers who are definitely *not* locals—"trying to stay up with the times and whatnot."

What she *really* means is trying to cater to a completely different clientele than she does any other time of the year. But I am *not* one of those frou-frou coffee people, even if I am no longer a Mistletoe permanent resident.

"Just black coffee is great, Nancy."

I scan the shop for any other changes I may have initially missed when I walked in while she gets to work on my drink, but I make the mistake of allowing my gaze to land on the table in the corner.

Where a certain *someone* always sits.

As she does right now.

Oh, Lord...

Bambi Burrell gives me a finger wave from her seat, then grabs her cup of coffee and plate and comes to join me, practically bounding across the small shop like the baby deer she's named after.

Shit.

48

She scoots into the chair opposite me, offering me a bright smile and a glint of mischief in her amber eyes. "So, I hear you saw Luke yesterday…"

For the love of all that's holy…

I try to keep my annoyance out of my voice. "How do you know that?"

She smiles and waggles her eyebrows. "How I know *every*thing that happens in Mistletoe?"

The gossip queen hasn't lost her crown since high school; she's just moved on to more *adult* stories.

I'd greatly prefer that my love life—or lack thereof—stay out of her list of discussion topics. But I've known Bambi long enough to understand that ignoring her question or trying to dodge it will only further stir the pot and cause her to interject her own suppositions and theories into whatever she blasts around Mistletoe.

I manage to avoid her inquisition most of the time when I come home to visit, but now that I made the mistake of stopping in for a sweet treat and dared to do it after something as exciting as a car accident and contact with the Grinch, I might as well have my head in a guillotine.

"Yes, Bambi, I saw Luke and—"

She shifts closer, hands clasped tightly around her mug, eyes wide and ears open. "And what happened?"

If you didn't interrupt me, I could tell you.

At least, tell her *some* of it.

Just enough to get her off my back.

And since Luke doesn't come into town anymore, I won't have to worry about him interjecting any other information into the gossip cesspool Mistletoe can become.

Nancy arrives with my coffee and plate of cookies, giving me a much-needed moment to consider how much to reveal to the woman who is walking word vomit and might twist anything I say into a coiled mess that no longer resembles the actual sentences that left my mouth.

"Thanks, Nancy." I accept the coffee and immediately take a sip, savoring the bitter liquid as Bambi drums her manicured nails on the Formica tabletop, waiting for me to spill. Grabbing a cookie, I smile at Nancy, who continues to stand next to me expectantly, like she, too, is waiting to hear whatever I have to say about my run-in with Luke. "This looks incredible."

Bambi's fingers move faster as I chew my first delicious bite.

The cookie practically melts in my mouth, the familiar flavor warming me just as much as the coffee does. But I can't put it off any longer, or Bambi might have an aneurysm right here, right now.

"Well, I saw Luke, and he was...difficult."

That seems like the most reasonable term for his attitude.

Anything else would only make me seem like a bitter ex looking to take a jab at the man who broke her heart any way she can.

Bambi snorts and shakes her head, lifting her mug to her too-red lips. "Isn't he always these days?"

I grasp my cookie a little too hard, cracking it slightly. "Is he really that bad?"

Why am I asking?

It isn't as if I didn't witness it myself yesterday.

Nancy exchanges a look with Bambi, then squeezes my shoulder. "Yeah, hon, he is. Anything you thought you knew about him pretty much went out the window the minute you left town."

Mom and Dad told me as much over the years.

Maybe I was naïve to believe he would have stayed the man I knew after so long, but it's impossible to accept that he could change so much. That he could have gone from the friendly, outgoing, funny, playful, helpful, and loving person I always knew him to be to…what I saw yesterday.

I take another bite to give myself a moment to consider what Nancy said. Holding up the final small piece, I smile at her. "I've missed these."

"You wouldn't have to if you visited more often or maybe even moved home…"

Leaning back slightly in my chair, I raise a brow. "Did my mom pay you to say that?"

She laughs and shakes her head. "No. It's just really nice having you here under more pleasant circumstances."

I try not to let the sorrow hit me immediately, but it's hard not to think about the last time I was here and saw her when she baked everything for Dad's wake.

"Honey?"

Blinking away the forming tears, I glance up at her. "What?"

"Your dad, he was super proud of you and what you've done with your career. He'd be happy you're home for Christmas, but he knew why you left and never wanted you to feel guilty about it."

It's the same thing he told me time and again. The very words Mom repeated after he died and I considered quitting my job to come home to be with her…

I didn't realize how much I needed to hear that from someone else, too.

"Thank you."

Some of the guilt about leaving that always weighs on me seems to dissipate as I devour the rest of my cookie and set to work on the second, sipping at my coffee and watching people scurry back and forth on the sidewalk outside, hustling to get ready for Christmas tomorrow.

"Is that it?" Bambi raises a brow. "He was difficult and…"

Shit.

51

I was stupid to think that would be enough to appease her.

"And he dragged my car out of the ditch and sent me on my way. It was a very brief, unfriendly encounter I don't hope to repeat anytime soon."

Her eyes widen slightly.

Crap.

That may have crossed the line into the bitter ex territory.

Forcing a smile, I sip my coffee. "But if I run into him, it'll be fine. It's been a long time since we were together. Ancient history."

Nancy nods with a smug grin. "Mmmhmm. Well, since that boy never sets foot in town this time of year, I think you're safe. Unless you go and decide to run your car off the road in front of the tree lot again."

"Very funny."

She chuckles and moves away to check on the other tables while Bambi watches me expectantly.

"What?"

Her eyes narrow. "You're not telling me something."

There's a *lot* I'm not telling her and never will.

"Nope. That's it!" I check outside again at the snow continuing to fall. "Are you heading to the ceremony tonight?"

She nods, still eyeing me. "I plan to…"

"Good." Excellent segue to a safer topic. "I'll see you there."

And walk the other direction as soon as I do.

Right now, it's time to ditch the bakery before she can grill me any further and do what I actually came into town to accomplish today.

I grab the box from the table and start to make my way

toward the counter to pay, but Nancy motions me away with a swift hand.

"Your money isn't good here."

"You know you're not going to be able to afford to keep that fancy machine if you don't let people pay."

She smiles. "I'll let other people pay. Not you, hon. Not when I changed your diapers."

"Oh, God. I don't need to be reminded of that, but thank you."

I slip back out onto the sidewalk. The sultry sounds of Bing Crosby piped over the speakers across Main Street in town square fill my ears, and I sing along as I walk the half block to Rose's.

Transferring the box to one hand, I tug open the door and step inside, welcoming the blast of warm air.

Bethany glances up from behind the counter. "Noel, welcome home!"

I smile and approach her, my hands trembling slightly around the box. "Thank you. It's good to see you."

And with *her*, I mean it.

Unlike Bambi, she's actually happy to see me home for reasons other than providing fodder for the town gossip mill.

"What can I do for you?"

I hold up the box. "Well, unfortunately, I broke my favorite ornament."

"Oh, no."

"I'm almost positive it was purchased here, and I was hoping you might have another one."

Even if I should let it go...

She holds out her hands. "Well, I can certainly take a look."

I pass it over the counter to her, and she sets it down and flips back the lid, staring down at the remains.

Bethany reaches in and pulls out the largest piece to examine it. "This is beautiful. Or...it was."

Like a knife to the chest.

"I know. It slipped out of my hand."

That was shaking.

Because I couldn't stop thinking about the man who gave it to me.

"I'm sorry, Noel, but I don't think this is one of ours."

"What?" I glance around the shop at all the handmade ornaments. "But it looks just like something you'd carry."

She nods, twisting the piece in the light to examine Santa. "The plain green globe might be, but this painting..."—she shakes her head and snags another chunk—"it doesn't look like anything I did."

"Well, this was from ten years ago. Maybe your mom?"

After all, it was Rose's name on the shop and had been since before I was born.

"Definitely not." Bethany leans over conspiratorially and peeks toward the rear of the shop, where her mother is probably lurking. "My mom kind of sucked at decorating these. I did most of the painting, or she paid others to do it. But I don't recognize this style. And please don't ever reveal that dirty family secret."

I bark out a laugh and quickly cover my mouth to try to stop it. Rose's shop has always been regarded as *the* place to get custom and high-end ornaments, which means she must have been hiring really great artists to get them done if she can't do it herself. "Well, I wonder where it could be from, then?"

Bethany sets the pieces back in the box, leaving the top tucked back and open. "I don't know. Why don't you ask whoever gave it to you?"

My throat tightens as I stare down at the shards, but I force a swallow through the lump there. "I'll do that."

She offers a sympathetic smile. "Anything else I can do for you?"

If only there were.

There apparently *is* no replacing what's in this box, just like there's no hope of ever seeing the old Luke again.

I step out of the shop onto the street, clutching the last remnants of who he once was in the open box and staring down at them.

Where the hell could the ornament be from?

This town might look like it puked Christmas, but when it comes to hand-blown glass and hand-painted ornaments, Rose's is the only place that has ever carried this quality.

I stand on the curb, watching a few cars trail by in the rapidly accumulating snow on the road, considering if there is anywhere else I haven't thought of, *any* other possibilities before I give up all hope.

The weatherman said the storm will hit tonight, closer to midnight, and this steady fall of heavy, wet flakes will increase until then as temps continue to plummet and winds increase.

Potentially as much as twenty inches of snow over the next two to three days—one of the largest blizzards we've had in decades.

And it has to fall on Christmas…

It seems the Grinch has gotten his way.

Luke is probably *thrilled* the town's holiday plans are likely going to be in shambles.

I can already see the difficulty everyone's having in trying to get set up for the ceremony tonight. Papers and garland float away in a blustery gust. Light strings don't hang properly and keep coming detached. Even the temporary dais they're setting up doesn't seem to want to cooperate—pieces haphazardly strewn near the top of the courthouse steps when it should be fully built and ready by now.

Would they actually cancel?

If they did, it would be a first.

But this storm feels different.

More dangerous.

Like whatever is coming will change things in a way no one in this sleepy town could anticipate.

Still, despite the nasty winds, freezing temps, my broken ornament, and even the gossip swirling thanks to my return home and run-in with Luke, I can't help smiling, staring up at the massive town tree.

The centerpiece of Mistletoe.

A physical representation of the Christmas spirit towering above everyone and everything.

Looking at it brings a flood of beautiful memories.

Decades of standing beneath it and watching Dad direct the decorating. Attending the Christmas Eve ceremony with Luke. Skating on the ice and playing pick-up hockey games with him and our friends.

Before I even realize what I'm doing, my feet carry me to the curb, and I glance either way before I hurry across crawling traffic, drawn to the tree the same way I always have been.

Snowflakes float around me, the crisp, clean scent mingling with those coming from the bakery and other shops lining the square on all sides. "Winter Wonderland" plays through the speakers, mixing with the laughter of children on the ice and running around the square.

My heart warms as I make it to the base of the tree and stare up at it. By far, it is one of the largest trees I've ever seen that wasn't still standing in the forests surrounding Mistletoe.

And it's absolutely perfect.

Stunningly symmetrical branches filled with fluffy needles and a strong trunk that supports its massive weight completely straight despite the wind's best effort to batter it into submission.

I can almost forget all the reasons I have *not* to be happy in this moment—

Until the hairs on the back of my neck stand on end.

And not from the wind.

This is a different kind of chill.

One brought on by the gaze of a certain man.

My body heats as someone moves up close behind me, and a familiar gravelly voice floats over me with his warm breath on my cheek. "I should have known I'd find you here."

6

THE MISTLETOE GRINCH

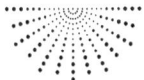

Noel flinches as if I've physically hit her, her back stiffening, shoulders tensing visibly even under the heavy pea coat she wears.

Hell.

I shouldn't have said anything.

If I had been smart, I would have just stood there across the street and watched her soaking in her joy in her favorite spot in town.

It would have been the right thing to do—for both of us. To give her peace and ensure my own by maintaining distance between us.

But I couldn't stop myself.

I never could with this woman.

Even when I was too young to know what it was, I was drawn to Noel like a moth to a flame.

In the classroom. On the playground. Anywhere she was —that was where *I* wanted to be. That never changed as we aged. If anything, that tether that kept me bound to her only strengthened until even a few hours apart became physically painful.

Noel always owned my heart and held it in her hands.

She cared for it. Nurtured it. Made promises to protect it.

And now, there's nothing left of what once beat for her.

Yet, I'm still drawn to this woman who broke me. I can't stop myself. Even with her reaction to my statement, the clear body language screaming that she wants nothing to do with me, I still inch closer until I can smell her light peppermint scent in the wind.

She remains stock-still for a moment before she slowly turns to face me, gripping a small box in her mitten-covered hands. Her blond hair spills out across her shoulders from under the matching cream-colored beanie with the little fuzzy ball on top that is far too adorable on her. "What are you doing here? From what I hear, you never come into town, especially now…"

While nothing she said is wrong, the judgmental tone stings worse than the flakes blowing into my face.

I scowl at her and cross my arms over my chest, then stare up at the tree that might be a true masterpiece. "My dad isn't feeling well. I came to the pharmacy to grab a few things for him. And believe me, I would have sent my mother to do it if I didn't think the roads were getting too dangerous. But the last thing I need is her sliding off into a *ditch*."

Lowering my gaze again, I meet hers, knowing full well what I just said will set her off.

Those icy-blue eyes of hers narrow, filling with a fiery heat I know all too well. "I *told* you; it was the rabbit's fault."

"Mmhmm."

Are we really going to have this argument again?

It wasn't what I intended when I came over.

Actually, I'm not sure *what* I intended.

I just walked, needing to be closer to her on the one hand while, on the other, knowing it was a dangerous prospect to approach after what happened yesterday.

Now, I've gotten us right back to where we were when we stood in the middle of that road—with the storm blowing around us and our annoyance with each other overshadowing everything. Even the shared history that should, at the very least, allow us to be civil in public.

She finally pulls her glare away from me and returns her focus to the tree, releasing a long sigh, as if she's letting go of that anger she just directed at me with the puff of air. Searching for her center and calm place. Something she always did, even as a child. "I hope your dad feels better." Offering a tight smile, she peeks over her shoulder at me. "Tell him he picked good this year."

"Picked what?"

Noel points up, balancing the small box in her other mittened hand. "The town tree."

"I would, but the compliment would be going to the wrong person because I picked it."

Her brows rise. "*You* did?"

I incline my head, watching for her reaction given the new information.

After what was just said, it wouldn't surprise me if she flipped a switch and withdrew the kind words, knowing they were now meant for me.

Her gaze bounces between the tree and me. "But your dad always picks the trees, every year…"

Shit.

She doesn't know.

Acid burns my throat, and I run a hand over my snow-dampened hair, swallowing it down as I glance at my boots rather than at her when I reveal this. "No, my dad has *never* picked the tree." Gathering all my remaining strength, I look back up to her, hoping her reaction isn't what I expect. Hoping I don't *crush* her. "*Your* dad always did."

Her soft brow furrows. "What?"

"Shit, I'm sorry, Noel. I thought you knew. Your dad would come down to the farm, and they'd go out all around the property until they found the perfect tree. Sometimes, they'd spend days searching. My dad would point out the ones he liked, but it was *always* your dad's call. He personally picked every tree that's been in this town square since...God, before either of us was born."

Those pale-pink lips of hers open and close a few times. "How did I never...I guess I just assumed your dad..."

She swallows thickly, her already pale skin going as white as the snow falling around us.

"This year, my dad..." *Shit. This is so much harder than I thought it would be.* "He couldn't bring himself to go out without your father. Said it didn't feel right to make that decision without him. So...I picked it."

Wondering every second what Russell Jolly would have thought.

Hoping I got it right.

For him.

And for the woman standing stunned, speechless in front of me.

Tears start to shimmer in her eyes, but she quickly turns away to stare back at the tree before they fall. "Oh, well, then...you did a good job."

A vise wraps around my sternum and squeezes so tightly that I have trouble breathing in the frosty air. I force myself to inhale, then blow it out before I respond—not with what I truly want to say. "Thanks."

An awkward silence settles between us, broken only by the squeals of delight from the children covering the rinks and the square and the ever-present Christmas music filling the air that I try so desperately to tune out.

This never used to happen.

She was the one person in the world I could spend hours with in silence and never once feel uncomfortable.

Everything was always so easy with her.

So effortless.

But now the tension is so thick it rivals the driving snow.

If I don't break *it* soon, it will break *me.*

"What are you doing in town? Are you and your mom ready for Christmas?"

She turns back toward me, gripping the open box in her hands. "Um, I guess…"

Her eyes dart up to meet mine like she wants to say something else and is gauging whether she should or not, but instead of voicing whatever she is thinking, she shifts the box from one hand to the other—the one farther away from me.

Almost like she doesn't want me to see it.

"Did you buy something?"

"Shit." Though muttered under her breath, I catch the curse before she continues. "No, actually I—"

I step forward and look down into the box, and even with the lid partially closed, I recognize it instantly.

The pain that hits me is like the dozens of shards of glass inside it being shoved through my skin at once.

Red-hot betrayal flares through my blood. Something I didn't think she could make me feel again, but here it is, just as thick and vile as the night she ended things. "Trying to get rid of all evidence I ever existed, huh?"

She glances up at me, eyes wide. "What? No, Luke, it isn't like that—"

"Don't bother." I retreat a step, then another, holding up a hand to stop her protests. "I think you made it very clear how you feel about me yesterday. There isn't any use in us pretending just because we once had a thing."

Her jaw drops. "A *thing*?"

Hell.

Regret at my knee-jerk-reaction choice of words slams into me.

Six years is a hell of a lot more than a thing.

Planning out your wedding is a hell of a lot more than a thing.

Talking about having kids and growing old together is definitely a hell of a lot more than a thing.

But I had to say it.

I had to be dismissive of what we shared because if I admitted how much she meant to me, how much she hurt me, I'm not sure my legs would keep me upright in this moment.

Not staring into her fathomless blue eyes.

Not watching her hair blow in the wind.

Not seeing the way snowflakes cling to her impossibly long, thick lashes and wanting to kiss them away so badly.

Her wide eyes stay on me as I retreat, but before she can say anything, I turn and walk away as quickly as my feet will carry me.

Across the street...

Dodging traffic and angry horns...

I duck into the pharmacy and release a shuddering breath, pressing my back against the door for a second to try to regain some semblance of composure I so easily lost out there with her.

Shit.

The door is glass, and she can probably see me.

I lurch forward, trying to find cover behind anything I can to avoid her witnessing how shaken I really am by a simple conversation with her.

Who are you kidding?

There's nothing simple about that woman.

Or my feelings for her.

Noel Jolly is the only person on this planet who has ever had this effect on me. Who can make me feel so much love. Who can cause so much agonizing pain—

"Luke?"

Shit.

Mr. Pierce peeks around the side of the aisle. "Can I help you find something?"

"Yeah." I force myself to focus my attention on him instead of out the front windows that overlook the square. "My dad has a really bad cough with a bit of a fever."

His bushy white eyebrows rise over his thick-rimmed glasses. "Oh, well, I can certainly help you there…"

He keeps talking, rattling off information about different over-the-counter treatments and pulling boxes from the shelf to show me.

I don't hear a word of it.

My gaze and all my attention keep drifting to the blonde across the street, still standing frozen in place, as if my words have rendered her unable to move. Kind of like what she said to me that night left me unable to move forward with my life.

"Just give me whatever you recommend, Mr. Pierce."

If I let him keep going, he'll talk for an hour, and I can't deal with being in town any longer.

The goddamn Christmas music infiltrating everywhere.

The smell of gingerbread and baking pies.

The bright, happy lights and smiles of anyone I pass on the street.

The stupid cheer everywhere I look.

All I want to do is get home, give this to Dad, go back to the cabin, and lock myself in it until after New Year's when Noel will be long gone—and all these feelings with her.

I follow Mr. Pierce to the register, still keeping my eye on the woman who I know will continue to haunt my dreams, even when she leaves Mistletoe.

She finally shakes her head as if she needs to clear it, then stares back up at the tree for a moment before she turns and makes her way toward her shitty rental car parked on the street.

Mr. Pierce rings me up, the click of his fingers on the old-time register loud enough to break through my obsessive stare. "I hear you had some excitement out your way yesterday."

You have to be kidding me.

I look over at him as I pull out my wallet. "Not sure what you mean."

He motions to the window and Noel slipping into her car directly across from us. "Noel have a little fender bender?"

Shit.

I clear my throat, trying to forget that moment of panic when I realized it was her and thought she might be hurt. "Nothing serious. She just hit some ice and slid off the road."

He raises a brow over his glasses. "Really? I heard it was a rabbit."

This is exactly why I don't come to Mistletoe anymore. The gossip is as bad as the music. And knowing that Noel is back, I won't make this mistake again.

I have enough supplies and books to last me weeks in the cabin, and if I desperately need anything, Mom and Dad will come get it for me rather than get into yet another argument with me about how I need "social interaction."

"No rabbit." I toss a twenty at him, grab the bag, and move toward the door.

"Wait, Luke, your change!"

Waving a dismissive hand, I push out onto the sidewalk. "Donate it."

I let the door close behind me and jog down in the opposite direction to my truck as Noel pulls away from the curb.

Her tires slip on the thick snow accumulating on the road—falling far too fast for the plows to keep up.

My breath catches, watching her regain control and make her way to the stop sign.

I climb into my truck and fire it up.

Don't do it, Luke.

I need to let her go, let her drive home in peace.

But envisioning the way she went off the road yesterday makes that impossible.

Only twenty-four hours ago, I threatened to follow her home to ensure she got there safely, but then I was so damn angry that I let her drive away and pushed aside that feeling in my gut that she needed my watchful eye.

Today, I'm not so sure I can ignore it again.

I tighten my hand on the wheel and pull out behind her.

She drives through the intersection of Main and State Street and starts to head out of town, back up the mountain. Where the roads are only going to get worse…

As is my anxiety.

I try to stay close enough to her that if there's any sort of issue, I can prevent her from killing herself in that stupid thing, but the shattered ornament in the box flashes through my head.

The pieces so representative of what she did to me.

She doesn't want your help, Luke.

She doesn't want anything from you.

She never did.

That old pain returns, the one that's always there but that I've somehow managed to push into the background over the last eight years without seeing that woman.

But that's impossible now.

Now that I've touched her, smelled her, felt her again.

"Fuck!" Before she can notice I'm following her, I slam my palm against the steering wheel and pull off to the side of the road. I throw the truck into park, watching her brake lights disappear into the snow. "Fuck, fuck, fuck."

This is why I don't do Mistletoe.

This is why I don't do Christmas.

This is why I don't do Noel Jolly.

7

NOEL

The longer I sit, staring into the fire, the more my eyes seem to drift from the flames to Nutsack on the mantle, then over to the empty space next to it, the corner where Dad's tree always stands.

Well, at least, his tree at home.

My gut twists, souring the coffee and cookies I had at the bakery a few hours ago.

How could I not know he was the one choosing the town tree every year?

It seems so obvious, something I should have known, yet that revelation has made not having the single thing he loved decorating the most in the house feel like a massive slap in the face to the man who *ran* Christmas in this town.

"Are you all right, dear?"

I glance over at Mom, who sits on the couch, knitting a new scarf while we watch *National Lampoon's Christmas Vacation*. Another one of our traditions I insisted we keep in Dad's honor, even if I've been unable to concentrate on anything happening.

The scene where their tree goes up in flames plays out on

the screen, and watching Clark Griswold's determination to replace it merely strengthens my resolve to do what will probably sound insanely stupid to anyone else, given the conditions outside right now.

It's bad enough that Mistletoe actually *canceled* the ceremony over the worry that the weather will deteriorate too fast for anyone to get home safely afterward.

That should be enough of a warning to toss my idea into the trash.

But next to putting out Nutsack on the mantle, the tree was always Dad's pride and joy. We would spend hours placing the lights and tinsel and picking the ideal spot for every single ornament, only to have him adjust things daily—sometimes even on Christmas Day.

It drove Mom nuts that he couldn't just leave things be, but he wanted it *perfect.*

And it isn't too late to get him that perfect tree this year.

I shift in Dad's recliner, unsure how to broach the subject with Mom when she was so upset yesterday about the mere idea of decorating the house without him. "Did you know Dad was the one who always picked the town tree?"

Her gaze darts up to meet mine, her brow furrowing. "I mean, I knew he and Bud always went out together, but I assumed Bud made the final decision, since he would know what trees looked healthiest, what would be the easiest to get out of their property and up in town square."

The same assumption I had made over the years.

And apparently, been very wrong about.

I chew on the inside of my cheek. "That's what I thought, too. But...I ran into Luke today."

Her hands still. "What did he say?"

Besides basically brushing off our six-year relationship as nothing?

"He said that Dad was the one who usually chose the tree, but he did it this year."

A wistfulness fills her eyes. "It is a beautiful tree. Dad would have loved it."

And that's the opening I had hoped for.

"Yeah." I push out of the chair and walk over to her.

She watches me with trepidation as I approach and squat in front of the couch.

"Mom, I know you said you didn't want a tree this year, that you couldn't bear the thought of putting it up without Dad, but"—I wave my hand toward the empty corner—"does this feel right? I mean"—the tears start to burn in my eyes, and I blink them away—"I know *nothing is* going to feel right without him here, but it definitely feels *very* wrong not to have a tree, not to decorate it, not to do the one thing he loved the most, just because he's not here. I feel like instead of avoiding it, we need to do it *for* him."

Her lips quiver, and she sets her knitting needles on her lap. "I know, but it's too late now. It's Christmas Eve, and—"

I push to my feet. "And you know Bud and Mary will have the lot open as late as they can."

Wide eyes dart to the windows along the back of the house that creak in the wind. "But the storm?"

"I've driven in worse."

She reaches out and snags my wrist. "Noel—"

I slide my hand over hers and squeeze. "Mom, I'll be all right. I'll drive down, snag a tree, come right back, and we can spend the rest of Christmas Eve decorating it, watching Dad's favorite movie. Okay?"

"The roads—"

"I'm only going two miles, Mom. And I know *that* road better than I do my own reflection."

She looks like she's ready to argue with me, but then her blue eyes drift to the empty spot in the corner. A resigned sigh slips from her lips. "You're stubborn, just like your father. If I said no, it wouldn't matter, would it?"

I lean in and press a kiss to her cheek. "Probably not. I'll be back as quickly as I can."

"Don't try to be quick." She gives me her best "mom" warning look. "Just drive safe. Maybe take my car. It has snow tires on it."

It would be a better option, if I could get it out of the garage.

"The last time I checked out front, there was a drift against the garage door. It would take way too long to clear it all and get your car out. I'll just take my rental. And don't worry so much, Mom. I could this drive with my eyes closed."

Mom offers a wry smile. "Please don't…"

After yesterday and what a runaway rabbit was able to do when I was *briefly* distracted by the Crisp farm, I don't think I'll attempt it with my eyes closed.

I step out of her hold and hustle toward the front door, where the foyer is now properly decked out in all the holiday regalia—as are we. Putting on the ugly sweaters felt like just one more "normal" thing we could do to keep Dad's presence with us.

With the added bonus of keeping us warm when Mother Nature seems determined to bury Mistletoe in a deep freeze.

Wind buffets the house, making the old wood creak in warning. Snow blows almost sideways outside the windows on either side of the front door, and as I zip my parka and tug on my books, hat, and mittens, I *almost* chicken out.

But we can't have Christmas without a tree.

And what I told Mom was true.

I've driven much farther in much worse weather for stupider reasons than fulfilling my dead father's Christmas wishes.

The moment I open the door and step outside, the blustery gale hits me, battering my face with icy flakes that make me cringe.

Shit, the storm really has picked up since the last time I was out here.

But the worst of it isn't supposed to come until after midnight, and it isn't even six o'clock yet. So, I have plenty of time to get down there and back up…as long as the road isn't too nasty.

That may take a Christmas miracle.

Maybe it isn't the smartest decision I've ever made, but I can't make it through this night and tomorrow without a tree.

It's bad enough doing it without Dad.

Which is why I'm willing to trudge through calf-deep, freshly fallen snow to the car, battling bone-chilling gusts and stinging flakes.

I brush the accumulation off the windshield with a mittened hand before I climb in and fire it up. The headlights flip on and illuminate how fast and hard the snow is really falling in front of me.

Not white-out conditions, but it will be before too long.

I better move fast.

Or, at least, as fast as possible in this car and this weather.

I throw the car in reverse and make a Y-turn to face the road.

Now or never, Noel.

Bitter-cold blizzard or…

I glance back at the house—the lights strung along the front eave and the warmth emanating from the bright windows.

Go back in?

The need to have the house complete on Christmas wins out over any concern about driving in these conditions or my earlier one about running into Luke if I *had* stopped for one earlier.

Of all the people in Mistletoe, the Crisps will understand why I need to do this and ensure I'm safely on my way with the perfect tree small enough for Mom and me to set up ourselves strapped to this tin can on wheels.

I inch down the driveway and out to the unplowed main road. Clearing Jolly Lane isn't a priority when only the Crisps and us live here. They'll get to it eventually, but the way the forecast is looking, it might be several days, which means getting down there and back up before it gets too bad is even more important.

Two miles.

It's nothing, really.

I slowly descend the mountain, telling myself that.

Blankets of snow flash across the headlights like I'm on *Star Trek*, going at warp speed when I'm barely crawling through the accumulation on the road.

My windshield wipers set on high fight the best they can to keep my vision unobscured, but it's a fruitless effort.

I grip the wheel so tightly that my fingers ache, trying to keep control of the car that seems to want to slip and slide around the slightest turn.

At least no one else is on the road, but as the little incident proved yesterday, there are other things to worry about around Mistletoe.

Like stray rabbits.

And moody ex-boyfriends.

Who hopefully won't be anywhere near the lot tonight...

I try not to think about the possibility that he will be as the normal three-minute drive to the farm any other day becomes thirty.

So many songs rotate through my playlist that by the time

"Last Christmas" starts, my hands ache from gripping the wheel so tightly to maintain control on the road.

When I finally see the break in the trees where the forest opens up onto the Crisp property, I'm almost ready to wave the white flag and give up.

Thank God.

I release a breath I've been holding as the multi-colored Christmas lights twining around their fence line and across the front of the barn come into view.

If everything is still lit, then someone is on the lot, even this late on Christmas Eve...

Which means I *will* get Dad a tree.

I turn into the farm, slowly advancing down the unplowed driveway toward where the lines of trees still stand, ready for any last-minute sales. But there aren't any other cars in the lot, nor is there any movement from anywhere on the property that I can see through the storm.

Even if the blizzard has driven Bud and Mary into the house, I can always go up there and have them come and help me. A quick in and out and back on the road.

If I can even find it by the time I get done here.

I park as close to the edge of the lot and the trees as I can, and climb from the car, leaving it running. Icy flakes blast me, a bitter warning from Mother Nature that maybe this wasn't the best idea.

"Fuck, that wind is cold..."

Shivering, I rush toward the barn that houses the sales office. That's definitely where I would be tonight, rather than waiting out here in case any customers come at the last minute.

Idiots like me who decided to drive in this for a tree.

I can barely see a few feet in front of me, but as I near the barn and safety from the storm, a flash of movement through the blowing snow makes me jerk my head up and skid to a stop.

Luke stands inside the open double doors, backlit in his customary sleeveless plaid shirt, unbuttoned and open to expose his muscle chest and perfect eight-pack.

Jesus Christ.

My eyes drift to a piece of mistletoe tied to one of the loops of his jeans, just above his crotch, then up to the Santa hat on his head.

Flashbacks of a different time when he wore the same thing and I had dropped to my knees for him infiltrate my mind long enough for a hot flash to warm me. But it's quickly cooled by the reminder of our earlier confrontation and his current reputation.

What the hell is he doing in that hat and with mistletoe?

For a brief second, bitter green jealousy spikes through my blood.

Is someone in there with him?

He steps toward me, axe resting across one shoulder, as if he just came in from felling trees during a damn storm. Hard eyes narrow on me, his lips twisting into what seems to be a permanent scowl. "Noel, what the hell are you doing here?"

His words get swallowed by the wind and barely reach me, but I can hear enough to catch the anger in them.

The feeling is mutual.

Luke Crisp is the last person I wanted to see tonight, on Christmas Eve, when I'm doing everything I can to stay in the holiday spirit and ensure Dad's memory is honored.

His constant snippy attitude will only sour everything.

Still, he may be my sole hope of actually accomplishing this mission.

I rush closer to him, bouncing on my feet, trying to stay warm. "I need a tree."

Those emerald eyes widen. "You drove down here in this storm to get a fucking *tree?*"

Okay, when he says it like that, it does seem a bit...unhinged.

"My mom didn't have the heart to get one herself, and I couldn't stand that living room without one on Christmas Eve. It all felt so wrong. I just…"

I let my rambling explanation trail off because the more I talk, the clearer it becomes how crazy I must sound to the man who already holds me in such low esteem.

He closes the distance between us and grabs my upper arm with his free hand. "You just decided to come to the farm in the middle of the blizzard of the century to get one?"

Eeep.

I open and close my mouth, my jaw snapping shut, surprised by how truly upset he seems to be. "Yes…" My gaze darts to the line of smaller trees leaning against the row of stands to our right. "Can you just put one on the car, and I'll head back home?"

Luke issues a low growl and drops the axe so he can grip me with both hands and spin me to face the rental car. "You mean the car you can barely see through the storm?"

Okay, he has a point there.

We're only twenty feet from it, and already, the gusting winds and heavy, wet flakes are starting to cover it. Even squinting, it's hard to make out, and I'm not sure I would be able to see it if I didn't already know where I had parked.

Luke sidles up behind me, pressing his hard body against my back and wrapping an arm around my waist, both holding me steady and keeping me warm while preventing me from moving. His hot breath flutters against my cheek as he leans in, sending a shiver down my spine unrelated to the cold. "I am *not* strapping a tree to that death trap and sending you back up the mountain on the unplowed road, Noel."

"What?" Breaking free of his hold—both physical and emotional, when it would have been so easy to lean into his touch and the way his gravelly voice ignites my blood—I whirl to face him. "But—"

A muscle in his clenched jaw tics, and he fists his hands at his sides, veins bulging on his neck and biceps. "Do you *really* think I'm going to let you just drive away?"

Coming from anyone else—or even observed by another person who doesn't know our history, who wasn't standing in almost exactly this same spot eight years ago—it might seem sweet, protective, downright chivalrous.

But not to me.

Not after what he did.

Not when I know the sheer hypocrisy of his statement.

Fighting the tears that so badly want to fall right now, I stare him down, preparing myself for the combat that seems to be coming. "Why not? You did before..."

8

THE MISTLETOE GRINCH

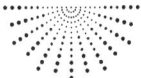

Her words make me stagger backward a step in the snow as a vision of her doing exactly that—driving away from this farm eight years ago and never looking back—slams into the forefront of my mind so hard that the pain almost doubles me over.

Watching her leave was the most agonizing thing I've ever experienced. Knowing she wasn't coming back. That I had lost her.

It still burns as hot today as it did back then.

And she threw it at me like an expertly wielded weapon.

One that cut deep.

But maybe I can't blame her after what I said earlier, calling us a "thing."

I did it to hurt her intentionally—the way she hurt me. Now, she's just lashing out, trying to get back at me, even though she's the one who put us in this position in the first place, the one who ruined everything all those years ago.

We had it all.

We were happy.

At least, I thought we were.

My reaction to her even now tells me nothing about my memories of us being together is imagined.

It was all very real.

Very potent.

Same as this need to protect her from herself right now.

I advance toward her and stop with my bare chest brushing against her parka, staring down into the eyes of the only woman who ever made my heart beat faster before she shattered it—the *only* one I would give a shit about driving out into the storm.

And to keep her safe, I have to ignore what she just said, no matter how much it hurt.

"You're not getting back in that car, Noel."

Her eyes widen, then shift from surprise into a fierce glare I almost never saw directed at me when we were together. "If you won't help me, I'll go find your mom and dad and get them to."

She tries to brush past me, but I wrap an arm around her waist, easily preventing her from advancing. Gasping, she looks up at me, her pink lips spread and harsh pants crystallizing in the air. "Luke Anthony Crisp, you let go of me right now!"

I growl at her. "Absofuckinglutely not!"

Before she can object again and lead us into a never-ending argument with no resolution, I dip my shoulder and toss her up over it.

She yelps, fighting against my hold across the back of her thighs. "Luke, what the hell? Put me down!"

"No."

I turn back toward the barn and stalk toward it, bending to snag my axe from the snow before I head to the path that leads back into the woods—straight to my cabin.

Noel pounds on my back. "Put. Me. Down. What the hell do you think you're *doing*?"

At this point, I thought that should be obvious.

"Saving your life. You're welcome."

"Saving my life?" She screeches over the wail of the wind battering the trees around us. "Oh, hell no. This is *not* happening right now!"

Icy-cold snow pelts my exposed skin, but I barely register it.

All I can concentrate on is the feel of her warm body pressed against mine, of holding her again—even if she is fighting me.

She lets out a frustrated groan and changes her tactic, twisting to apparently tug off one of her mittens and dig her nails into the exposed skin on the back of my neck.

I flinch at the bite of pain and pull away instinctively, but the rest of my body doesn't mind it in the slightest. Instead, flashes of nights we spent together in the very cabin I'm bringing her to, that I shouldn't be allowing to invade my brain, overtake it. "If you think that's going to stop me, you must not have a very good memory, Noel."

She stiffens in my arms, all her fight leaving her with one simple statement.

Shit.

Maybe it was unwise to bring up our sexual history after that comment she just made about me not stopping her, not to mention the fact that I'm currently storming through the woods with her tossed over my shoulder like a damn caveman.

"Luke, you can't *do* this!"

"Watch me."

This is for her own good.

She's already proven her inability to control that piece-of-shit rental car, and the roads weren't even as bad yesterday as they are now. The fact that she made it down here tonight at all was probably luck.

And luck wears out.

Especially when the storm is only going to get worse over the next two days.

I can't be responsible for letting her drive away again into *this*.

I couldn't live with myself if anything happened to her.

Back here, with the high, thick trees offering some protection, the accumulation isn't as bad, and the well-worn path I take back and forth every day makes it fairly easy for me to carry her toward my place. But once the storm hits in full force, it won't be so simple to navigate the property, and certainly not the roads.

I still can't believe she drove down in this.

What the hell was she thinking?

She wasn't.

She was acting with her heart instead of her head.

And deep down, I can't really blame her for it.

Not when I know how important the tree always was to her dad, to the family—decorating it together and having it be the center of their family holiday.

Plus, after what I told her today, going home and not having one at the house probably pushed her over the goddamn edge and made her show up here when she should have remained safely inside, watching *National Lampoons Christmas Vacation* and sipping eggnog.

So, really, I'm at least partially to blame for her stupid decision.

And the current consequences of it.

She continues to pound on my back, and the faint light from the single bulb above my front door finally breaks through the swirling snow and trees.

I stomp the last few yards to it, push open the door, step in, and kick it closed behind me with my boot before I set her down on her feet.

Noel wastes no time getting out of my reach. She staggers back a few steps, glaring at me with an intensity I only ever saw from her one other time. "What the fuck do you think you're doing, Luke? You can't keep me here!"

Sucking in a long, slow breath, I turn away from her and lean my axe against the wall, then turn back for the showdown I know is coming. "Yes, I *can*. Because if I send you out onto that road, you're going to *kill* yourself. I already pulled you out of a goddamn ditch once. I'm not going to do it again —this time to find your mangled body inside."

She flinches and retreats another step, apparently not wanting to be reminded of what could very well happen if she tries to drive home—let alone with a *tree* strapped to the roof of that car. "But it's Christmas Eve. My mom is expecting me back. You can't—"

I release a frustrated growl, then turn back and tug the door open.

This is getting us nowhere.

And staying here to argue won't change anything.

"Luke! Where the hell are you going?"

I don't answer her, just pull the solid wood slab closed behind me and quickly snag the key out of my pocket to twist it in the lock.

Of course, she can unlock the deadbolt from the inside— but after eight years, I don't know that she'll remember the trick of how to get it to unstick.

Hopefully, she won't.

But even if she manages to find her way out, there isn't anywhere to go but back to the lot or Mom and Dad's house —and she'll have to make it past me to get to either place.

I shove the key back into my pocket and trek out into the storm, my body heated despite the blustery chill and the freezing cold spray hitting me—both from the exertion of carrying Noel up there and the way she *always* affects me.

As soon as the trees open up, it intensifies to near white-out—already worse than it was twenty minutes ago when she arrived.

She fucking drove in this?

Her irrationality, where this whole thing is concerned, equally pulls at the part of me that loved her and infuriates the other half that has lived with her destruction for years. And now, it's on *me* to call her mother and give her the bad news about her holiday plans.

I make my way down to the barn and slip into the office to use the landline, dialing the number I know by heart with a shaky hand.

It rings twice before her mom answers. "Hello?"

Releasing a little sigh, I summon up the courage to tell this poor woman she's going to be spending Christmas alone. "Hi, Mrs. Jolly."

"Luke? Is that you?"

"Yes."

"What is it? Why are you…Oh, God, Noel was coming down there. Is she all right? Is—"

"She's fine, Mrs. Jolly. But the way the storm has picked up, there's no way I can let her back out on that road. It isn't safe…"

She releases a heavy sigh only a mother can make, followed by a long silence. "I figured as much. She's been gone an hour now, and it looks pretty nasty out there."

"It is." I glance out the open barn doors to where her car is parked, now completely hidden behind a wall of white. "There's no way she should have driven down here."

"I know. Believe me, I tried to reason with her, but—"

I squeeze my eyes closed and drop my forehead into my palm, scrubbing it across my face. "There is no reasoning with Noel when it comes to things like this."

When it comes to anything Christmas.

Noel is obsessive.

She wants everything perfect.

Exactly the way it's always been.

And that's impossible this year with her dad gone.

She's reaching for something she can't attain and, in doing so, making decisions that are putting her at risk.

The woman who was like a second mother to me issues a little laugh. "No, there isn't. That's why I didn't want to press the issue and get into an argument with her on Christmas Eve. I knew I would lose, and she'd go anyway."

My chest tightens at having to say these words to her. "I don't think she's going to get back tonight…"

"I know, Luke."

Bile burns my throat, crawling up as I gear up for the final devastating blow. "And the way they're talking about this going, she likely won't be there tomorrow, either."

She releases a long, deep sigh, and I can feel the weight of it on my chest from two miles down the mountain. "If I can't have Christmas with her, at least she's getting to spend it with you…"

The words are like an axe straight through my chest—the warmth in them, the affection that has always been there, and that lingering hope that something might change even though that's an impossibility. "I don't think she's too happy about it, Mrs. J."

Her laughter floats through the line. "I'm sure she isn't. But I appreciate you keeping her safe, even if she hates you for it."

"Oh, she hates me all right…" *But for a completely different reason. Or now, for this, in* addition *to that.* "I'll get her home as soon as I can in the truck."

"I'll be here. I'm sure not going anywhere in this."

"Stay warm."

"You too, kiddo. And Merry Christmas."

85

"Merry Christmas."

She ends the call, and I drop the phone into the cradle and sit back to stare at it.

What the fuck did I just do?

Locked your ex-girlfriend in your cabin during a blizzard...

Shit.

I wince and rub at my temples and the growing headache there.

It could have been so much worse, though.

If Dad wasn't under the weather and Mom wasn't taking care of him, he would've been the one out on the lot tonight, and he wouldn't have had the strength to stop her from leaving the way I did.

I guess I should count my blessings.

But right now, Noel doesn't seem like one. More like a pissed-off viper, ready to strike the minute I throw that door open.

9
NOEL

My throat burns from screaming for Luke for so long, and my hands and fingers ache from pounding on the door and trying to unlock the deadbolt he used to imprison me in here.

There was some trick to getting the thing unstuck, but it's been eight years since I've been in this place. And while some memories remain painfully crystal clear, the secret to getting the old metal to slide free isn't one of them.

Admitting defeat, I step back from the door, release a heavy, annoyed sigh, and tug off my hat and jacket, tossing them onto the couch with the mitten not already shoved in my pocket as I scan the place where I once spent so much time with him.

I barely recognize it.

Stark.

Empty of anything but the basic necessities.

Lifeless.

Not at all the way his home was when we were together—especially this time of year.

Luke always went overboard with his decorations,

87

decking out the entire cabin with garland, tinsel, holly, wreaths, lights, and *always* with the most beautiful tree he could find on the property.

He always joked that it was the *one* perk of being the owners' son—he got the pick of the lot. But I was *never* to tell Dad that because it would have become a competition between them to get the best tree.

That version of Luke had a holiday spirit that rivaled my own.

Now...there isn't a hint of Christmas anywhere to be found. Just like the man I loved in these walls has disappeared, replaced by one who would throw me over his shoulder and lock me in here simply to prove a point.

Another blast of wind rattles the old windows.

I move over to one that faces the front of the cabin and squint outside, the light from the single bulb above the door reflecting off the snow blowing almost horizontally.

Shit.

My hands curl into fists, and I slam them against the window frame, unleashing some of the building frustration.

I hate to admit it, but Luke may have been right.

It was stupid for me to drive in this.

Even if it is only two miles down the road, I likely never would have made it home if they had taken the time to strap a tree to the car. With the weight on it, coupled with the lack of snow tires or four-wheel drive, that mountain incline would have won.

And I might have ended up wrapped *around* a tree instead of putting one up in Dad's memory.

"Goddamn him."

As if called by my curse, Luke's dark form materializes through the snow, still decked out in a Santa hat and a barely there cutoff shirt, despite the subzero temperatures and blizzard enveloping him.

"And he calls *me* insane…"

It's freezing outside, and it never seems to bother him. But he'll have something else to worry about when he gets in here—a very angry me.

I move to the door to greet him—but definitely *not* the way I used to. There will be no throwing my arms around him and getting him naked to warm him up. For a brief moment, I eye the axe he left, but the lock flips open, stalling any revenge plans for the blade.

He pushes the door in, and I cross my arms over my chest, tapping my foot as I glare at him the second he steps through the jamb.

The evergreen eyes as deep and fathomless as the forest surrounding us stare back at me, now more grinchy than the stunningly beautiful I always found them before. He slams the door behind him and throws the deadbolt again, securing us inside.

Snow melts on his warm skin, water dripping down across his bulging biceps, pecs, and abs.

He reaches up and swipes it off his face.

"Where the hell did you go?"

Scowling, he tugs the hat off his head and tosses it unceremoniously against the wall near the door. "To close up the lot and call your mother."

My anger at him evaporates at the mere mention of her, replaced instantly by the heavy guilt of knowing I've left her to spend Christmas alone.

"You called my mom?"

He offers an annoyed glare, wiping away more of the melting snow from his body. "Of course I did. Did you really think I was going to let her worry about you?"

"Well, no, I…"

Honestly, I hadn't thought about what he might have stalked off to do.

I was so angry at his caveman antics that I hadn't even considered how I would get in touch with Mom since cell phones don't work on the property.

He runs a hand through his hair, rubbing at the back of his neck where I dug my nails into him as hard as I could. "She knows you're here and that you're safe."

At least from the storm.

Being stuck in this small cabin with this man feels very, very unsafe at the moment.

"Did you tell her you kidnapped me?"

He snorts, letting his hand fall to his side. "I did *not* kidnap you."

"Really?" I raise a challenging brow. "And what would you call refusing to let me leave, throwing me over your shoulder, and locking me in here with no means of escape?"

Luke studies me for a moment, his gaze drifting from my soaked boots that are tracking water all over his wood floors, up my now-wet leggings, and over the ugly sweater Mom knitted for me, finally settling on my face. "Doing what you couldn't for yourself—keeping you safe. Your judgment was—"

"Was *what?*"

He drops his head back, staring at the high ceiling of the A-frame for a second before he returns his gaze to me. "You couldn't be objective about this." That hardness in his eyes breaks slightly, the tiniest hint of something resembling what I used to see there peeking through. "Not when it's tied to your father's memory."

Anger heats my blood as I take a step toward him. "What would you know about my father's memory? You couldn't even be bothered to come to the funeral."

His jaw tightens, a muscle there ticing violently. He fists his hands at his sides—opening and closing them a half dozen times as he examines me as if he's contemplating offering a response.

But I don't know what he could possibly say.

We were together romantically for six years.

Beyond that, he's known my father since the day he was born, and he couldn't put aside his grumpy, reclusive, asshole-ish behavior to come say his goodbyes and pay his respects. To offer any hint of concern for Mom or me. To show at all that he ever cared.

Finally, he releases a long sigh. "I was there, Noel…"

"Where?"

"I was at the funeral."

"No"—I shake my head, running through every single minute of that day in my head—"you weren't."

I may have been in a haze of despair, but I most *certainly* would have remembered Luke Crisp being there.

It would have been impossible to forget.

"Yes, I *was*, Noel." He shakes his head, his broad shoulders rising and falling. "But I didn't know if you wanted me there. I didn't want to upset you further. So, I stayed up on the hill behind the old oak near the mausoleum, watched from there, and I took off before you could see me."

My heart stutters in my chest as he continues.

"I loved your father, too, Noel." He swallows thickly. "I wanted to say goodbye to him—"

"But you couldn't to *me*?"

The question comes out on a sob I can't keep down anymore. Eight damn years of anguish finally boiling over— impossible to keep bottled up anymore. Not now that we've been placed in this pressure cooker.

He flinches, squeezing his eyes closed.

"You never actually said those words, Luke. You never said goodbye, just dumped me like I meant nothing. Like we were just a 'thing' that you had outgrown and were over."

I toss his words from yesterday back at him like a poisoned arrow, hoping it hits the mark and that it hurts him as much as it did me.

When he reopens his eyes, his brows draw low, but it isn't pain that darkens the green to an almost black. It's confusion. "What do you mean, when I broke up with *you*? *You* broke up with *me*."

I gape at him, my mind spinning. "I most certainly did not."

Luke takes a step toward me, his huge body trembling enough to be visible.

Apparently, we're going to do this now.

Right here.

When we have nowhere to run and no way to get away from each other.

We're finally going to hash it out and say what we should have a long fucking time ago.

"I did not *end* things with you, Noel. You *left*." He motions backward, vaguely in the direction of the highway. "You drove away and didn't look back, started your new life in a new fucking country without me."

I snort and throw up my hands. "You say that like I moved to Bali. It's Toronto. Canada is closer to Wisconsin than most of the rest of the United States is."

He grits his teeth, as if biting back words he doesn't want to say. But he clearly has some crazy, warped recollection of what happened that day because nothing he is saying is making *any* sense.

"And I didn't just drive away, Luke. I *begged* you to come with me, and you said no."

He throws up his hands this time and shrugs. "What was I supposed to do there, Noel, in a massive city like Toronto, while you were at work every day? Sit around and twiddle my thumbs?" His arms spread wide. "*This* is my life. This farm, Mistletoe, helping Mom and Dad. And you wanted me to walk away from all of it, to go sit there and do *nothing*."

"It was my dream job, Luke. It still *is* my dream job—"

"You could work PR anywhere."

Frustration boils over, and I stomp my still-booted foot. "Not for an NHL team! You *knew* how much I loved hockey. How I always dreamed of working for one of the teams. I can't believe you expected me to give up that opportunity."

"Oh, no…" He holds up a hand, shaking his head. "Don't do that. Don't put that on me. I didn't *expect* anything. I *wanted* you to choose me, to understand how important the legacy of this farm is to my parents and to me. I've never done *anything* else, Noel. All I know how to do is grow trees and swing an axe." He scoffs. "Seriously, how did you imagine that going? Me in Toronto with you?"

I open my mouth to respond, but I don't have an answer to that question.

"Exactly." He scowls. "You have no idea."

My lips quiver, all the pain of our breakup rushing back like a tidal wave that threatens to drown me. "We would've figured it out. That's what I told you then, too. We could have made it work. You wouldn't even *try*. That's all I was asking. I was asking you to choose *us*."

I didn't intentionally use his own words to make my point, but they seem to hit the mark.

His shoulders sag slightly, his whole body softening with a resignation that I have felt for years—the realization that it was a fruitless effort.

He sighs and bends down to untie his boots, remove them, and place them beside the door before turning back to me. "And we're right back where we were that night, aren't we? In the same fucking spot, having the same argument that has no resolution."

It certainly appears that way.

Same positions.

Same argument.

But nothing about this place where we're having it looks like it did back then.

I scan the cabin—not because I haven't already examined almost every inch since he locked me in but because continuing to stare at Luke is making it harder to regain control over my emotions. "I love what you've done with the place. So festive."

He stalks past me to the kitchen, opens a cabinet, and pulls out a bottle of bourbon and a glass.

"It seems a lot has changed. You certainly have."

Turning slightly, he glances over his shoulder at me. "You've been gone a long time."

I have been...but this isn't just a little shift. Not natural growth or changing preferences.

This is like someone else who merely *looks* like the Luke Crisp I knew my entire life snuck in during the night and replaced that one, took over his life without regard for anything he once cared about, and did everything he could to push those people away and destroy anything tangible.

"The Luke I knew loved Christmas, loved working the lot with his parents and tending to the trees. But you, you don't even have one in here." I glance at the Santa hat on the floor near the door. "And my guess is that hat and mistletoe on your jeans were your mom's doing...an insistence that you show some holiday spirit if you were potentially coming in contact with customers on the lot, rather than anything you *wanted* to do."

He pours a drink and downs it, hissing slightly before he sets the glass on the counter. "You're right, Noel. A lot has changed." Pushing off the butcher block, he turns to face me fully. "You don't have the right to come in here and criticize me anymore, to question how I live my life. You gave up that right when you left."

"And you gave up the right to toss me over your shoulder like a fucking caveman and treat me like a child you need to protect when you didn't come after me."

Something flashes in his gaze, and he smacks his palm on the counter, making me flinch. "Come after you?" A sardonic laugh slips from his lips, and he shakes his head. "Oh, God, Noel, you have no fucking idea."

"I have no idea what?"

Muttering something under his breath, he pours himself another drink and glances back at me, trepidation filling his gaze more now than anger. "I did come after you."

My back stiffens, his words taking a minute to really register. "What? No, you didn't. I left the next day, and I never heard from you or saw you again until yesterday."

He sighs and runs his hands through his hair. "You didn't see me, but I saw you."

What the hell is he talking about?

Nothing is making any sense, and the more he talks, the more twisted my head becomes around the memories I have and the things he's saying that seem so impossible and wrong.

"What do you mean?"

His hand tightens around his glass. "I came to Toronto."

My gut twists. "When?"

"A week or so after you left, right before New Year's, after I had helped Mom and Dad take down the sales lot."

I stand speechless, staring at him, waiting for some sort of explanation.

"I got your address from your mom, and I showed up at your place up there." He lifts his glass and takes a drink, staring into the amber liquid rather than looking at me. "And

I saw you coming out of the building as my cab pulled up outside."

"Why didn't you stop me, let me know you were there?"

Luke peers up and offers a tight smile that doesn't reach his eyes. "Because I saw how happy you were to be there. You were laughing and smiling, talking with somebody on the phone." His shoulders rise and fall again. "I came up there to try to convince you to come home, but once I saw you like that, I knew I was going to fail. You didn't seem at all affected by the fact that we had broken up, or fought, or whatever the hell we did. And I knew in that moment that I'd already lost you."

A single tear slips from my eye and travels down my cheek, and I reach up with a trembling hand to swipe it away. "I..."—I release a heavy breath—"I had no idea."

"Why would you?" He takes a long pull from his glass, leaning back against the counter and watching me process what he just told me. "You never would've come back. There was no point in telling you."

"But my mom and dad didn't say anything, either."

"Probably for the same reason."

His gaze meets mine, and I choke on the inevitable question, struggling to get it out.

"Would...would you have stayed? If you had gotten out of the cab, if we had spoken, if I had asked you to, would you have stayed in Toronto with me?"

Luke squeezes his eyes closed, his grip on the rocks glass tightening so much that his knuckles whiten. He remains like that for so long that my legs begin trembling hard enough for me to grip the back of the couch for support.

When he opens his eyes again, I know what his answer will be before he even says it, but it still doesn't prepare me for the single word that destroys me all over again.

"No."

10

THE MISTLETOE GRINCH

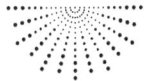

Noel sucks in a sharp breath, staggering back a half step. Her already pale cheeks whiten even more, as if my answer sucked the very life from her. She presses her hands over her chest—smack dab on the grinning Santa's face on that damn ugly sweater.

It should look ridiculous on her.

Because it is *really* fucking ugly—with the gaudy fluff balls dangling all over it, the oversized rose-colored cheeks on the big man, and the silver and gold yarn Mrs. Jolly used to make it reflecting the orangey glow from the fireplace.

But Noel could be wearing an old potato sack and make it look like a damn ball gown—or nothing and make me completely forget all the reasons I said "no" in the first place.

She's always been one of the most beautiful and strongest women I've ever known, but now she's acting like I cut straight through her mom's knitting work to her heart with that single word.

Fuck...

I regret how my answer hurt her, but it's the truth. Lying

97

to her about it, telling her I would have stayed, that things could have been different, won't change anything.

Not then.

Certainly not now.

We would still be standing here at an impasse. Hurting each other by doing what's best for us individually but destroys us as a whole.

I take another long sip of my drink, trying to figure out how to deal with this woman now that we're trapped in this space together, forced to confront the past we both ran from.

Her to Canada; me to this cabin where I could hide.

Lot of good it did...

All it took was her lifting her head and meeting my gaze from inside that car on the embankment for every wall I've built to protect myself over the last eight years to crumble instantly.

Tears stream down her cheeks, and she swallows in a way that almost looks painful. "I knew you wouldn't stay. Just... hearing you actually say it hurts a lot more than I thought it would after all this time."

There are so many things I want to say in response.

Words that have burned like acid inside my chest for almost a decade. But telling her any of it would only make this already tense situation worse—for both of us.

Instead, I ask her the question I know the answer to already. Because maybe—just maybe—once *she* voices the truth, she'll understand that this isn't something we can simply talk out. That I am not the only one to blame for how we fell apart.

"Would *you* have come back with *me*? If I had approached you that day, if I had begged and told you how much I loved you and needed you here. Would you have returned to Mistletoe?"

I brace for impact.

Steel myself for what is coming so she won't see me break down in front of her.

Noel presses her lips together in a firm line, wrapping her arms around herself and hugging tightly, like she's trying to physically hold herself together as much as I am. "No."

And there isn't any further explanation needed.

I wouldn't have stayed.

She wouldn't have come back.

It absolutely would *not* have mattered if either of us had done anything differently then—or now.

That doesn't make it hurt any less or make it any easier to be in this room with her.

I need space.

Air that isn't filled with her peppermint shampoo scent.

Some way to get my head around the fact that wanting Noel, even loving her, will never, ever be enough to make it work.

"Yeah…" I down the last of my drink and release a heavy sigh, dropping my head low. "That's what I thought."

I push off the counter and make my way to the bathroom without looking at her again. If I did, I might go to her, pull her into my arms, bury my face in those luscious golden waves, and breathe her in. Then do something far worse…

Like let myself love her again.

I close the bathroom door and lean against it, clenching my eyes closed and listening for anything from her.

She doesn't make any sound out in the living room.

All I can hear is the blood rushing in my ears from the pumping of the heart I wasn't sure I possessed anymore as it thunders against my ribs.

The need to wash away the pain, to cleanse myself of these feelings, wants, desires, and needs that will only make the agony worse, finally draws me across the small bathroom and to the glass-enclosed shower.

I flip on the water as hot as it will go and strip, stepping in while the spray is still cold enough to sting my heated skin.

Maybe it's exactly what I need to wake myself up from this nightmare I've brought upon myself by bringing her here.

You should have taken her to Mom and Dad's...

Hindsight is twenty-twenty.

It might have been the best course of action to keep her as far away from me as possible, but then again, it would have exposed her to whatever crud Dad has and risk her getting sick when she's only home with her mother for a week.

There's no way to undo it now, anyway.

Not with the way this storm seems intent on keeping us trapped in this cabin together for the foreseeable future.

Going outside again in this would be insane, even for me.

So is bringing the woman who broke your heart to the place where you spent your most intimate shared moments with her...

"Fuck..."

And as the water finally starts to heat, I allow the warmth to soak into my sore muscles, releasing the tiniest bit of the tension that has felt like it would make me snap since the moment she drove back into my life yesterday.

Christ, was it really only one day ago?

It feels like I've been tortured by her presence for years instead of a few dozen hours.

And I thought I had eradicated that part of me that cared.

I believed I had completely swept away those little shards of my heart that she shattered, and I was *confident* there was nothing left of it. But *one fucking day* of having her back in my life has undone all the work I've put into the last eight years.

Releasing a frustrated groan, I turn to face the shower-head, letting the scalding-hot water beat against my chest and flow down to my cock that doesn't seem to want to get on board the "you can't have her" train.

No amount of chastising myself for it will make the traitor go down.

My attraction to that woman will *never* die.

Not until the day I do.

Which makes the fact that I can't take my aching cock in my hand and do anything about it a thousand times more painful.

"Fuck! Fuck! FUCK!"

I lash out, knocking free the bottles from the small cutout shelf to clatter near my feet, then slamming my palms against the tile in front of me and dropping my head under the spray.

The bathroom door flies open almost instantly, like maybe she followed me and had been standing just on the other side when I lost my shit.

I jerk my gaze toward it, frozen in place by what I find.

Noel stands there, wild, concerned eyes scanning the small space until they land on me.

They flare wide.

She sucks in a sharp breath but doesn't move.

My cock twitches under her assessment, and I reach out and swipe my hand over the fogged glass to better see her. Those baby blues of hers follow the movement and linger over my body as if she's examining a work of art.

Silence broken only by the water pelting the tile and the bottles fills the few feet between us.

"Noel?"

"Shit." Her eyes flare, and she spins around, shaking her head as she reaches out to grip the doorjamb. "I'm so sorry. I heard a crash and—"

"And thought you needed to come to my rescue?"

It would be funny under any other circumstances...

If having Noel in here while I'm naked and hard and wanting her wasn't so agonizing.

"Umm..." Noel glances over her shoulder, keeping her eyes on mine instead of letting them drift lower, as they had before. "I was just worried..."

I push off the tile, rising to my full six-five height, and turn to face her—nothing but the single pane of glass and a few steps separating us. "You don't have to worry about me, Snowflake. I'm a big boy."

Her gaze drops, and she quickly jerks her head back to face the main cabin, her fingers tightening on the wooden doorframe. "Even big boys can still get hurt...at least, those who let themselves feel anything."

That final added comment kills any playful retort I had.

She really believes that...

"You think I don't feel anything? That it didn't hurt me, too?"

"That what didn't?"

"Us. Breaking up. Losing you." I release a humorless laugh that echoes off the tile. "It fucking destroyed me."

Her back stiffens. "You seem to be doing pretty fine."

"Fine?" I snort and shake my head, fisting my hands at my sides as the water cascades over me, keeping me warm as the conversation and her belief that I'm "fine" chills my blood. "Turn around, Noel."

A shiver rolls through her, and her nails bite into the wood under them, as if she's using it as an anchor to keep her from following through with my request. "I don't think that's a very good idea, Luke."

The waver in her voice makes my hard cock throb.

"Why not? It isn't anything you haven't seen before, and I don't like talking to your back."

Seconds tick by.

Then a minute.

Almost two before she finally releases her death grip on the door frame and slowly turns to face me.

Pink colors her cheeks—a flush caused by the heat and humidity in the tight space or perhaps by the eyeful she's getting.

"Do you think *this* is *fine,* Noel?" I spread my hands out wide, absently referencing my life in general. "Do you think how I live is? You want to know why I hate Christmas so much? Do you want to know why I can't stand to be around the people and the music and all the merriment?"

She doesn't answer, just stands silent, watching me like I might somehow pose a threat.

Maybe I do.

God knows she does to me.

The worst one I've ever faced.

Far more serious than any mountain lion or bear or coyote that might wander onto the mountain. This woman won't maul me—she will devour my soul again.

"I hate Christmas because it reminds me of *you.* Because this whole damn town reminds me of you. You were always the walking personification of Christmas spirit, and I didn't have the strength to think about you and not fucking crumble every day."

Her whole body trembles as she absorbs my words.

"Shit." I scrub a hand over my face and force myself to look away from her, up at the hot spray to let it wash away the regret.

Because I shouldn't have said all that.

I shouldn't have made such a stupid admission when it won't change anything, when it never could.

Finally, her soft, unsteady voice floats to me over the sound of the rushing water. "But you loved Christmas, too."

I shake my head, returning my gaze to hers. Any hope I had of keeping those unsaid things that way completely gone now. "No, Noel. I loved *you*. I loved spending Christmas with you, doing all those things together. Going to the tree lighting. Wrapping gifts. Singing carols. All the stupid bullshit that now nauseates me because every fucking minute of it, I think about you, what I had, and what I lost. And God"—I release a sardonic laugh—"it's been almost a decade, and I can't get over it. I can't get over *you*."

And now the truth is out there, hanging somehow frozen in the warm, humid air.

She stares at me for so long that I wonder if she's actually going to say anything. So long that I reach out and flip off the water, sliding the glass shower door open to step out onto the mat. So long that I have time to grab a towel and wrap it around my waist before she finally shows signs of life again.

Her tongue darts out across her lips, and Noel approaches me slowly, tentatively, like I'm a wounded, caged animal and she's worried I'm going to lash out at her if she unlocks the gate and unleashes me.

She's probably not far off.

That's how I felt since the moment she left, since the minute she said she was taking the job in Toronto: wounded, utterly fucking destroyed.

Like I'm half a man, half the person I was when she was here with me.

Like I'm not fully human.

Like my goddamn heart is three sizes too small.

Or maybe I don't have one anymore.

Maybe she always held it, and when she left, she took it with her.

Noel stops just short of reaching me, twisting her hands together in front of her like she doesn't know what to do with them. Her eyes shimmer, but she manages to hold back her tears as she examines my face carefully. "Do you really mean all that?"

"Fuck, Noel…"

I squeeze my eyes closed and release a heavy, deep breath that I feel all the way into my bones. When I open them again, she's shifted closer, and I can feel the heat of her body radiating into my damp skin.

Her bottom lip quivers. "Do you?"

It feels like a trap.

Bright-red warning lights flash in my head.

Alerting me of the danger.

Cautioning that moving forward will be at my own risk.

But I can't see any of it when I look at her, so nervous as she awaits my answer.

"That's how I've always felt about you, our entire lives, Snowflake. You know that. The fact that we didn't get together until we were sixteen had more to do with me not thinking I was good enough for you and nothing to do with me not wanting you before that. I wanted you *always*. So, yes, I meant every fucking thing I said."

And my body urges me to do something really stupid.

I reach out and caress her cheek, the skin so soft and flawless against my calloused hand.

The feeling is so familiar.

So goddamn good.

It's like a drug seeping into my veins.

My cock twitches against the towel, my still-wet body primed for the very bad idea that has taken root in my head.

The only question is whether or not Noel wants to take the trip to fuck-ourselves-over-ville with me.

11

NOEL

Rough calluses skate over my skin, sending shivers down my spine. The familiarity of those gritty patches makes me lean into Luke's touch when, really, I should be pulling away.

Just like I never should have come into this room.

I should have left him alone.

Because he can certainly take care of himself.

His rock-hard, work-honed body proves that—at least physically.

But the way he talks proves he's as vulnerable and feels just as deeply as I do.

And it's too late to regret letting him touch me now, too late to go back when I'm standing in front of him and he has this yearning in his eyes, the same one that always unraveled me, that I don't stand a fucking chance against.

His intention is abundantly clear—as are the reasons we shouldn't.

"I…but…what about—"

Luke slides his thumb across my lips, silencing me, and

instinctively, I open and let it slip between them, biting down in a way that makes his hard cock jump against me.

"Whatever you were about to say. Don't."

He's asking me—no *begging* me—to forget all the reasons this is a terrible idea, all the reasons we should never have gotten back into each other's orbits, let alone allowed ourselves to be drawn in this close.

I so badly want to go along with it.

To fall back into his arms.

His care.

To experience his touch and his kiss again.

To have all those things I lost and never regained in the eight years we have been apart.

To take what he always so freely gave me.

He pulls his thumb from between my lips and glides his other hand down to my hip, squeezing there gently. "All you have to do is say the word, Snowflake."

Damn him.

Another shiver arrives with the old nickname, which seems so fucking ironic now, considering how we got into this situation. The storm that has us trapped together—confronting the past and our feelings for each other—continues to rage the same way the war inside me does.

He dips his head, feathering his lips across mine.

A question.

Not demanding anything I wouldn't freely give him.

And all it takes is that soft touch, that whisper of a promise for me to unravel completely.

Any willpower I may have had to resist him, any anger I may have harbored for how things went down, any lingering doubts…all of it evaporates the moment I push up onto my tiptoes and press my lips to his fully.

He groans into my mouth, using his strong arm to tug me up against him completely. His cock twitches between us, and heat flares at the apex of my thighs, the ache confirming my body is clearly one hundred percent on board with what my mind has decided is somehow a good fucking idea.

Even when we both *know* it isn't.

This won't change anything.

About where we are in our lives.

About where we stand with each other.

It's simply giving in to old feelings that we maybe never resolved.

I should be more worried about it, but I can't be as one of his hand tunnels through my hair to support my upper back and he uses the other to reach down and lift me easily into his strong arms.

My crotch settles against his, and I wrap my legs around his waist, groaning when his hard length presses in *exactly* the right place to make me throb.

The pressure there only builds as he stalks from the bathroom out into the main room of the cabin, but instead of heading for the bed against the far wall, like I would have anticipated, he beelines for the fireplace.

What he knows has always been my favorite spot.

Both just to sit and read.

To soak up the warmth.

And also, to make love.

Something about the bearskin rug spread out in front of it and the heat emanating from the crackling fire has always fueled my passion.

Luke apparently plans to take advantage of that—and I have no plans to stop him.

It only takes a few steps to get us there, and he easily sinks to his knees, then uses his hand at my back and behind my head to lower me down gently while his mouth takes mine torturously.

Long, languid strokes of his tongue drag a little frustrated mewl from deep in my chest, and I grind up against him, seeking more friction, more of *him*.

He grins against my lips, then pulls back, his eyes filled with lust and the tiniest hint of trepidation.

I know why it's there, after what he just said to me. The true pain I felt emanating from every single word is still very real for this lumberjack. Now I understand that Luke was destroyed by me leaving, by the end of our relationship, maybe even more so than I was, and that agony never left him.

It was something I always carried deep inside my chest— a scar that wouldn't heal. But for him, it was so much more— a gaping wound that festered and became infected with the bitterness I've seen from him since I arrived back in Mistletoe.

And all of it was my fault.

The real pain still etched on his face as he stares down at me makes my breath catch.

Luke really was suffering, and I never made any attempts to ease his pain, to bridge that chasm I created by leaving him and this town.

All this time, I let myself believe he wanted it to end, that he sabotaged us by refusing to even consider moving with me. But that decision killed him just as much as it did me.

I reach up and thread my fingers through his thick, dark hair. "Can you ever forgive me?"

If he had been the one who left, if I had remained in Mistletoe as miserable and hurt as he did, I'm not sure I could easily forget. Clearly, he hasn't. But I *need* his forgiveness as much as I need him to understand that I never meant to hurt him.

Luke slips his leg between mine, wedging it up until his hot skin presses against my core—the thin material of my leggings allowing that warmth to seep through easily. He dips his head, grazing his teeth along the shell of my ear.

A full-body shiver makes me arch into him, my clit brushing against his thick, heavily muscled thigh as his cock presses into my belly.

His breath flutters the hair at my nape. "That depends on how well you beg…"

"Beg?" The word comes out breathy, almost a moan, but my brain struggles to process what he's asking for. "Beg for forgiveness?"

His tongue snakes along my neck, raising goosebumps in its wake as he grasps my hip tightly in one hand and fists the other in my hair. "No, Snowflake, for my cock. I want Mrs. Parsons to hear you at the base of the mountain."

"B-but that old bat couldn't hear a freight train barreling down on her…"

Luke nips at my ear, sliding his hand from my hip to my waistband, then down the front of my pants to cup my already embarrassingly wet pussy that he can undoubtedly feel through the thin barrier my thong offers. "Then you better be…*Really*." Nip. "*Fucking*." Another. "*Loud*."

He bites down hard enough to make me jerk under him.

Oh, God…

This is the Luke I've missed.

The confident, rightfully arrogant, masterful lover who always gets what he wants but ensures I get mine first.

He always demanded so much from me, yet he *never* left me wanting. Ensuring my own pleasure over his.

But only if I complied.

He pulls back long enough to tug the waistband of my leggings and my thong down my legs and toss them to the side, leaving me in my sweater in the firelight. "You still have far too many clothes on—though, I really do want to fuck you in this thing." He flicks Santa's bulbous red nose with one finger playfully, then grins. "Maybe next round."

Fuck.

Luke is already planning *rounds.*

That means I am in big, *big* trouble this Christmas.

He grasps the hem of my sweater and tugs it up and off, letting it crumple next to us on the floor. His blazing green eyes rake over me in the dancing light from the fireplace, the heat in them matching that emanating from the stone hearth.

How did I ever think they looked cold?

His warm, hard body pressed to mine proves he's not the man who gave me that icy reception back to town. He's gone, replaced by the scalding inferno of shared need.

Bracing himself over me with one hand, he drifts a rough palm up my inner thigh. Goosebumps break out across my skin, and I tremble as he inches closer to the spot I want him so badly.

He reaches my slick core and slips two thick fingers inside me easily, curling them up in a come-hither motion and slowly gliding his calloused fingertips along the perfect spot only he's ever been able to find.

"Luke..." I moan and shift, lifting my hips to give him better access even as I need to voice my protest. It's been so long. I can't disappoint him. I won't. "I don't know if I can—"

He feathers his lips across mine, sliding his thumb across my clit and making me buck on his hand. "You *can*, Noel. You used to come so beautifully like this all the time for me."

Only, this man isn't trying to make me come.

Luke is trying to make me *squirt...*

"I haven't since—" I bite back the admission, tightening my thighs around to try to stay his sensual assault.

His eyes meet mine, dark brows furrowing. "Since when, Snowflake?"

A single tear trickles from my cheek—all the pent-up need and anguish about to boil over. "Don't make me say it."

He kisses it away. "I need to hear it, Noel. Just like I need every whimper, every moan, every gasp, every scream. I need them all."

"I haven't come like *that* since the last time we were together."

A slow grin spreads across his face. "Then loud shouldn't be a problem."

Fuck.

I am in so much trouble with this man.

The moment I let him touch me, I knew I was done for.

And I'm right.

He has always played me so well, using his hands and wielding his cock as expertly as he does his axe. Driving to exactly the right spot. Sinking deep. Striking over and over again until I split in two.

Which is clearly his goal now.

The glint in his eye is one I recognize means trouble for me if I want to maintain any semblance of control.

But who am I kidding?

I gave over control to him the moment I fell in love with him, and I never got it back. Evidenced by the way my body so easily responds to his ministrations. How quickly it remembers that calloused touch and what it can do.

How it yearns for it.

Aches for it.

Demands it.

My hips roll up against his hand, seeking more as he glides his thumb around and across my clit. Coiling me tighter. Drawing me higher. His fingertips deep inside me working that magical spot.

He watches my face, his brow furrowing. "I'm not hearing you, Snowflake. Stop biting that lip and let it go."

Hell.

I hadn't even realized I was doing it.

But sure enough, my bottom lip aches where its pinned under my teeth, and I release it at his command.

Almost instantly, a needy, undignified groan slips out, and he captures it in his mouth in a soul-searing kiss that steals my remaining breath.

When he pulls away, that grin returns. "That's better." He dips his head low to flutter a barely there kiss across my lips. "And I know what will really get you to open back up to me."

Open what?

My mouth.

My legs.

My heart?

His intent is clear on the first two, but it's that final one that makes me tense under him.

I don't know that I'd survive giving *that* to Luke Crisp again.

But I don't have time to consider it any further before he slides back and pushes my knees wide with his strong, broad shoulders. He drags the flat of his tongue across my clit in one long, slow motion that almost snaps me in half.

I arch into it, seeking more, needing it all in one greedy instant. "Oh, fuck!" I gasp, struggling to suck in any air. "Oh, God! I need…"

The words fail me, replaced by a strangled groan.

Yet I know he will give it to me.

That was one thing Luke *never* failed in—providing mind-bending pleasure that bordered on pain. The kind of hot, sweaty sex that left me boneless and floating in a haze I never wanted to come out of.

We were practically kids then—only twenty-two when we parted ways. I can't imagine what new tricks he must have learned since then that he plans to torture me with.

He swirls his tongue in tiny, tight circles over that nub, his fingers gliding back and forth inside me, applying hard pressure perfectly to ensure he will get what he wants—me screaming as I come down his throat.

It's already starting.

That low heat that slowly spreads out until it ignites into an inferno that can't be contained—a rush that the man crushed between my thighs can never get enough of.

The wind buffets the cabin, rattling the windows and whistling down the chimney, but all I can hear is the sound of my own unsteady breaths, Luke's approving moans, and the needy mewls that keep slipping from my lips.

Luke laps at me around his fingers, moving them faster, dragging harder, flicking his tongue against my clit rapid-fire until my head is thrashing back and forth against the bearskin rug beneath us.

I bury my hands in his hair, tugging on the strands as I cry out an anguished plea. "Please. Fuck! Just…fucking hell, Luke…"

He chuckles against my flesh, clearly enjoying the way he has me dangling over that dangerously high precipice. "Come for me, Snowflake." Another flick over my most sensitive spot. "I'm dying to taste you again." A languid glide across it. "To drink you down." His searing gaze meets mine, holding me captive as much as his strong body is. "I'm a fucking parched man who needs the life-giving waters your cunt provides."

Sweet, bloody Christ.

There it is.

That spark.

That rush of heat.

The snap of the tension before it explodes.

My head drops back, my mouth falling open on a scream as I finally come, unleashing everything that's been pent up for the last eight years on the man who demanded I do just that.

Luke groans his approval, drinking me down, lapping up every fucking drop of my orgasm as he continues to work his fingers inside me and across my hypersensitive clit to drag out my release longer than I thought possible.

Before I even start coming down from it, he shifts over me and pulls away his hand, replacing it with the head of his cock.

He pushes inside me in a single, hard thrust.

12

LUKE

Noel's cunt still ripples, her orgasm continuing as I drive into her. I bottom out, and her head falls back, mouth dropping open on a strangled moan that rolls over me like a tidal wave. My entire body trembles, and she clenches around me so tightly that I almost come on the spot.

Eight fucking years without this woman.

Without this feeling.

Without her kiss, her touch.

Without *her.*

It takes every ounce of willpower—more than I ever thought I possessed—not to unload deep inside of her immediately, not to take that pleasure for myself instead of giving her more.

But it's all I've ever wanted.

To make her happy.

To see her eyes light up and pleasure cross her face, the same way it did today staring up at the tree in the town square, when she looks at me.

I draw my hips back and plunge into her again, and the

way she gasps and tightens around me assures me I'm doing just that. But I need to *see* it, too.

"Look at me, Noel."

She whimpers, and I still my hips until she complies, allowing her lids to flutter open. "Please, Luke, don't stop…"

"Oh, Snowflake…" I drop my head and capture her mouth and her next groan as my hips slam into hers and I grind my pelvis against her engorged clit, ensuring the most contact possible. Reluctantly tearing my lips from hers, I brush my thumb across them. "I have absolutely *no* intention of stopping until you have to spend all of Christmas Day on this rug or in my bed because you can't walk straight."

Lust flares hot in her gaze, that burning desire I feel raging through my body now reflected back at me.

Her hands score down the back of my neck, making my cock twitch inside of her. "That's your plan?"

I raise a brow at her, stilling my hand on her cheek. "Do you have a problem with it?"

A coy smile tilts her lips slightly, and she wraps her legs around my back, angling them to allow me to slip the tiniest bit deeper.

"Fuck…"

Noel feels even better than I remember, better than I thought possible.

Every dream.

Every memory I ever had of this woman was such perfection that I convinced myself none of it could be real, that the memories were fake. Something I built up and created in my head because nothing that perfect could possibly exist.

But what I had in my head was nothing compared to the real thing.

I take her mouth again, needing that connection as much as the one currently linking us together.

She tastes like she smells.

Peppermint, lust, and everything I ever wanted.

I pull back and plunge into her again, eliciting a throaty moan that almost undoes me.

Touching her was a terrible idea, bringing her here, thinking there was any chance we wouldn't end up like this, that I wouldn't want it. And now that my cock is buried deep inside her, now that I've tasted her again and felt her, I don't know how I'll possibly let her go.

I tunnel my hands into her hair and tug her head up off the floor. With her eyes closed again, I've lost that confirmation I so desperately need that this is *real* and not some mirage brought on by exhaustion and desperation after seeing her yesterday.

"Open. Your. Eyes, Snowflake."

My voice comes out rough, gravelly, full of the desire currently consuming me, and the frantic struggle to keep my body under control long enough to make her come again before I do.

She mewls, rolling her hips to meet mine as I maintain a languid pace. Her lids finally flicker open, and she stares up at me, the light from the fire dancing across her blue orbs, lighting one side of her face so beautifully in the soft glow that she looks like a fucking angel sent here to destroy me.

"You know what I want, Snowflake. What I need you to do…"

I roll my hips and drive up with a hard snap, then withdraw incredibly slowly, only to do it again, the methodic, languid rhythm designed not merely to slow myself down but also to get her there again.

Not in a wicked-hot rush.

A slow build that will rush through her even harder than before.

"I don't think—" She swallows thickly, struggling to keep

her eyes open as I keep moving my hips almost mindlessly. "Luke, I-I-I don't think I can."

"Oh, Snowflake…" I flutter a kiss across her brow, then lock my gaze with hers, holding her there while I continue my long, hard thrusts. "I know you can."

I kiss her deeply, gliding my tongue along her lips until she opens for me and greets mine with her own, twisting and warring, her frustration building to find the thing I want to give her so badly, the thing I never thought I could offer her again.

"You *are* going to come again for me, Noel…and it's going to be as beautiful as the first time, but you're going to do it on my cock. Because I want to feel it." I nip at her bottom lip. "I want to feel your cunt squeezing me, desperate for it."

She twitches against me, nodding her agreement.

And if I keep going like this, it *will* get her there.

Torturously slowly.

But not just agonizing for her.

My cock has never felt so hard. I've never been so close to losing all control. Not in all the years we were together. Not in all the times we did this. Not during my most frantic moment in the past.

I want to drag it out, but I am weak.

A man desperate to see her come again. To allow myself to release everything I've held inside for so long. To fill her and feel complete again.

And I know what she really needs.

What will get her over that edge again, the one that she's fighting so hard to dance along without toppling over it because she fears what it will mean for her heart as much as I do.

Dropping my head low against her ear, I drag my teeth along it, and she bucks. "Get ready, Snowflake."

She whimpers, and I pull back and slip out of her.

Her eyes fly open, her mouth falling agape in protest, but I smack the side of her bare thigh and wait.

I don't need to tell her what I'm asking for.

Noel knows, her eyes flaring as she moves without hesitation, flipping onto her stomach and pushing up onto all fours, offering herself to me the way we always both loved.

And fuck is she stunning.

A Christmas angel...

The fire light dancing across her pale skin, glimmering in her golden hair, flashing off her brilliant, silken ass. I glide my palms over it and across her lower back, up along her spine, and to her shoulders. Every brush of my palms leaves goosebumps and makes her shudder in the best way.

I take her hair in my hand and wrap it around my left wrist, jerking her head back.

She gasps and looks back at me the best she can, cheeks flamed and lips half open, ready to beg.

My free hand collides with her right ass cheek, hard enough to rock her forward, but she comes right back for more.

This time, I give her my cock.

I fit it to her slick core and drive into her again. Only my arm wrapped around her waist and my hand in her hair keep her from collapsing under the force and weight of my thrust.

"Oh, God..."

Her words echo around the space—part plea, part prayer.

And I draw my hips back and do it again.

I angle her back slightly so the head of my cock will hit and drag against that perfect spot deep inside her. She gasps, dropping down onto her forearms and burying her face there.

Jerking on her hair again, harder this time, I force her back up. "No, Snowflake. I want you like this so I can see your face, so you can see mine and you'll know who's fucking you." I lean forward, pressing my chest to her back, kissing her neck. "So you'll never fucking forget it. Never forget me."

It's as stupid an admission as the one I made in the bathroom earlier.

A far more dangerous one, considering she'll be gone in a handful of days and I'll be left with nothing more than the memories of this snowstorm and how she gave herself to me one final time.

Noel shakes her head as much as my grip allows, and a single tear trickles from her eye down her soft cheek. "I never forgot you, Luke—" A little mewl slips out as I drive into her. "How could I—" She gasps as I bottom out deep. "I couldn't ever. I—"

Again and again, I steal her words.

Not because I don't want to hear them or that I don't believe them, but because I'm on the brink of losing control. It's slipping the same way my cock is in her first release.

So fucking slick.

Her body accepts me and everything I have to offer her.

She clenches down on me with each retreat, her body struggling to keep me inside her.

I know she's almost there.

Each slam of my pelvis into her lush ass, each grind deep, drawing her closer.

Her legs start trembling so badly that she has trouble staying up.

I tighten my grip on her waist and her hair, pinning her and holding her steady, watching my wet cock glide in and out of her. "I wish you could see this, Noel, how fucking beautiful you look taking my cock, how soaking wet you are for me." Leaning forward, I kiss the back of her exposed neck, all the way to her ear, as I snap my hips again. "I wish you could feel your cunt. How hot and tight it is, how fucking perfectly you fit me. I wish you knew what fucking torture it's been to be without you…without *this*."

She whimpers at my words, squeezing so hard that I feel that first spurt of cum start to make its way out.

I twist her hair harder and jerk her head back. "I'm not ready for that yet. Not ready to let you go."

And I don't want to examine what I *really* mean by that.

Instead, I pull my hips back until just the head of my cock stays inside her, trying to rein myself in long enough to regain control.

Her eyes flutter open, and she looks back at me, an almost pained look pinching her brow. "But I need it, Luke. I need you. Please give it to me."

"Fucking hell."

That thin cord of control snaps, and I drive into her hard, tightening my grip until I probably bruise her hip and might come away with some strands of her hair, too.

Each slam and retreat grows more frantic, more demanding.

Until her gasps and my own fill the air along with the rattling wind.

Until all I can feel is her cunt and her need and my own.

Until she finally comes, crying out and drawing my own orgasm free with her grasping pussy.

Until I bury myself so deep inside of her that I hope I never find my way out.

It's a beautiful dream, but one that can't last forever.

She sags in my hold, and I can't keep her up anymore, my own body feeling boneless and my head hazy in the after-glow of the cataclysmic release.

Releasing her hair, I wrap my arm around her chest, tugging her fully against me so I can roll to the rug on my side and take her with me without her slamming into the unyielding wooden boards.

My still-hard cock twitches inside her, and she moans and rubs back against me in a way that could get me ready for round two before round one even clears my head.

I nip at her ear from behind her, releasing a little growl. "Stop that."

She peeks over her shoulder at me through thick lashes. "Why?"

"Because I already told you I want to fuck you in that sweater next, and I am not ready to let go of you long enough for you to put it on." I cup her breast in her bra, brushing my thumb over the taut peak, pressing against the silky fabric. "I'm good right where I am for the moment."

A little gasp falls from her lips, and then she giggles. "You were serious about the sweater?"

I bark out a laugh, my body shaking. "I was...it reminds me of that time when you and your mom came to help my mom make Christmas cookies—"

"And we snuck out to the barn for a quickie between batches."

Burying my face in her hair, I inhale that peppermint scent and tighten my grip on her. "You were wearing—"

"The one with the silver bells sewn onto it."

The laughter returns, and I nuzzle her. "That sound every time I slammed into you still rings in my ears."

As do those sounds *she* made before I slid my hand over her mouth to keep her silent in case either of our mothers came looking for us.

Her body goes impossibly still. "That was...our last Christmas together."

A heaviness settles over us, one I feel deep in my soul.

I squeeze her, then pull free with a wince, urging her onto her back so I can prop myself up on my elbow and really *see* her.

"What is your Christmas wish, Snowflake?" I cup her chin

in my hand and tilt her head up, forcing her gaze to meet mine. "What do you want that I am capable of giving you?"

Because there are two things I know I can't do that would be at the top of her list.

I can't bring her father back, and this storm will not let me get her back to her mom in time to celebrate the holiday unless we wake to some miracle.

Noel pulls her bottom lip under her teeth again, considering my question, then relaxes against me, resting her head over my heart. Her breathing evens out, growing softer as she nears sleep. "I just want to have Christmas. A real one…"

NOEL

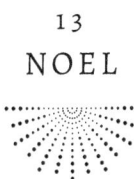

The soft knock on the bathroom door as I'm towel-drying my hair draws my lips into a grin I can barely see through the fogged mirror over the sink.

I reach over and turn the handle, tugging the door open, laughing softly at the almost hesitant look on Luke's handsome face. "Aren't we a little beyond knocking at this point?"

Especially after what he did *in* the shower to me before he climbed out and told me to enjoy the hot water myself for a bit.

Which is precisely what I did for probably far too long.

Even though I could barely stand anymore on my wobbly legs, I accepted his offer for what it was—a chance for me to relax and regroup, maybe to get my head around what had so rapidly happened over the last several hours.

Maybe that's why he's looking a little...different.

Maybe he's questioning everything, too.

Luke grins, that dimple I wasn't sure I'd ever see again popping in his right cheek—a cheek that looks very pink compared to how he appeared when he left me under the scalding spray. Even after another round against the tile and the heat and humidity in here, his skin wasn't this red.

"Luke…what's going on?" Concern suddenly knots in my stomach. "Are you all right?"

He nods slowly, his green gaze traveling over me in the red-plaid flannel shirt he left out on the counter for me —*with* sleeves, considering how cold it is outside and my feelings on his cut-offs. "Everything is perfect. But if you plan on walking around here in just *that*"—his focus dips to my bare legs, the hem of the shirt falling only mid-thigh —"*then* I might be in really, really big trouble."

I already am.

It almost slips out as I stare at the man to whom no other has ever compared.

Not that there have been many.

But the handful of men I've dated since our split never measured up—in any category—to the one devouring me with his gaze.

And even after all this time, I know it isn't merely his lust surging again.

He's up to something—more than just ogling me.

His still-damp hair looks mussed and disheveled, and that pink tint to his cheeks dissipates the longer he stands in the doorway of the steamy bathroom.

I narrow my eyes on him, not allowing his deflection from my original concern. "What's going on?"

He holds out a hand, those deep calluses dark and rough and waiting for me to accept them. "Come see."

What the hell is he up to?

Luke was always great at surprises, but he also knows I hate them.

The anxiety of not knowing what's coming always makes me feel almost nauseated before the big reveal.

And it's starting to churn my stomach now.

I rehang the towel I had been using on my hair, swallowing past the unease, and slid my palm into his unusually cold one.

All night, his touch has been scorching hot, as fiery as his passion.

I open my mouth to ask him about it. Before I can, his grip tightens, and he tugs me up against him firmly. Aligning his entire body to mine, pressing into me like he can't get close enough.

The scent of crisp snow, freshly cut pine, and that masculine musk Luke always carries with him invades my breath.

Luke stares down at me, his eyes glimmering with mischief, as well as the kind of heat he hasn't stopped looking at me with since I got here. He lowers his head, brushing a feather-light, barely there kiss over my forehead. "I know this isn't the Christmas you anticipated, definitely not the one you wanted, but I hope this helps."

"What?"

He pulls back and drags me from the bathroom out into the cabin.

My eyes immediately land on what looks to be about an eight-foot pine now standing in the corner, which was sad and barren when I came into this bathroom. "Luke!" I whip my head around toward him. "What did you do?"

His broad shoulders rise and fall nonchalantly as he watches me with a hint of trepidation in his gaze. "I got you a tree."

I stand awestruck, staring at him, unable to form any sort of words while my head tries to wrap around what he's done.

He steps in behind me and slides his arms around my waist, lowering his chin to the top of my head and squeezing me tightly.

The wind howls, the windows vibrate, and that sharp, high-pitched sound that has been our constant soundtrack since the moment we arrived at the cabin, comes down the chimney again.

I point toward the door. "You went out in *that*?" Luke nods, and I glance up at him. "All the way down to the lot?"

He chuckles low, his chest vibrating against my back, his body heat keeping me warm as much as the fire roaring in the fireplace does. "God, no. I never would have made it in this."

"Then..."—I pull out of his hold and turn to face him —"where did the tree come from?"

One corner of his lips twitches, and he inclines his head toward the front window.

Narrowing my eyes on the storm outside, I slowly make my way across the wooden floors to the same place I stared out, looking for him only hours ago—when I was so fucking mad at him for locking me in here.

Frost coats the glass, and I swipe it away so I can see the forest.

Even with the porch light on, the white-out conditions have taken over, and I can barely see a few feet beyond the cabin.

But what I can make out causes my breath to catch.

The landscape looks very different than it did the last time I stared out this pane. Or maybe I didn't see it because I was too blinded by my rage at the man standing behind me silently now.

A true winter wonderland greets me—the kind of white Christmas my heart always sings for.

Rabbit prints in the fresh accumulation in front of the cabin.

Icicles hang from every snow-covered tree.

And one is missing.

Footprints in the snow lead to a slightly dug-out area...

and a fresh stump where a tree once stood, just in front of the small building Luke calls home.

I glance near my feet next to the door where his wet boots and axe lean, then up to the jacket hanging on a hook above them, dripping from the melting snow sloughing off it.

Oh, my God.

He didn't...

My hands shaking, I turn back to him, utterly speechless. My chest tightens so much it makes it difficult for me to even draw in a breath. "You went out and chopped down a tree for me." I motion over my shoulder with my thumb. "In *this*."

Luke offers another nonchalant shrug, the white T-shirt he put on after our shower pulling tightly across his muscled chest and biceps with the move. "A lot easier than trying to make it down to the lot and drag one that was already cut up here…"

Tears sting my eyes. "Luke, you're insane. Certifiably crazy."

His lips twitch as he shakes his head. "I'm not." The gaze he levels on me doesn't hold any humor, though. He looks dead serious about whatever he's about to say. "What would have been crazy was standing by, watching you be miserable on Christmas Eve, when I could give you the very thing you came down here in *that* for."

He inclines his head toward the tree in question—the absolutely perfect, proportional, postcard-photo Christmas tree standing in the corner. Water drips from it, the snow he wasn't able to remove before dragging it in falling to the wood floors the same way my tears are about to.

They finally slip from my eyes, and I close the distance between us and practically launch myself at him, wrapping my arms around his waist and burying my face against his strong, broad chest.

Luke catches me, presses his face into my hair, holding me tightly and breathing me in.

He doesn't say a word.

He doesn't need to.

A little sob slips from my lips, muffled by his chest. "You really didn't have to do that."

Luke kisses my head, squeezing me. "I really, *really* did."

"But it's freezing out there…"

He chuckles low again. "It definitely isn't pleasant, even for me, who usually wouldn't complain about a little snow and wind, but it would have been worse to have to sit in here and watch you be miserable because I don't have any Christmas spirit."

I pull back and look up at him, pressing my palm against his cheek. "I think we can find some more."

One of his dark brows rises slowly, his skepticism evident. "Do you? I don't have lights or ornaments or any of that anymore. You're lucky I even kept the tree stand out in my shed at the side of the cabin to put that thing up."

That tiny hint of grinchiness seeps into his gaze.

But seeing that only makes my grin bigger. "You *greatly* underestimate my ingenuity…"

He presses a kiss to my lips, letting his linger there, like he's savoring the moment. "Oh, I never underestimate you, Snowflake, but I have no idea what you're talking about or suggesting."

I reluctantly pull out of his hold and walk backward toward the bathroom, my mind racing, ten steps ahead of where I was a moment ago. "I know for a *fact* that there are several things you always have in this cabin this time of year."

He narrows his eyes on me, watching me retreat. "Not sure where you're going with this, Snowflake."

No doubt, the many years he's spent avoiding anything and everything to do with the holiday has left him a little atrophied when it comes to his Christmas decoration knowledge.

"You will…" I slip into the bathroom, pop open the medicine cabinet, and snag what I need from there, then practically giggle as I run to the kitchen and throw open the top cabinet on the left.

"Snowflake…"

The warning and questioning tone in the way he says my name only makes me laugh harder, and I turn back with the jar of popcorn kernels and hold up the dental floss I just snatched.

His eyes widen slightly.

I keep grinning as I set them on the counter and move to the refrigerator, pausing with my hand on it. "Though a lot of things have changed in the last eight years, Luke Crisp would never *not* have his favorite tart holiday treat stocked inside his fridge."

His lips twitch, proving I'm right, and I tug open the refrigerator door and find exactly what I need—a giant Tupperware filled with fresh cranberries from his cousin Dean's farm.

I grab it and hold it up. "I assume he dropped these off a few days ago."

He crosses his arms over his chest and leans his shoulder against the wall, watching me with that grin that could melt off my panties—if I were wearing any.

"So, we have popcorn and cranberries to string, and…" I dart to the other side of the kitchen and tug open a drawer, not at all surprised to see that he hasn't moved anything. Pulling out a package of aluminum foil and the ball of kitchen twine, I hold them up for him. "Foil wrapped around twine would make incredible strings of faux tinsel."

"Plus…" He interrupts my excited ramble and holds up a finger.

I freeze as I wait for him to continue, to see what he's thinking.

He pushes off the wall and walks over to the antique roll-top desk that once belonged to his great-grandfather and has always sat in the far corner of the cabin. I hold my breath as he pulls open a drawer and holds up a stack of white paper and a pair of scissors. "Cut out snowflakes."

My heart stops.

It literally *stops* in my chest as I see the old Luke standing in front of me.

The one who loves Christmas.

The one who loved me.

The one who walked out in a goddamn blizzard to chop down a tree for me...

"I bet it's been a long time since you've made those, Luke."

He laughs as he approaches me and drops a kiss on my forehead. "You have no idea..."

"Oh, I think I do."

I have *no doubt* that Luke hasn't touched *anything* Christmas related since the moment I left for Toronto.

To see him now...

My giggle increases, picturing what the residents of Mistletoe would say if they saw him. "God, could you imagine what anyone would think if they knew that the Grinch of Mistletoe was up here about to string popcorn and cranberries, make homemade tinsel, and cut out snowflakes to decorate a tree and his cabin?" I grin and waggle my eyebrows. "Bambi will have a field day with it. Absolutely scandalous."

He rests his hip against the counter and sets down the paper and scissors, examining everything we have laid out. "If you really want to scandalize them, I can do one better."

I raise a brow at him. "Color me intrigued."

"Do you have your phone?"

"Yeah…but it doesn't work up here."

If it did, I would have been on the phone with Mom instantly instead of having to leave it to Luke to call her and tell her I wasn't coming home for Christmas. A tiny part of me is still annoyed he didn't take me into the office to do it right away or bring me back down there with him. But honestly, I probably would have tried to run back to my car.

And he knew it.

He nods slowly. "I know, and I don't have the internet—intentionally—but what I do have"—he points to a speaker on top of the desk—"is that and what I know *you* undoubtedly have on your phone." He wraps an arm around me and tugs me up against him. "That incredible Christmas playlist of yours, which I'm sure has been updated to reflect all the new songs and versions that have come out since we last listened to it."

Okay, that's it…

I'm going to melt into a puddle on the wooden floor, just like the snow is melting from the tree and his jacket and boots next to the door. "You'd be right."

No matter how many times I hear them, sung by countless different voices in a thousand unique styles, I never get sick of Christmas songs. And I will add every single one that releases to my list the moment I can get my greedy hands on it.

Something Luke is abundantly aware of.

He offers a smug smile and kisses me, slow and deep, like he's trying to say something without using his words. "I'm right about a lot of things, Snowflake."

14

LUKE

L*ike the fact that I never ever stopped loving her and never could.*

She gazes up at me with so much affection, appreciation, and wonder in her eyes that it's hard to remember that she isn't mine anymore. Not really. As soon as New Year's rolls around, she'll be gone, heading back to Toronto and her dream job and life there…

Until she comes back again for her annual summer visit and then disappears again for another six months before next Christmas, when I will be able to feel her presence even from two miles down the mountain.

A vicious cycle that only seems to get worse for me each year.

Knowing she's coming back, knowing she won't stay.

It was hard enough before tonight, before I made the mistake of letting her into my cabin and my heart again.

Come next year, I don't know how I'll even stay in Mistletoe while she's here.

I might have to take my first vacation ever—maybe somewhere warm like Bali.

She reaches up and brushes her fingertips across my forehead. "What's wrong? Your brow just furrowed *very* intensely."

Noel always was far too observant.

Able to read me like an open book.

In tune with what I was feeling and able to anticipate what I would need.

It was what made us falling apart so much worse.

I force a smile I'm not feeling at the moment, but I won't ruin this for her.

It may not be the Christmas she wanted—actually, I *know* it isn't—but it's what she's stuck with. And the least I can do is make it as happy for her as possible without bringing down the mood by mentioning the truth that's hanging over our heads and will come crashing down as soon as the storm stops.

This is only temporary.

A few days at most.

Just long enough to rebreak my heart.

"I'm fine, Snowflake, just trying to remember how to do the cut-out-snowflake thing."

She narrows her gaze on me, trying to read me while I put up the strongest wall I have. Apparently, she buys it because she leans up and presses a kiss to my lips quickly. "I'm going to grab my phone. You make the popcorn."

"I can handle that."

It gives me something to do—something to take my mind off the sense of impending doom that settled over me.

That won't do.

Not tonight.

When she's so happy in this moment.

Noel practically skips across the cabin to where her jacket lies draped across the couch and digs in her pocket as I grab the pot, pour in the oil, and light the stove.

I can't keep my eyes off her for very long.

The amount of joy she exudes, despite all the reasons she has not to be filled with it right now, reminds me of why I fell in love with her in the first place.

Even as kids, I was drawn to her—her lightness, her smile, the way she could always make the best out of any situation. And like I told her, I always thought she was too good for me, too good for any man, actually.

But that Christmas, when we were sixteen…

I swallow thickly, remembering our first kiss, that surprised look on her face when she realized what it meant.

When we both did.

I knew then that I was hers forever.

I just never imagined forever would only last six years.

I thought we'd spend a lifetime here, building our lives in Mistletoe.

It never even crossed my mind as a possibility that she might leave—her parents, this town, or me.

She moves over to the desk, and I shake my head to try to clear away the memories and darker thoughts as I pour in the popcorn kernels.

A few seconds later, "Have a Holly Jolly Christmas" fills the cabin, and instead of my usual response—a gut-twisting agony and gagging, the desire to flee as far away as possible and clasp my hands over my ears to try to drown out the sound—I actually smile.

Something I don't think I've done in years.

Yet somehow, I've done it a thousand times since I locked Noel in here.

Maybe kidnapping her was a good decision...

Noel slips up behind me and wraps her arms around me, pressing her face into my upper back. "Is that the Grinch of Mistletoe, smiling and listening to Christmas music?"

Busted.

I laugh as the kernels start popping and I shake the pot to ensure they don't stick or burn. "I told you, Snowflake, I never hated Christmas. I just hated Christmas without you. This one is different than the last eight…"

And what the rest will be like without her.

She releases a little sigh, lifting her head from my back to look around. "If we do all this decorating tonight, what are we going to do all day tomorrow? You don't have a TV, or—"

"I don't need a TV. I can think of plenty of ways we can keep ourselves occupied on Christmas Day." I glance over my shoulder at her to find wide blue eyes. "Things I'm not sure sweet, little, innocent baby Jesus would be too pleased with."

The flare of pink in her cheeks coupled with the sight of her in my shirt makes my heart turn as riotous as the popcorn in the pan.

The popping finally slows and stops, and I incline my head toward the lower cabinet. "Grab the big bowl."

She slips her arms from around me and snags the big plastic bowl we've always used for popcorn. "How do you want to divvy up this work?"

I dump the popcorn and nudge the hot pot to the back of the stove so we don't accidentally knock into it.

Noel grabs a few pieces and pops them into her mouth, chewing as she examines the cabin, then taps her chin with her finger. But my eyes drift down to her exposed legs.

The creamy skin of her lower thigh.

To her shapely calves and ankles.

And her adorable feet with her red and green toenails.

"I think I should do the stringing because my fingers are smaller and it might be easier for me. You can cut the snowflakes, and then, we'll both work on the tinsel."

I lick my lips, remembering how good her skin tastes. My cock strains against my jeans.

"Luke, did you hear me?"

Slowly, I lift my gaze to meet hers. "Oh, I heard you all right, Snowflake. I was just wondering if this can wait another hour or three."

She playfully swats at my shoulder and smiles. "It can't. I want to be done before that clock hits midnight."

I glance up at the clock on the stove that reads 9:30 and groan, my already semi-hard cock aching at the thought of having to put off being inside her again, even for a few hours.

After so long, I want nothing more than to spend every waking moment I get with her wrapped around each other.

But this is important to her, which means it's important to me.

I press another kiss on her forehead. "Whatever you want, boss."

"Ooh, I like that." She does a little shimmy that makes her loose breasts sway under the flannel fabric of my shirt and her thighs jiggle. "Call me 'boss' anytime you want."

I grit my teeth, fighting the urge to bend her over this counter and fuck that sass right out of her. "Don't do that again."

Noel raises a brow, playing coy. "Do what?"

Shaking my head, I scowl at her. "You know damn well what you just did, woman."

"Do I?" She turns to the counter and leans over it, pretending to stretch and allowing my shirt to ride up and expose her completely bare ass…and pussy.

Fuck.

"Jesus Christ, you didn't put your underwear back on."

It never occurred to me that she wouldn't. I put her thong and leggings in the bathroom with one of my shirts and her sweater after I got out of the shower and found them dry.

So that isn't why she's left herself bare.

She shakes her head, pulling her bottom lip between her teeth and batting her thick eyelashes. "I sure didn't." Twisting back to face me, she pushes up on her bare toes and presses a kiss against my neck, just below my ear. "That's your incentive to work hard and fast so you can do me hard and fast when you're done."

A growl rumbles in my chest, and she chuckles and snags the popcorn and cranberries and rushes over to the couch before I can get my hands on her.

"I need you to grab me a needle from the sewing kit."

Maybe I can stick it in my cock to get it to go down?

"What makes you think I still have one?"

She gives me an incredulous look. "You may cut your sleeves off your shirts like a fucking madman, but I also know that you can sew a button and would *much* rather do it yourself than take it all the way down to your mom."

I hate—and secretly love—how well she still knows me after all this time, after so many years of apart.

She's spot-on about the sewing kit and the fact that I hate asking Mom to do *anything* for me.

That woman is a saint who already has to deal with enough bullshit from me. I will not go to her with any tiny inconvenience, like losing a damn button off one of my flannels.

Noel watches me make my way to the small linen closet next to the bathroom, tug it open, and pull out Grandma's old sewing kit box with her name engraved on the top.

I let my fingers drift over the letters, remembering sitting on her lap while she darned socks and fixed tears in my clothes from running around in the woods and ripping every single piece of clothing I owned.

Of all the things she could have left me when she passed, this was the most unexpected.

And what meant the most.

Noel's eyes are on me when I turn back to her, and she grins when she sees what's in my hands. "I knew Frances would never let us down."

She runs her hands reverently over the top of the box, then flips it open, snags a needle from where it's pushed into the puffy pin-cushion top, then begins to string it with the dental floss.

"Why don't you just use the thread?" I motion to the several different colors in the kit. "Wouldn't that be easier?"

Noel raises a blond brow. "Are you questioning my methods?"

I take a step back and hold up my hands. "I would never question you. I value my life too much."

And right now, keeping her happy and her spirits lofty, knowing her mother is two miles up the mountain, alone on Christmas Eve, take priority over arguing with her about something so trivial.

Especially when I'm sure she has a valid reason.

She smirks. "I'm using this"—she holds up the dental floss —"because it's waxed and it'll slide through easier, even though it's thicker than thread."

Damn.

That's brilliant.

I never would have figured that out or even *thought* about it. Yet, she seems so confident in her plans. Like she hasn't just done this before, but recently.

"When was the last time you did that?"

Noel's shoulders stiffen slightly, and she clears her throat, tucking her bare legs under her and settling deeper into the couch. She starts threading on a few pieces of popcorn, followed by a cranberry, only to repeat the pattern again. "The team actually hosted a Christmas kids' night last year.

Right before I came home for the holiday. I took charge of activities." Her gaze darts to mine, concern darkening the blue. "This was one of them."

My gut churns, and acid crawls up my throat. "Oh…"

The thought of her doing this *there*.

Celebrating Christmas somewhere else.

Maybe *with* someone else.

It's enough to make me want to walk out into that storm again.

"Have Yourself a Merry Little Christmas" flips on the speaker and allows me an excuse to walk away from her before I say something I shouldn't. I turn it up slightly, then think better of it. "Do you want me to change the song?"

This was one of her father's favorites.

Always an emotional, sensitive man, Russell would often tear up just hearing those first few lyrics.

And Noel always followed suit.

So much like her dad.

She gives me a tight smile and shakes her head. "No, I want to hear it."

No matter how painful it might be, Noel wants to remember her father. All the things about him. The things he loved.

"Whatever you want, Snowflake."

I hesitate, considering sitting next to her and pulling her into my arms to comfort her, but she seems engrossed in what she's doing. Her fingers moving deftly to glide the popcorn and cranberries on with precision and ease.

My attempt to console her could result in pushing her in the wrong direction, into despair instead of toward the holiday joy I've been trying to stoke tonight.

Instead, I move over to the kitchen and set to work on the paper snowflakes, knowing full well this was another activity she did with the children last year.

Just like we always did it when we were kids.

Before love and life complicated things.

I hold up the triangle shape and turn the folded paper toward her. "Am I doing this right?"

"Wow." Her blue eyes widen. "You remembered."

The corners of my lips twitch despite the uneasiness that's settled between us momentarily. "We did make them for what...twenty years?"

I can still vividly remember cutting paper with those tiny plastic scissors that had the rounded blades.

Noel grins, quickly returning to her work. "Probably close to that."

Another memory flashes through my head when I unfold my first attempt—that isn't great.

The awkward, uneven cutting and patchy holes remind me instantly of the one Russell always hung on their tree. One Noel made him in preschool and he cherished as much as he did that horrible Nutsack that always graced their mantle.

I glance over at Noel. "Your dad always loved these..."

Her hand stills, and she closes her eyes, sucking in a sharp breath. "I know." She gives me a tight smile. "Even with all the expensive decorations and the lights and the store-bought crap, handmade things like this"—she holds up the few inches of garland she's created—"were always his favorite."

"That's because you made them."

Her eyes flick up to meet mine.

"Just like me, your dad loved Christmas so much because you did."

Lips trembling, Noel shakes her head. "I don't think that's true. He grew up here, surrounded by all this." She waves a hand absently. "It was bred into him."

I work on cutting out another snowflake, careful to avoid

snipping where it's held together in the middle, while trying my damnedest to make this one more even. "That may be true, but he always looked the happiest when he was with you and your mom, doing anything together around this time of year, especially the tree lighting."

She releases a heavy breath. "I still can't believe they canceled it…"

"Can you blame them?" I look up and out the front window, though I can't actually *see* anything but a wall of white—snow reflecting off the cabin light. "This storm is the worst I've seen in a long time."

As if to prove its point, the sound of a massive tree branch cracking somewhere outside cuts through the air.

Noel flinches, head whipping toward the sound. "Oh!"

"Don't worry, Snowflake. I took care of all the widow-makers."

Shit.

Poor choice of words, considering that's what her mother just became.

Her eyes cut over to me again, but they don't hold any of the animosity over what I said, just relief. "You did?"

I nod and motion outside with the scissors in my hand. "I may not like spending time around people. May not like going to town, but I don't have a death wish, Noel."

The words come out a little snippier than I intended.

But there are definitely people in this town who *would* think I wished something like that to happen.

Because I never gave them any reason not to.

"Well…"—she releases a long, relieved sigh—"that's good to know."

We both get back to work, each of us silent and in our own heads as her playlist continues to cycle through all the classics.

Sometimes, she sings softly to herself; others, she's silent and focused on her work.

I have no idea what that woman is thinking.

Whether it's happy memories with her father or me.

Or terrible ones that will remind her of why we broke up in the first place.

15

NOEL

"There…" Luke secures the final side of the snowflake chain to the edge of the doorjamb so it hangs all the way across the entrance to the cabin. "All done."

He steps back and examines his handiwork, scanning the entire cabin, which is now decked out in well over one hundred hand-cut snowflakes and a tree drenched in foil tinsel and popcorn and cranberry garland. Complete with an origami star on top that I learned to make a few years ago.

Though I never imagined it would come in handy for something like this.

I never thought I'd spend Christmas anywhere but at home with the people I love the most.

Now Dad is gone.

And Mom is there alone.

But I try not to dwell on it at this moment.

Not when everything is so damn beautiful.

Luke props his hands on his hips. "What do you think? How did we do?"

I lean back against the kitchen counter, allowing my eyes to linger over every single piece we've put together tonight.

That damn tension that always comes before I cry returns to my chest, and I try to relieve it by drawing in a long, deep breath and releasing it slowly. "Everything looks perfect."

He raises a brow as he approaches slowly, almost like he's stalking me. "That's pretty high praise coming from Miss Christmas herself."

I scowl at him. "I am *not* Miss Christmas. But I am incredibly impressed with your ability to put aside that attitude you cling to so tightly, and touched that you'd actually do all this for me."

His gaze softens as he approaches and cages me in with his hands on the counter at either side of my hips. Lowering his lips to mine, he presses a chaste kiss there. "I would do anything for you, Snowflake."

Except move to Toronto.

The words sit on the tip of my tongue, so close to coming out that biting them back actually hurts and burns like acid in my mouth.

But I can't say them.

Not after he just did all *this* for me.

"We finished." His eyes drift over to the clock. "And barely in the nick of time, too."

I follow his gaze...

11:59.

This time, it's my turn to raise a brow. "We've really been at this for that long?

He nods slowly. "Two and a half hours." His head dips until his warm breath flutters against my neck. "Though it has felt like so much longer."

My spine stiffens. "Because of how much you've made yourself hate all this for so many years?"

Luke shifts even closer until his chest brushes mine and I can feel his hard cock pressing into me. "No." His lips feather across my skin. "Because you've been prancing around this cabin, bending over, reaching up, doing everything you can to flash that sweet ass and glistening pussy of yours at me. And I've been walking around with a painfully hard cock the entire time."

I suck in a sharp breath, and he draws his head back, grinning.

A few seconds tick by, then several more, but he doesn't move.

Doesn't say a word.

Just watches me like a predator, waiting for the perfect time to strike.

"What are you doing, Luke?"

The question comes out breathless, like I, too, can't wait for whatever is about to happen. And given the heat flooding my body, the ache between my legs, I know if he doesn't make a move soon, I might.

His grin deepens until that dimple pops again. "I'm waiting for that clock to tick over to midnight so we can start that Christmas Day stuff I mentioned earlier that baby Jesus would absolutely hate."

Hell...

My pussy throbs at his words, at the promise in them and in his gaze.

He glances at the clock again, and when his eyes return to mine, he doesn't have to tell me what it reads.

The absolutely feral glint in the green that stares back at me is all I need to know that it's *officially* Christmas.

"Merry Christmas, Snowflake." His hand captures my cheek. "Now…I would very much like to get my present."

I raise a brow at him. "What present?"

He reaches to the right on the counter next to me for something just out of my line of vision, then pulls it out in front of me—the bottle of bourbon he left out from earlier. "I want to know what this tastes like...on you."

My legs quiver under me at the low gravel in his voice, and I squeeze my eyes closed, gripping the counter behind me.

Luke pops the cork off the top of the bottle—the sound somehow loud even over the music still playing. He sets it back on the counter beside us with a soft clink of glass against the butcher block.

A calloused palm slips from my knee up along my thigh and between my legs to my already slick core.

His rumbled groan of approval vibrates through me. "So wet for me already, Snowflake?" He barely brushes my wet flesh with a fingertip. "Did you get hot? Walking around without your panties on, teasing me like that by flashing your ass and pussy at me..."

Luke barely grazes my clit with his thumb, making me twitch, and I bite my lip to keep from crying out.

"Did you?"

He presses his thumb there hard, not moving it, literally pinning me in place with one single digit and a question.

I allow my eyes to flutter open to meet his and find the determination there that I'll never be able to break.

Luke won't let me go until he knows.

Until I've come clean.

"Every time I caught you watching me, I felt like I was in a porn...about to be split wide by the smoking-hot lumberjack and his...weapon of choice."

A grin spreads across his face. "Then we better get working on those things that'll make baby Jesus cry."

I bark out a laugh, and he captures my mouth, swallowing it down, along with my breath, his hand shifting again so he can slide two thick fingers up inside me.

"Fuck..."

Clenching around them, I wrap my arms around his neck, trying to draw him even closer, but he pulls his hand free and backs away slightly.

"What?"

Luke slides his glistening fingers into his mouth to lick them clean before he grips my hips and lifts me up onto the counter. He pushes his flannel shirt up across my stomach to fully expose me and spreads my legs wide. "So beautiful."

His compliment washes over me like a soothing balm.

Wiping away all those stupid little thoughts that have popped up during our night together.

Ones I do *not* want to think about or consider until faced with the harsh reality of the world outside this cabin again.

Luke dips his head and drags his tongue through me, making my entire body clench and arch as he grabs the bottle. "Two of my favorite things in the world." He wiggles it in front of me, the amber liquid sloshing. "This one is sweet and fiery, and so are you."

Angling the head of the bottle just above my clit, he pours, then dips his head, catching the liquid, not allowing a drop of it to spill as he laps at me and his favorite drink.

The bourbon stings against my pussy slightly, but Luke's hot, wicked tongue tempers it immediately before he probes inside me, groaning his appreciation.

"Fucking hell, Noel, better than I ever imagined, better than I ever dreamed."

I tighten my grip on the edge of the counter, trying to find my breath as he continues to pour and lick, to suck and drive into me with his mouth and fingers. "You-you…you dreamed about this?"

Somehow, I manage to get the words out, and his eyes immediately flick up to mine, dark, almost obsidian now, full of need and something else.

"Of course I did. I dreamed about you every night when you were gone."

Shit.

Might as well drive an axe straight through my ribcage and into my heart.

The pain in his statement, coupled with the pleasure of his tongue and fingers on me, is enough to make me come in a hot rush so fast I don't even see the orgasm until it's hitting me full force.

"Fuck!" I gasp. "Luke!"

I clutch his hair, tugging on the long, thick strands as I buck against his face, grinding there as he continues to suck and nip at my clit in a way that just keeps dragging it on impossibly long.

The white spots behind my lids flash as my breath rushes from my lungs, and then he's there, kissing me, devouring me, allowing me to savor what I taste like.

My release mixed with the bourbon.

And he's right—it is incredible.

But it isn't what I'm craving.

I nudge at his shoulders, urging him back, and gasp for air as he tears his mouth from mine.

His brows rise. "What?"

It takes a second to catch my breath as he watches me, searching to ensure that I'm okay and for any reason that I might have stopped him. "It isn't fair."

His brows draw low. "What isn't?"

ANY of this.

I want to scream it at him, but there's one thing in particular that's been bothering me since the moment he got his mouth on me the first time earlier tonight.

"That you get to taste me, but I haven't been able to kiss you properly yet."

A frown pulls at his lips, mixed with the confusion in his hooded gaze. "What are you talking about, Snowflake?"

I urge him back with a nudge to his shoulder, and he retreats a step, then two, and I release my death grip on the counter to slide off onto shaky bare feet.

The shirt slips down again to cover my throbbing pussy, and my eyes zero in on their target—with a piece of mistletoe still tied directly above it.

He glances down, following my gaze, then back up at me with wide eyes. "Snowflake…"

His voice cracks slightly as he says it, but I reach out and unbutton his fly, dragging the zipper down with a playful grin as I sink to my knees.

"Your mom has a real sense of humor."

He chuckles, running his fingers through my hair. "I forgot that was even on there. She told me that I should tie it to the Santa hat when I was working the lot. But I told her that I'd rather get kissed elsewhere." That dimple appears with his laughter. "Just to mess with her, I hung it here."

I grin up at him as I tug his jeans down, allowing his cock to spring free directly in front of me.

God, he's hard and thick everywhere.

He grips my hair and pulls back on it, urging me to look up at him. "You don't have to do this, Snowflake. This isn't a quid pro quo."

The deep concern in his gaze and voice only makes me more intent.

"God, I know that, Luke. I want to. I-I've been dying to."

A slow smirk curls his lips. "Well, when you put it like that…"

His cock twitches in anticipation, and I reach out and smack him on the outer thigh, urging him to turn around and lean against the counter so he doesn't crumple in the middle of the goddamn kitchen once I start.

As soon as he's leaning back, I angle forward and slowly glide my tongue along the underside of his cock. His fingers tangle in my long strands, tugging as his hips buck forward and a low grunt slips from him.

I blow air lightly along the same track, over the damp, warm skin, then do each side just as slowly, intentionally avoiding the tip.

Toying with him.

Building him up the same way he does me.

By the time I finally get to that most sensitive spot, his body is vibrating so violently that I know I made the right decision to make him move. The knuckles on his left hand gripping the counter have turned white, and the fingers in my hair sting my scalp as he struggles to hold on to control.

"I'm going to suck your cock now, Luke." I glance up at him to find hooded, fiery eyes staring back at me. "And I want you to come down my throat."

"*Fuuuuck.*" The word comes out more growl than anything else, and he opens his mouth to say something else. "Noel, I—"

I lean forward and suck him down in one smooth motion, relaxing my gag reflex and taking him all the way to the back of my throat. He squeezes his eyes closed, his mouth falling open on a silent gasp, and he tugs on my hair violently, pushing himself slightly deeper.

"Sweet bloody fucking hell…"

He grits his teeth, and I moan around his hot, hard flesh.

"Fuck, Snowflake. You keep doing that and you're going to get your wish pretty damn fucking fast."

His words sound frantic, worried, as if he's concerned coming fast is somehow an insult to me or something to be embarrassed about instead of proof of just what I want.

For him to give himself to me.

Fully.

I reach up and wrap my hand around the base of his cock as I slowly withdraw until only the head remains in my mouth. Gliding my tongue around it, paying special attention to flicking against the underside, in that sensitive spot that makes his hips thrust forward, I push him to the brink.

And he drives deeper.

Hips surging.

I moan my approval, not wanting him to stop because he fears he might gag me.

I want to see him come undone.

I want him to fall apart the way he makes me fall apart.

I want him to forget everything except this moment, the way I've been trying to, no matter how hard it might be.

My pussy still throbs, aches to have his cock there instead of in my mouth, but the familiar flavor of his hot skin dancing along my tongue and knowing he's about to explode is enough to urge me forward, to make me suck and twist and glide until his hips are moving with me and he's fucking my mouth.

He lifts his hand off the counter and buries it into my hair, angling my head so he can drive harder and down my throat even farther.

And I let him take over.

Encourage him to take the lead.

Beg him with my body and mouth to take what he wants.

Because tonight, he gave me what I needed, what I wanted.

He comes on a roar that rivals that of the wind outside.

Hot spurts of cum hit the back of my throat almost violently.

I swallow them down greedily, savoring his familiar flavor and relishing the knowledge that I can still make him like this.

A quivering *mess*.

His body relaxes slightly, and he sags back against the counter.

He releases my hair and drifts his palm down under my chin to tilt my head up as he watches his cock slip free from my mouth. His thumb brushes over my lips. "That might have been the single most fucking beautiful thing I've ever seen, Snowflake. Next to you."

16

LUKE

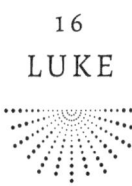

Bacon sizzles and pops in the pan. The aroma fills the cabin, mixing with that of the other breakfast items I already prepared, and makes my stomach rumble.

After the night we had, I'm starved, ready for a big breakfast on this cold, blustery Christmas morning.

I flip over the browning strips just as Noel starts to stir on the bed. She releases a long yawn and stretches, arching her back off the mattress, arms up toward the headboard.

Even though she's wrapped in the heavy comforter and I can't see anything, merely *knowing* she's naked underneath there makes my cock twitch against my sweatpants. "Good morning."

She lazily pushes up on one elbow with another yawn and narrows her eyes on me. "Do I smell bacon?"

I grin and motion down to the pan with the tongs. "In about three minutes, you'll have a full lumberjack breakfast —eggs, pancakes, potatoes, and bacon."

"Wow"—her eyes widen slightly—"you went all out."

Noel shoves her hand back through her mussed hair, trying to flatten the unruly mass that doesn't want to comply.

Fuck, she's stunning like this.

In my home.

In my bed.

Where she fucking belongs.

"You know"—she grins at me playfully—"I would think after the last, what twelve hours, that I would be a foregone conclusion. There's no need to wine and dine me."

I snort as I move the bacon around in the pan to avoid it settling on one of the hot spots. "I don't keep wine in this house."

"Oh, I know." Her sing-song tone warms me far more than standing next to the stove does. That she can be so relaxed, so seemingly content on the day she should be absolutely destroyed, tells me more about how she feels right now than she ever would verbally. "You greatly prefer sweet and fiery bourbon..."

I dart my gaze over to hers to find that coy smile that makes my balls draw up tight and a low rumble of approval roll through my chest.

She enjoyed that as much as I did.

And fuck did I.

I'll be jerking off to that memory 'til the day I die.

And to the one of her on her knees with my cock down her throat in this kitchen, begging me to let her swallow my cum.

Hell.

I reach down and adjust my growing erection now to a more comfortable position and turn as I hear her approaching footsteps on the wood. My body tenses in anticipation of her touch.

Please let her be naked.

It's selfish.

It might make me a greedy asshole.

And I woke with her tangled around me and promised

myself I wouldn't touch her for at least a few hours today—to give her a break and not make our Christmas together only about the mind-blowing sex.

But I desperately want to see her beautiful body this morning.

It would be the best way to start the holiday—a true gift.

I glance over my shoulder, but instead of endless smooth, peachy skin and that ass I could grab and kiss and lick and worship all fucking day, one of my flannels covers her to mid-thigh again.

Though I'm confident she still has nothing on under it.

She comes into the kitchen and loops her arms around me, pressing her lips against my bare back. The warm brush makes my stomach tighten. "Merry Christmas."

"Merry Christmas, Snowflake." I turn off the pan and move the bacon to the platter on the counter where I ate her last night and want to so badly again, then motion toward the oven. "Do you want to grab the eggs, potatoes, and pancakes out of there? I was keeping them warm."

"Sure." She drops another kiss on my heated skin. "I'm starved."

I snort. "I wonder why."

Completely my fault.

I kept her up longer than I should have last night. I've probably taken her too many times. Definitely took advantage of how sweet, hot, and receptive she has been to my obsession with making her come. But Christ, I couldn't keep my hands off her.

And it wasn't like she wasn't a very willing participant.

She couldn't keep hers off me, either.

Something I will *never* complain about.

It was like we were eighteen again—those young kids just starting out in our "real" lives, trying to figure it all out.

Seems we failed at that.

But at least we're still good at the sex part...

She grabs oven mitts from the counter, pulls out the platters from the oven, and sets them on the small table in the corner of the kitchen that seats two.

And she's the only other person who has ever sat across from me at it.

She slides into what was always her seat and glances up at me as I bring over the bacon and two empty plates, setting one in front of her. "What? Why are you looking at me like that?"

"I'm not looking at you like anything."

At least, I was trying not to.

But seeing her back in this spot, where we shared so many meals, where we shared our plans and dreams, might be the hardest part of this entire situation so far.

Because she looks *right* in that chair.

Like she's home.

She offers an annoyed little scowl, grabbing the knife and fork from the table and shaking her head as she examines the spread of food. "I hate when you do that."

"Do what?"

Her icy-blue gaze cuts to mine. "Don't tell me what you're really thinking."

I clench my jaw hard enough for the teeth to actually hurt.

There are so many times in the last two days since she literally crashed back into my life that I haven't said things to her.

Ones I've kept back.

Clung to as tightly as I always have.

Because this might be the only time I get with her.

It likely will be.

And I don't want to waste a minute of it, even if it means she's going to decimate me again when she leaves.

I bend down and press a quick kiss to her lips, trying to stop the conversation before it becomes a Christmas morning argument that doesn't need to happen. "What I'm thinking can wait."

She grins, waggling her pale brows and shifting on the chair slightly to expose more of her bare thigh. "Something else sweet, innocent baby Jesus would hate?"

Laughing, I snag two mugs from the cabinet and pour us each a cup of coffee. I set one in front of her and start serving both of us from the platters. "Oh, there are definitely other plans, Snowflake, but I have something else in mind."

Noel takes a sip of her coffee. "Like?"

"You'll see."

Her eyes shift to the clock on the stove. "It's almost 9:00. That's late for you. What have you been doing while I was being lazy and probably snoring and drooling in bed?"

I slide into my seat, take my first bite of eggs, and chew, watching how the storm-filtered morning light coming in the window beside us dances across her face so beautifully. "You were not being lazy, snoring, or drooling."

Far from it.

She looked…peaceful.

Content.

Free.

Something I'm not sure I've felt in eight years.

Despite my days filled with endless manual labor, I certainly haven't ever slept as well or as deeply as she did last night.

I sip my coffee, watching her over the brim as she smothers her pancakes in the fresh maple syrup I put out. "In fact, you were incredibly enticing and made it very hard for me not to climb back under the covers and join you."

Noel swallows the bite of eggs she's chewing. "Why didn't you?"

"I have incredible restraint."

A scowl twists her lips. "What we've been up to has been *restrained*?"

Grinning, I cut off a chunk of pancake. "You have no idea, Snowflake."

She shudders slightly, then grasps her mug between both hands and sips at her coffee. Her gaze shifts to the front door and my boots, jacket, and axe. And the water under them. "Did you go back outside?" She glances toward the window. "What's it like?"

"Shitty." I shove in a few bites of food, then point to the radio with my fork. "And I listened to the weather report. I'm surprised you didn't hear it."

Her laugh lights up her face as she tears off a piece of bacon and pops it into her mouth. "I was pretty exhausted, if you remember…"

"Oh, I definitely remember, Snowflake." It would be impossible to forget *how* she got so exhausted. "The weatherman said as much as another eight inches today and tonight."

Her eyes bug out. "Seriously? Eight inches?"

I struggle to keep my face neutral and not burst out laughing. "You handled more than that just fine—many times. In multiple places…"

Noel gasps. "Luke! You cannot be so filthy this early in the morning, and definitely *not* on Christmas."

"I can't?"

"No." She takes a bite and leans back slightly, crossing her arms over her chest. "What would your mother say?"

This time, my laugh floats out, filling the cabin. "My *mother* isn't here, so her thoughts on the topic are irrelevant. The only thing she is worrying about this Christmas is taking care of my dad, who is a terrible patient. She knows I'll dig their house out once I can get down there."

Noel's face suddenly falls, her brow furrowing. "My mom…"

"I already warned your mother that you probably weren't going to make it back up there today."

Her shoulders slump slightly, but she shoves a rather aggressive bite into her mouth. "How did she take that?"

"About as well as could be expected." I shrug. "She's a smart woman, Noel. She knew what this storm could do and that you probably weren't coming back as soon as I called."

"So…we really are stuck here all day, huh?"

I shove a big bite of pancakes into my mouth, chewing as I watch her. "Is that really so bad?"

She stops with her fork full of eggs halfway to her mouth. "What? No. God, no. I mean, this has been"—she releases a long, heavy breath—"I don't even know what to say. This has been…"

"I know what you mean; I can't find the words, either."

Unexpected.

Complicated.

Wonderful.

Heartbreaking.

Disastrous.

All those things rolled into one.

All because I could never get over this woman, no matter how hard I have tried.

We eat in silence for a few moments.

Her eyes never leave me, a thin thread of tension still hanging there. "What else did you do this morning besides listen to the weather report?"

She knows how early I always get up—well before dawn—and then I'm usually out the door and out onto the property, checking on the saplings, fertilizing, doing whatever else I have to in order to help Mom and Dad keep this place running year-round.

"I didn't stray too far from the cabin, if that's what you're asking. There's no way to get down to the barn right now and not end up with either frostbite or lost in the goddamn woods."

She snorts and takes another bite of her eggs. "You could never get lost in these woods. You know them as well as you know my body."

I set down my fork and lean back, crossing my arms over my chest. "And how well is that?"

Heat blooms across her cheeks, and she ducks her head slightly. "Are you fishing for compliments, Luke?"

I grin at her. "Not really."

Just trying to change the subject so she doesn't keep asking what I was doing all morning.

Letting my gaze fall down to her plate, I find another topic. "Did you get enough to eat?"

She glances at her half-empty plate and nods. "I did."

"You didn't take very much."

Sipping at her coffee, her slender shoulders rise and fall. "I'm not much of a breakfast person anymore."

I raise a brow. "Really? It was always your favorite meal."

She offers another little half shrug. "Still is. I do breakfast for dinner all the time. But my schedule is such that I'm sometimes eating at weird times and rarely this early in the morning."

Her schedule.

Her job.

What drew her away from Mistletoe and me so easily.

I shouldn't ask—for my own sanity—but I do anyway, unable to stop myself. "You're still liking it?"

She leans back, too, cradling her mug between her hands. "What? My job?"

Nodding, I toy with the edge of the table, where the old

wood has started to wear and splinter slightly from things banging against it over so many years.

One of her blond brows wings up. "Do you really want to know?"

Shit.

I don't.

I really, really don't.

Unless the answer is, "No, I fucking hate it and I'm coming home." But given the look on her face, I don't think that's going to happen.

"I do."

Because despite everything that's happened, despite the way I feel about her and how intensely I want her to stay, I want to know she's happy—even if it can't be with me.

She sighs and drums her fingers on the side of her coffee mug. "I do love it. There are three people on the main PR team, and when I moved up there, I was the noob, the American."

I smirk at her.

No matter how knowledgeable she is about hockey, I can only imagine the shit she must have received up there for being from south of the border.

"They didn't want to really trust me with much. I drafted PR releases, handled a lot of grunt work for the first couple of years. But something about being there in the arena, the crowds, the energy, and the team, I don't know, it's electric."

My body tenses the longer she talks and the more I can hear the true joy in her voice.

She really does love it.

And I know she's fucking good at it.

Even when she was just doing PR for the local high school teams and the community college, she was brilliant.

Coming up with campaigns to draw people to their games and get students enrolled.

Noel is always going to be good at whatever she does.

"And now that I've been there for this long, I'm not the noob anymore. In fact"—she swallows thickly—"my boss, the head of the department, is retiring in February, and there's a good chance I'm going to be promoted to his position."

"Head of PR for the Leafs?"

She nods.

"Wow, that's pretty impressive. I'm happy for you."

Her brows arch. "Are you?"

Shit.

I push back my chair and make my way over to the sink to start washing the dishes without answering her question.

And maybe that, in and of itself, is answer enough.

No matter how badly I want Noel to be happy, I'm still a selfish bastard who wants her to be happy *here* with *me*.

Not a thousand miles away in another country.

I throw on the faucet, letting the water warm before soaping my plate and silverware. Noel approaches and stands next to me, handing me her plate without another word.

It was so dumb to bring that up.

And now there's this tension again that I had hoped to avoid.

At least until it gets closer to the time when she actually has to leave and our little snow globe where we can pretend our futures aren't so divergent shatters.

She takes the washed plate from me and snags a towel from the drawer handle to dry it.

We work in silence for a few moments before I can't take it anymore.

This isn't how I want to spend today.

It's Christmas.

I can't let anything interfere with making this special for her.

Peeking over at her, I watch her set the clean and dry dishes on the counter. "I know how we can spend the day—at least, part of it."

Her lips twitch. "That won't insult sweet, little baby Jesus?"

"I don't think he'd have a problem with this."

Turning toward me, she tosses the towel onto the counter. "Well, now I'm intrigued."

I incline my head toward the bed. "Go in the top drawer of the nightstand."

Narrowed eyes on me, holding slight trepidation, she nods. "All right." She pads over on bare feet and pulls open the top drawer. A tiny gasp slips from her mouth, and then her gaze darts up to meet mine. She reaches in and pulls out the leather-bound book. "You kept it?"

I got rid of anything and everything related to Christmas or Noel.

I couldn't bear to have any of it in my home, in my space.

Any reminder of either only felt like the pain of her leaving was fresh again.

But that book in her hand—that would have felt like throwing away an actual piece of me.

And I just couldn't do it.

"I kept it."

Tears glisten in her eyes as she flips open the first page, and I know what she's reading there. The inscription she wrote before she gave it to me that Christmas when we were sixteen—the one that changed everything.

"Merry Christmas to my favorite person on the planet. I never want to spend another one without you."

If only we knew what was coming.

If only there had been some way to avoid the storm.

17

NOEL

The book feels heavier now than it did when I bought it for him all those years ago, or maybe that's the weight of the conversation we just had and the tension it created between us. That almost suffocating pressure of our pasts and the things we aren't saying that threaten to crush my chest.

It's unavoidable.

We can't spend every minute together while we're stuck here and not acknowledge the thing that drove us apart in the first place.

But God, I'd love to try.

Especially standing here, in his shirt, next to the bed where I spent a magical night in his arms again.

Holding *this.*

I run my fingers over the inscription, remembering how surprised he'd been that I bought this for him and what I wrote in it.

He hadn't thought I noticed the way his eyes lit up when he saw it in the used bookstore.

Nor did he know that I felt the same thing he had in the months leading up to that Christmas Eve.

We'd been friends for so long, basically since birth. Almost always together, since our parents were such great friends. Laughing, playing in the woods, chasing each other into the pond in the summer and onto the ice that covered it in the dead of winter.

But things changed that year.

Looks lingered longer.

A little spark started to arc between us each time we touched.

Luke and I stopped seeing each other as just friends.

And the gifts we gave that night led us down the path that got us to where we are today—broken and wanting so badly to put things back together with glue that will never hold.

"You know, yesterday"—I gulp, remembering the pain on his face—"at the tree..."

He finally turns to face me fully, shoulders tense, jaw locked. Luke is bracing himself for whatever I'm going to say, already anticipating that it will hurt, given what happened standing in the town square and what I held in that box.

"Luke...I need you to know that I was in town to try to replace the ornament you gave me. I didn't break it on purpose. I wasn't trying to destroy the memory or—"

His gaze softens. "I know you didn't, Snowflake. I only said that because..." He sighs and runs a hand through his slightly disheveled hair. "I don't know why I said it."

That isn't true.

He does.

We both do.

Because he was hurt.

He still is.

And lashing out at me over something like that made it easier for him to walk away.

I hold up the book. "Do you still read it?"

He offers a little half grin. "Every year. It's the only Christmas thing I still do."

"I'm surprised." I run my hand over the old, worn leather cover I've held so many times that I practically have every nick and crack memorized. "I would have thought it was the one that would be the worst."

A muscle in his jaw tics, and his hands tighten around the edge of the counter. "It is."

Shit.

I close the book and hold it to my chest, wishing we could go back to that night, knowing what we do now and maybe make different decisions.

Luke holds my gaze. "But I still do it…"

That little shiver runs through me.

The one of anticipation mixed with the longing and need I've always had for him.

I squeeze my eyes closed.

Why?

Why does he still do it even though it hurts?

Either the man is a masochist and I just never noticed it, or he's willing to bear the pain in order to experience those fleeting memories of loving me.

Before that got tainted by my ambition and need for life beyond Mistletoe.

I open my eyes to meet his and find him staring at me intently. "You're going to read to me?"

"If that's what you want, Snowflake. It isn't a long book. Should only take a few hours, and then, there are always those other things to occupy the rest of our time."

My cheeks heat, but there is no fighting my grin as he

approaches the side of the bed where I stand and holds out his hand for the book.

Our fingers brush as I turn it over to him, and that same little spark I felt when I was sixteen zaps between us again.

So much stronger now.

Impossible to ignore.

There's no way he didn't feel it, too.

"Come on." He takes my hand and tugs me with him over to his massive leather chair in front of the fireplace. "Our usual spot."

Hell...

Between fucking on the rug last night and now this, the man is certainly doing what he can to remind me of how much I love this place.

And him.

He settles in the worn leather and tugs me down onto his lap so I'm lying across it. My bare legs drape over his arm, and I drop my head against his shoulder and snuggle into him.

Exactly like we used to before I left.

Countless hours spent sitting here, reading to each other, talking about life, enjoying the fire.

He grabs a blanket and tosses it over my legs, though the fire roaring beside us keeps me plenty warm, along with his body heat. His warm breath flutters across me. "If I keep catching flashes of your bare pussy, we aren't going to get very far into this."

Grinning, I wiggle on his lap, pretending to get comfortable when I really just want to relish in the control I have over him in this moment.

Luke presses a kiss on my forehead. "I know what you're doing, Snowflake, but I'm going to let it slide. For now." His eyes darken slightly. "Are you ready to meet the Ghost of Christmas Past?"

Gosh, that's a good question.

It feels like that's what we've been doing this whole time I've been here.

Confronting our past that is so inextricably tangled with Mistletoe and Christmas.

All those memories bottled up in this one place we can't escape from.

They won't go away until we face them.

Until we vanquish the ghosts.

"I think I can handle it."

This story won't be easy to hear—for so many reasons— but the warm memories it holds have to outweigh the pain.

They just have to.

"All right. Then, here we go."

Luke dives into *A Christmas Carol*, his deep voice floating over the words in the most soothing manner. Inflecting the humor the story holds and mixing in the horror and super- natural elements with his tone.

No matter how many times I've heard the story or seen it on the screen in its many different variations, my heart still races in the same spots, my chest tightening and gut twisting as the characters suffer the consequences of their actions and learn their fates.

The book is almost two hundred years old, but the themes, the messages, the things that are taught through Ebenezer Scrooge, Bob Cratchit, Tiny Tim, the ghosts, and everyone else have stood the test of time.

Even now, they make me question a lot of things that I hadn't much allowed myself to before I came back here and heard the words from Luke Crisp's lips.

Did I make a huge mistake?

He pauses and squeezes me, knocking me out of the spiral I was starting to make in my own head. "You okay?"

I glance up at him and nod. "Yeah, why?"

"You haven't said a single word since I started, and I'm almost halfway through the book."

Halfway?

"That far already?"

He nods, his brow furrowing as he brushes his rough fingertips over my cheek. "Should we take a little break? I need to throw some more wood on the fire, and I think you could use another long, hot shower."

My body aches at his comment and not just between my legs.

Everywhere.

The way he worked me over, twisted me, turned me inside out since I got here, and I know I'll feel him for months after this. Though the emotional toll will linger longer.

"That probably wouldn't be a bad idea..."

Especially if he has other scandalous things in mind for later today.

He presses a kiss on my forehead, then lifts me easily from his lap and sets me on my feet, swatting my bare ass. "You go hop in the shower. I'm going to go grab more wood from the shed."

I glance over at the fireplace and the massive stack of wood already piled up next to it. "Okay..."

It feels like he's up to something.

Why did he go out this morning in this storm?

The winds seem to have died down, at least temporarily, but the steady blanket of snow that continues to fall outside the comfort of the cabin should have kept *anyone* indoors.

But he went out.

And seems intent to do it again.

Unless I can convince him otherwise.

I slowly back away toward the bathroom. "You're not joining me in there this time?"

A lazy grin spreads across his lips, and he advances toward me slowly, book still in one hand, middle finger slid between the pages to mark our place.

That shouldn't be so sexual, but my pussy flutters, watching it, knowing what he can do with those fingers and that hand.

"Do you really want me to, Snowflake?"

The gravelly tone has returned to his voice, the one that acts as a warning.

He doesn't have to say what will happen.

It's *more* than implied.

I offer a little half shrug, as if I'm not ready to bend over or otherwise spread my legs and offer myself to him again without question. "I wouldn't mind the company."

Because despite everything, all the reasons I shouldn't, I've become addicted to Luke Crisp again.

To his touch.

To the way his eyes light up every time he looks at me.

To how he worships me.

To the way he makes me feel complete, even when there are so many reasons not to.

And to how he makes me forget and remember at the same time.

He stops his advance suddenly, as if remembering he's supposed to be doing something else and not me—again. "I'd love to join you, Snowflake, but I really do need to take care of that fire."

I purse my lips and dart my gaze between him and the wood.

Definitely up to something.

I just offered him a free Noel buffet and he's turning it down.

Maybe he's getting sick of me.

Maybe six—*or is it seven?*—times is too many.

Even for him.

If I were less confident, I might believe that. If I couldn't see the pure lust shimmering in his gaze or hadn't felt his cock hard against me when I sat in his lap, I could consider it a remote possibility. But knowing what I do, I'm more convinced he's trying to get rid of me long enough to do something he doesn't want me to know about.

"I promise, Snowflake; I'll join you later."

And make it hard for you to walk.

Again.

His dark-green eyes tell me that as much as words could.

I release a little breath that sounds far too needy for a woman who has been thoroughly fucked senseless for hours and hours. "You better."

Paused in the doorway, I watch him for a moment.

He holds my gaze for the longest time, for longer than would make most people comfortable, even around a man they're intimately involved with.

I am barely dressed as it is, but it's like he's stripping me bare, seeing everything I try to fight and hide. Like he can see my soul and still hold on to it, still control it, the way he did when we were just kids.

"You better go get in that shower."

Or else.

I should. "I won't be long."

"Take your time, Snowflake. I'm not going anywhere."

Those words twist like a knife in my chest.

He said them to me for so long.

All those times I felt insecure in high school and college, when I felt like I wasn't good enough or pretty enough, he was always the one lifting me up. Assuring me that I was his fucking goddess. Telling me that I was brilliant and endlessly listing all the other things he loved so much about me. And promising he would *always* be there. That he would *never* leave me.

He was always my rock.

And I smashed it.

Tears prick my eyes, and I close the door quickly, before Luke can see them, and slowly slide down it.

I bury my face in my hands and press my palm tightly over my mouth to contain the sob that threatens to slip out, one he would undoubtedly hear with us being in such tight confines.

This Christmas has turned into a storm worse than the one outside.

Losing Dad.

Sliding off the road because of a damn rabbit.

Confronting the man I have avoided for almost a decade.

Making a stupid decision that cost me my time with Mom and left me trapped here with him.

And the worst part…

Like opening the door to the frigid winds and biting snow outside…allowing my heart to reopen to him.

What the hell are you doing, Noel?

I wish I knew.

18

LUKE

By the time Noel opens the bathroom door and steps out, I've managed to regain a little bit of my composure and take care of what I needed to without her around.

It's been so long since I've had anyone here, constantly in my space, that I had forgotten how hard it can be to find any time alone.

To think.

To try to accomplish anything without someone looking over my shoulder or asking questions.

Even when she slept last night, her presence was so intense.

Each breath.

Every brush of her skin against mine.

All of it filled more than just my bed.

The only way I managed to leave her this morning was by convincing myself it was worth it—for the end result.

Assuming it goes the way I hope it will…

I recline on the bed, back pressed against the headboard, watching as she steps out from the bathroom, scanning the small cabin for me as if she's worried I won't be here.

Her eyes meet mine, and my spine stiffens. Worry twists a knot in my stomach, seeing how red and puffy it is around the blue.

She's been crying.

Why?

At this point, there are so many possible reasons.

The pain of losing her father.

Distress over missing Christmas with her mother.

Frustration at being stuck here with me.

My first instinct is to go to her to tell her everything will be okay, but I can't do that because I don't know that it will.

I can't do a damn thing about the first two issues, and when it comes to us…

A vise tightens around my bare chest, and the longer she stands in the doorway, staring at me, the harder it becomes to ignore what we've been doing.

Pretending.

We've fallen back into what we were *before,* ignoring what we can't be *after.*

It's a shitty situation.

No matter how hard either of us tries to pretend everything's normal and the snow outside is creating a fresh page for us to write a new chapter on, the past and everything that comes with it lies just underneath that first layer of pristine icy white.

Come tomorrow—or whenever the storm dies out—we're going to have to fully face what waits beneath the surface.

Even if both of us would rather go along pretending that isn't the case.

"Come here."

I pat the side of the bed, half expecting her to reject my offer, given the uncertainty in her gaze and the evidence she's been crying so vivid and fresh.

Could I blame her?

If she's ready to end our charade and keep her distance—as much as possible in this tight space—until she can leave, there isn't a damn thing I can do about it.

She smiles softly, then moves off the jamb and approaches with another one of my shirts covering her.

Christ...

There's something about her wearing them that makes my heart thunder against my ribcage violently. That possessive caveman thing that overtook me when I threw her over my shoulder and dragged her up here in the first place rekindles every damn time that plaid hits her skin.

Though, I can't deny how much I enjoyed her sweater and fucking her in it last night, as I promised…

This is far more enticing.

My cock stirs against the soft fabric of my sweatpants as she approaches.

She climbs up on the bed and crawls toward me in a way that makes my hands itch to reach out and snag her, to draw her up and over me. But I have no idea where her mind is at.

Or where mine is.

Besides the obvious desire to kiss her, touch her, and make love to her as many times as possible during our time together, the rest of my head is a jumbled mess of conflicting thoughts.

Some heartbreaking.

Some terrifying.

Many too intense to even *consider* addressing.

I force myself to resist the desire to ravage her, instead holding up the book as she settles next to me. "You ready for more?"

Her brow rises as her gaze darts between the yellowing pages and my very obvious erection straining against my sweatpants, with no real way to hide it. "Of you or the book?"

A grin tugs at my lips, knowing she's still very on board with the former. "Either."

Noel hesitates for a moment, chewing on her bottom lip in that way that makes me want to take it between my teeth and take *her*. "I don't think we should leave Scrooge hanging."

"Agreed."

As much as I'd love to roll her under me right now and make her come—plus do something about my aching cock—we need to take a breath.

She snuggles up to me, pressing her head against my bare chest, and wrapping my arm around her. I open the book to where we left off and begin reading again.

My other hand finds her hair, dragging through the damp, silky strands darkened by the water, but they'll be bright again in an hour or so once the heat of the cabin dries them.

The same kind of bright and sunny she has always brought into my life.

There was a time when I never thought I would feel this kind of warmth again, this kind of easy affection because God knows she's the only one who ever gave it to me.

I never wanted it from anyone else.

Never even tried to find it after she left.

No one would ever compare to Noel.

And now, she's in my arms, lying here so comfortably on Christmas Day, trapped inside this cabin by a storm that seems intent on keeping us together when life has driven us apart.

Noel leans into my touch and trails her fingers over my bare chest and abs in slow, lazy motions that make my muscles tense under her.

It isn't sexual.

Far from it.

But it's the closeness I've been missing, that I've been dreaming about.

The sex is incredible, but *this* type of intimacy—simply snuggling up together to read and absently touch each other because it feels natural and right—it's what I crave the most.

She has to feel how hard my cock is pressed against her, but she doesn't mention it, and neither do I, both of us putting aside the passion that has overwhelmed us since yesterday to focus on just *being* instead.

And the most classic of Christmas stories—besides the original one.

As Scrooge searches for meaning with the three ghosts and the other characters suffer from his greed and uncaring nature, I can't help but search for some meaning or something to learn in what is happening with Noel.

Why bring her back to me only to tear her away again?

It seems cruel.

This whole thing has played out so much like the book, that as I read the words, my heart aches more and more.

Like the Ghost of Christmas Past forcing Scrooge to remember a time when he was so innocent, I'm forced to remember years with Noel when we didn't see a world beyond Mistletoe and our love for each other.

When we were happy.

Content.

Loving in a way people only dream about.

But just like Scrooge never realized Belle was slipping away from him, I never saw it happening with Noel.

I never expected her to leave.

When she did, it left me as cold as the man in the story became.

Everyone always calls me a grinch. And they aren't wrong about that.

I've become bitter.

Secluded myself in this cabin on the mountain.

Avoiding any social interaction.

Ignoring that my heart once beat instead of feeling like a broken, hollow hole in my chest.

Yet the more I read, the more I see parallels on the page that I never did before. All the times I've delved into these words since she left, I only ever felt one thing —pain.

Glaring agony at having lost her.

But this time, with her snuggled against me, listening to me in the warm calm of the cabin while the blizzard rages outside, my plight seems to mimic Scrooge's.

This—last night and today—is the Ghost of Christmas Present.

Seeing what could have been if things had been different —if we had made different choices.

This is how it should *be.*

Spending Christmas together, wrapped around each other, happy.

The past two days have shown us what we could have again if things change...

"Luke?"

Noel's voice cuts through the endless questions running around my head.

"Yes, Snowflake?"

She spreads her palm flat over my heart. "You seem tense."

I set the book down next to me and tilt her face up so I can see into her eyes. Concern lingers there. The same I've held for her with everything that's happened.

But I'm not ready to come clean with her.

I'm not mentally prepared to let it all unravel by revealing how the story on these pages feels like it's speaking directly to me.

It's so much easier to fall back on something that I can pretend is not about *feelings* and is only about *feeling.*

I drag my thumb across her bottom lip. "Maybe because your touch is about to make my cock explode."

She laughs lightly, grinning. "I'm sorry. I'll stop."

"Dear God, don't do that." I dip my head down and kiss her, savoring the sweet maple flavor still there from breakfast. "Please, please don't."

"I won't." She whispers the words against my lips, then pulls back and shakes her head, laughing again. "Do you remember the year my dad thought it would be a great idea to read this on Christmas Day?"

It would be impossible to forget.

"I do."

Shaking her head, she sighs and drops it against my chest again. "That was one very long Christmas, but I still loved it."

"Me, too."

Her father did it with different voices for each character, almost acting it out in a way that made it impossible not to enjoy it—even though it became an almost all-day ordeal with us and my parents as his audience.

She releases a little wistful sigh. "He did a great Scrooge."

"Are you saying mine sucks?"

The way things have been playing out, I feel like I *am* the man.

Noel shakes her head, grinning up at me. "No, but you were never the theatric type…"

"No, I wasn't."

Though I certainly became more reclusive after she left, I never particularly enjoyed being the center of attention before that. Not like how Noel glows and lights up even more around people and in the spotlight.

Everyone says opposites attract, and when it comes to the two of us, that seems to have been true.

But even the strongest magnets can be pulled apart.

It just takes a tremendous force—like her desire to leave and mine to stay colliding with a catastrophic impact.

I drop my head back against the headboard, running my fingers through her hair as she resumes her teasing, soft touches over my chest and stomach.

A comfortable silence falls over us for a moment before she tips her head up. "What do you think he's doing right now?"

Her question freezes me in place unable to move.

What if I say the wrong thing?

Losing her father is still so fresh.

The wound still so raw.

And today, being Christmas, is likely similar to rubbing salt into it.

But one answer comes to mind, and it seems like the right one.

"Probably watching over the town tree to make sure it doesn't blow over in the storm."

I feel her grin against my chest. "You're probably right…"

Burying my face in her hair, I pull her against me tighter. "He'll also be watching you, too, though. Always."

"I know." She draws a little circle over my heart, then drags her fingertip across it, creating an invisible pattern that I realize is a snowflake. "I think that's why I've been able to function at all, just knowing he's watching over me. How proud of me he was. Though, I do worry about Mom. She's up there all alone. What if something—"

"Hey"—I shake her gently until she looks up at me—"your mom is fine. My dad and I went up to the house a couple of months ago, checked the roof, all the trees around it, helped her with a few little repairs. We made sure she was ready for winter since she was going to be there alone for most of it."

Her eyes soften, tears forming in them. "You did?"

I nod and tilt her chin up. "I should have told you before, so you wouldn't have worried. Just because I abandoned this town and wanted nothing to do with it didn't mean I would ever abandon your mother, Noel. She knows I'm always here, and so are my parents. If she needs anything during this storm, she'll call either them or into town if they can't get to her. But I'm confident she's okay, and we'll check as soon as it's possible to get down to the lot and the phone."

Noel releases a long, slow breath. "You were always so good at that."

"At what?"

"Talking me off the ledge."

I couldn't that night, though.

I couldn't talk her out of leaving.

Even though we haven't reached that part yet, the Ghost of Christmas Yet to Come and what he shows Scrooge races through my head.

That is my future.

Living alone.

Being called a grinch or a Scrooge—or worse.

All because I'll be losing her again.

She stares up at me for what feels like an eternity, her cheek still pressed to my chest, hand splayed next to it, naked leg thrown over my sweatpants-clad thigh.

All my muscles tense in anticipation.

I don't know what she's thinking or what she's going to do.

But something about the look in her eyes tells me it's going to *mean* something.

Noel pushes up onto her knees and slides her leg across my waist to straddle me, looping her arms around my neck. My body thrums, my cock hardening against her core as she aligns them with only the thin fabric separating us.

It can't block the scalding heat of her pussy along my length.

And despite all my best efforts *not* to fall back into bed with her like this—at least, not for a while—it seems she has something else in mind other than finishing our book.

NOEL

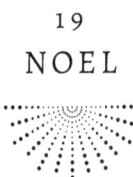

L uke issues a low, rumbling growl of warning, his hands tightening on my hips where they're spread across his.

I see the hesitation.

The concern.

The conflict raging inside him that also lives and breathes inside me.

I press my fingers across his lips, silencing him so I can get out what I need to so he can understand. "I know we keep doing this as soon as we get cleaned up." A little laugh slips out at the absurdity of how many times we have ended up having sex in less than twenty-four hours, and he grins against my fingertip. "But Christ, Luke"—I lean forward and press my forehead to his, pulling my hand away from his mouth—"I just need it. I need you. Again. I don't care if it makes me look like some wanton slut—"

"Whoa!" He threads his fingers through my hair and tugs my head back, forcing me to meet his gaze. His brows draw low over his darkening eyes. "Don't ever think or say anything like that again, Noel. You want what you want, as much or as little as you want it. There's absolutely nothing wrong with that, or you, or us, or *this*."

He rolls his hips up, which pushes his hard cock even more intensely against my pussy.

I bite back a moan, sagging onto him slightly. "I've just never…"

"You've never what, Snowflake?"

Squeezing my eyes closed, I rally myself to make the admission I never thought I would to this man. To tell him how truly and completely he affected my life and ruled my heart even after I left Mistletoe and him behind.

When I reopen them, now fighting tears, I know I can't get away with not finishing the thought now that I've opened the door.

"I have never wanted *anyone* the way I do you. Not then. Not over the last eight years…"

And I probably won't in the future, either.

I can't imagine how I ever could.

My lips trembling, I hold his heated gaze, watching his eyes warm at my admission. "Are we crazy?"

He nods slowly, never looking away from me, still gripping my hair and holding me in place so I can't try to hide. "Yes."

"Stupid?"

His head bobs again. "Yes."

"Shit."

I squeeze my eyes closed, unable to accept what we both know.

That we shouldn't keep doing this to ourselves.

That it will only make it hurt more when it ends.

But his lips feather over mine gently, like he's seeking permission to take something that's always been his.

I gasp at the zing of electricity that flows through that simple act, the way it ignites that fire that was merely smoldering before. My nails curl into his chest, and he groans, taking my mouth with his brutally.

Seeking and exploring like he doesn't already know everything.

Claiming me in a way that screams *forever* when we both know it's really only *for now*.

Until this storm blows over.

Once it's gone, so will be my reason to stay in this cabin.

I'll go home to Mom for the next few days until New Year's rolls around and I have to return to work and my life in Toronto.

And the message he conveys with the way he holds me, the intensity of his kiss, comes through loud and clear—I am not the only one struggling with all these feelings being here has dredged up.

HE'S in exactly the same boat.

With no engine.

No sail.

No paddle.

Surrounded by a dark, stormy sea, or in this case, a white-out blizzard.

There's no hope of rescue unless we do it ourselves, but we're both drowning in this lust, these memories, this place, and I don't know how either of us will come up for air when it's over.

Maybe we won't.

And I can't seem to care.

I roll my hips, grinding myself down against his length, and he groans into my mouth, his bare chest rumbling under my palm. He releases my hair, and his hands slide down to unbutton the flannel shirt, freeing my breasts and belly. Exposing them to the warm yet somehow chilly air.

Goosebumps pebble across my skin, and Luke cups me almost reverently, brushing his thumbs across the taut peaks, sending a jolt straight to my clit and making me clench.

Moisture floods my core, and I gasp against his lips, shuddering as that tight, coiling spiral already starts to build low in my belly.

He alternates his caresses, soft, gentle, sweet, then suddenly pinching and twisting my nipples in a way that almost makes me come on the spot.

"Fuck…"

The word tumbles from my lips and into his mouth, and he catches it with an appreciative groan. Kissing me everywhere. Touching anywhere he can.

But I need more.

I fumble between us for the waistband of his sweatpants and shift back as he lifts his hips to allow me to slide them down and off, freeing him. His scalding gaze rakes over me so hot my skin ignites.

A fire surges across every inch of it—outside, inside, all the way down to my soul.

"Take what you need, Snowflake." Low and gravelly, his voice holds the evidence of his own barely restrained desire, but he's pushing it aside, putting me first. "Whatever you need, however you need it, Noel, I'm yours, and I always will be."

Oh, God.

His words make a sob climb up my throat, and I straddle him again, grasp his hard cock, and drag it through my arousal, then sink down on it slowly so I can pretend the sound is merely a response to feeling so full rather than to what he said.

"Always yours."

It's what we used to say to each other.

For so many years, even before we were boyfriend and girlfriend.

We swore we were best friends for life, and it all fell away so easily, the same way I'm falling away now—from all my worries, from all my fears—just by giving in to what I want from this man.

I finally sink down to the hilt and catch his groan with a kiss. Luke drops his head back, his hands tighten on my hips, and I roll them and grind down, pushing my clit against his pelvis. Seeking that delicious friction.

His body jerks under mine, and I rest my hands on his shoulders to use them for leverage to push myself up, then ever so slowly sink back down on him again.

Allowing myself to feel every solid inch.

Achy and clenching for it.

Luke's jaw tightens.

A muscle in his neck strains like it might snap.

He shifts his grip on my waist to help lift and guide me, allowing me to set the pace we both want.

Rising and falling together, a dizzying maelstrom more disorienting than getting lost in those woods outside.

The cracking and popping of the wood on the fire, the random gusts of wind battering the small cabin outside, and the two of us coming together, our gasps and moans of pleasure, of contentment, of desire create an intimate soundtrack.

I ride him desperately, in frantic movements that keep his cock inside me as much as possible, the head dragging against that deep spot. His hands dig into my hips almost painfully, and each time I drive down, he grits his teeth harder.

He finally lifts his head and meets my gaze, then pushes himself up from the headboard, slides one hand to my nape, and plunges his mouth into mine again.

A brutal, soul-searing kind of kiss.

One that tells me how fucking starved he is, despite how many times we've already had each other.

It's almost animalistic, feral, the way he takes it as I take him.

The slap of my pelvis against his.

That slow, beautiful grind of my clit to his flesh.

The flashes of light and sensation that ripple and course through me as he drives his tongue along mine, as he devours me more intensely than he ever has with his face between my legs.

Christ...

He was right, and so was I.

This is so crazy and stupid.

It will hurt later.

The kind of agony that lingers for years.

The kind we're both so familiar with.

I can't put on the brakes now, though. Not when my body is barely my own, when it belongs to him. Even though he turned over control to me—something he never does, especially where sex is concerned—he still owns me, owns this.

It's an illusion of control when he holds my heart in his calloused hand.

All it would take is one sharp twist to wrench it from my chest.

He plants his feet and drives up into me, pushing himself that little bit deeper and making me gasp against his lips.

"Christ, Noel. I thought watching my dick disappear in your cunt was beautiful." He leans back and feathers his fingers across my lips. "I thought watching you take it down your throat was, but nothing compares to watching you ride me. To the look on your face every time my cock goes deep like this."

He thrusts up again, and the groan I release sounds as inhuman as some of his have.

I don't even know how to respond to that or that I could, even if I tried.

My head spins, and my body buzzes.

Only his cock embedded deep inside me, the constant roll of our entwined bodies, and his hand at my hip keep me grounded.

He twists my hair around his wrist and tugs, angling my neck back as he dips his head to kiss his way up the column, then slowly grazes his teeth over my pulse point.

The move makes my clit throb and my hips twitch, and I lose the rhythm, groaning in frustration.

My legs start to ache from the position and all the work it entails. But he gave this gift to me, told me to take him.

I don't ever get the upper hand with Luke Crisp, and I don't want to lose it.

He licks over that spot where my pulse thrums wildly, then down lower, bending me backward with his tug on my hair until I'm arched toward him, my breasts an offering in front of his hot lips.

Luke takes one peak into his mouth and sucks, and I arch even more, like a bowstring strung so tight that it's ready to snap.

My hips falter yet again, but the buzz of pleasure his mouth on my nipple creates almost makes me forgo caring. He keeps moving inside me, and I try to find control, regain it, but he grazes his teeth across that sensitive peak, and I lose all ability to think or speak.

He kisses his way across my chest to the other breast, flicking his tongue across it, then blowing cool air, twisting it between his fingers before he scrapes his teeth along it and sucks away the pain.

Sweet.

Hot.

Harsh.

Agonizing.

Luke continues to move, pushing his cock up into me, even though I can barely do anything on top anymore, then pulls his head away from my breast. "How do you want to come, Snowflake? On my cock or in my mouth?"

My eyes fly open to meet his, and I can see the plea there.

I can *see* what he wants.

Or maybe I just know the man well enough to understand it.

Swallowing through my dry throat, I struggle to suck in enough air to speak. "Both."

A grin spreads across his lips. "Greedy and fucking beautiful."

He lies back so he can get a better position, and I can angle forward and find the friction I need. We return to the driving rhythm. Luke pumping up and me grinding down until the world finally—*fucking finally*—shatters the same way the ornament he gave me did.

I gasp, losing my breath and control over my limbs, and he wraps his arm around my back, pulling me to him as he continues to thrust up wildly. His hips buck and drive into mine. Plunging deeper and harder with each movement until he groans low against my ear, his body twitching under me as he comes deep inside.

My strangled moan falls from my lips as my orgasm finally abates and I collapse against him fully.

He wraps his arms around me and holds me tightly, kissing my temple. "Don't fall asleep, Snowflake."

I lift my head to meet his hooded gaze, still hazy from his release as I am from mine.

"You promised me I was going to taste your cunt and make you come again."

"But—"

"Now." He doesn't leave any room to argue with him. "I'll help you stay upright. Come sit on my face."

Fuck.

I clench around his still-hard cock, my pussy rippling and clit aching at the promise.

Slowly, I shift, letting his cock slip out as I shift up his body until I'm kneeling directly over his face. My legs spread across his broad shoulders, knees on the bed above them.

I grip the headboard as his rough hands find my hips.

He stares up at my cunt as if he's staring into the sun, like it's the most beautiful thing he's ever seen, then lifts his head and licks through both our releases.

Good God, he was right about baby Jesus hating us today.

LUKE

F or the first time in days, bright sunlight filters through the windows, completely unobscured by the gray clouds or the constant snow that has plagued Mistletoe.

Not that I'm complaining.

That storm brought more than nasty winds and massive snowdrifts; it brought me something I never thought I would have again.

Her.

Even if it *was* literally kicking and screaming.

One of those beams of light falls across the bed, inching closer and closer to Noel's sleeping form the longer I watch her, warning me that the day is slipping away even though it's still relatively early.

Wasting *any* time with this woman feels shameful.

Not to mention agonizing.

Because this is my final day with her—and I don't even know how long it will last.

How many more chances will I have to hold her? To kiss her? To hear that little hitch in her breath that completely undoes me?

I ignore the tightness in my chest as I hang my coat, untie

and kick off my boots next to the door, and pad across the wood floor to her.

Temptation to let her sleep longer, to allow to her enjoy the peace she seems to have found in her dreams and in my bed for a few more minutes creeps in—especially knowing I can crawl in with her and hold her until we're finally forced to come up for air.

But I don't want to spend what little time I have left with her just sleeping.

There are *other* things we could in that bed, but I want to see her face light up with the kind of joy that it has over the last few days...one last time. Without my cock in her or my mouth between her legs.

I want to know it isn't just lust that brings that brilliant smile and happy tears.

And that means waking her up.

This is the last time Noel will be here...

Fighting through the physical pain that knowledge brings, I climb onto the bed and slide in behind her, wrapping my arms around her waist and burying my face in her neck. Smooth, warm skin that always somehow smells like peppermint brushes my lips, and I let my mouth linger there.

Inhaling her deeply.

Tasting her.

Never wanting to move from this spot.

She groans slightly and shifts back, pressing herself into me more tightly. Her firm, bare ass aligns against my cock, and if my jeans and plans weren't in the way, I could so easily slip inside her—for just *one* more time. "What time is it?"

I don't bother looking at the clock.

After spending a lifetime in Mistletoe and on this "mountain," the angle of the sun is more than enough to tell me how much time is slipping away.

"Just after eight."

Her eyes flutter open, and she glances back at me. "When I fell asleep, it was still Christmas."

I grin at her, feathering my lips across that sensitive spot behind her ear. "When you fell asleep the first time…"

If memory serves me correctly—and it does since crystal-clear images and vibrant memories flash through my head—I woke her up twice in the night to taste her again and take her.

And my entire body throbs, thinking about each time.

"You need to get up."

She pushes up on her elbow, her eyes drifting to the closest window. "Is the storm over?"

Such a loaded question.

Noel is referring to the blizzard that changed her holiday plans and allowed us to have this incredible time together, but I can't help but think of her as the storm.

This feisty, brilliant, funny, kind, caring, stunning blonde spun back into my life on a slick road and brought with her a cyclone of emotions I didn't know I was capable of anymore.

And when she disappears again, the damage she will leave in her wake won't be easily repaired.

It can't be.

Eight years have proven that.

"Just some flurries now." I incline my head toward the door. "The wind is almost completely gone."

Her bright eyes meet mine. "Then I can get home to Mom."

She starts to push up out of the bed, but I tighten my arm around her waist to drag her back down, rolling her onto her back and settling my body over hers.

"No, you can't. You know Jolly Lane won't be plowed until the rest of the town is done, which means probably late this afternoon or dinnertime before even *my* truck will get up to your mom's house."

Those pretty pink lips of hers purse, her annoyance making the blue in her eyes sparkle.

I chuckle, kissing the corner of her mouth. "Don't look so disappointed, Snowflake. I have something planned to occupy our time."

She frowns slightly. "Can we at least go down to the lot and call my mom?"

God, she's so sweet.

I shake my head. "I tried to go down there earlier, but the path is completely gone. Snowed over. If we stepped off it, we could get trapped in a deep bank or, even worse, in a tree well. You wouldn't make it."

Earlier, I wasn't even sure *I* could make it safely and turned back, and I have made that trek a thousand times in my life.

All it would take is one misstep to get sucked so deep in the snow that there would be no way out, and even if we were together, I won't risk her life when, in a few hours, we can get down safely.

The corners of her lips twitch. "You could just throw me over your shoulder caveman style, like how you got me up here in the first place."

I smirk at her and dip my head to nip at her plump bottom lip. "I could do that, but I worry with the snow as deep as it is, I could trip or step off the path, and you'd end up hurt. And I would never forgive myself."

No matter the hard feelings I held over our breakup, or the ones I'm trying to keep at bay now, knowing she'll leave *again*, the thought of anything ever happening to Noel sends a shiver through me worse than any brutal Wisconsin winter wind could.

Her blond brows rise. "So...then, how are we going to get out of here?"

"My mom and dad will clear the path up here with the plow attachment on the snowmobile."

"Why can't we use that on the road?"

I bark out a laugh. "You really can't wait to get away from me, can you?"

Her eyes widen, her mouth falling open. "No, I'm worried about my mom."

"I know, Snowflake." I kiss her gently. "I'm just messing with you. But seriously, that tiny little plow isn't going to do shit for what's on that road, and you know that. You're just intentionally being difficult this morning."

She offers an annoyed little harumph sound. "Fine, so we're stuck here until at least this afternoon, huh?"

I nod, brushing the hair back from her face. "Probably, unless my mom and dad manage to shovel themselves out of the house, get to the barn to the snowmobile, and get the path up here cleared faster than I'm anticipating."

Something seems to click in her head, and her brow furrows. "Why didn't you bring the snowmobile up on Christmas Eve?"

Shit.

It isn't a bad question, and one I hoped she wouldn't ask.

"Because I was afraid you'd remember how to unlock the deadbolt on the door, manage to get out of here, jump on it, and be reckless enough to try to get all the way home."

Her eyes widen, her jaw gaping open. "You really *did* kidnap me and try to hold me captive."

I shift my knee between her legs and press up until she issues a little gasp at the contact of my jean-clad thigh on her bare cunt. "Was it so bad being my captive?"

She shakes her head and grins. "No, you are a *very* accommodating captor."

"I do my best." I twist a strand of her hair around my finger and tug lightly. "Now, as for our plans today…"

Noel looks at me through thick lashes. "I'm so interested to know what you have in mind."

The sultry tone in her voice tells me exactly what she's anticipating. But this isn't about getting where my thigh is right now.

It's about giving Noel a gift she doesn't even know she needs.

But despite how long she's been gone, I still *know* this woman, what lies deep in her heart of hearts.

I shake my head. "Not that. We're going out."

Her brows fly up. "Outside?"

I nod. "The temperature is actually perfect, and...I have a surprise for you."

"Another one, besides the beautiful holiday meal you cooked me last night?"

The playful barb lands, and I snort and shift back, holding out my hand to tug her up and against me on our knees on the mattress.

"You know"—she feathers her fingers through my hair —"I don't think I've ever had Kraft macaroni and cheese for Christmas dinner before."

I chuckle and kiss her gently. "Well, I would have had a whole plate of food for myself from my parents' house under normal circumstances."

Her brows draw low. "You don't eat with them anymore?"

Arguments I've had with Mom about this very thing replay in my head.

Years of her begging me to spend Christmas with them, to come for dinner and open gifts.

Too many rejections of her offers to count.

Almost a decade of staying in this cabin pretty much the entire months of November and December, locked away from any potential "contamination" by Christmas spirit.

I swallow thickly as I avert my gaze from hers. "No, I can barely stand to be in their house this time of year."

"Shit." Any humor she has disappears. "I'm sorry, Luke, I didn't mean—"

"Stop apologizing." If I hear her say I'm sorry one more time, I might snap. "Get dressed. You're going to need your mittens and your hat, too."

She pulls that plump bottom lip of hers under her teeth. "Where are we going?"

"You'll see."

Her gaze narrows on me as I slide off the bed and make my way over to the door. I tug my boots back on and pull my jacket off the hook, then shove my arms through.

She watches me intently for a moment, like she's about to argue and try to get information from me.

That won't happen.

Something she seems to accept with an annoyed sigh before she climbs to her feet.

I tug on my gloves as she snags her pants, socks, underwear, and sweater from where they've been sitting near the fire. She takes them into the bathroom with her while I lean against the door and wait.

This could backfire, big time.

After our breakfast conversation yesterday, it may not be the smartest idea I've ever had, but it was always one of our traditions after a big snowfall, and I know she hasn't been up there even once in the last eight years.

She must miss it.

It's impossible *not* to miss something when you love it so much.

When she opens the bathroom door again, her hair has been somewhat tamed and spills around her shoulders over that silly, ugly Santa sweater. The big man stares back at me, looking jolly as fuck.

I can't fight the smirk that pulls up my lips as she approaches.

One of her blond brows flies up. "What's that look for?"

I grin and swat her ass as she bends over to tug on her boots. "That sweater." Leaning over her, I wrap my arms around her waist, growling low into her ear. "So many new memories to add to the ones of that day with the sweater and the ringing sleigh bells."

She releases a sharp laugh and pushes back against me to get me to stand and release her, then turns to face me. "My mom can make you one, you know."

"She has. Many times."

"And I'm sure those are in the trash somewhere, aren't they?"

Hell.

They are.

And that makes me feel like a real fucking asshole for having literally thrown away the sweaters her mom hand-knitted for me over the years.

Even if Mrs. J made me a new one, once Noel is gone again, God knows, I won't want to put it on.

Still, I force a tight smile, sidestepping the question. "Maybe she will make me a new one."

Noel slides on her jacket, and I reach up and grasp the deadbolt, pounding gently to the left of it so that it will slide more easily when I twist.

Her mouth gapes open. "So *that's* how you do it."

I chuckle as I tug the door open. "It's a good thing you didn't remember, or you might be frozen solid on the side of the road somewhere between here and your mom's place."

She scowls as she pulls on her mittens and then tugs the hat down over her wavy, blond locks. "You're not going to tell me where we're going?"

"There aren't many places to go up here, Snowflake."

And if she *really* thought about it, I bet she could guess.

Eight years might have passed, but Noel still knows this mountain and the special places that hold a piece of my heart —and hers.

I usher her out in front of me and pull the door closed behind us.

Noel sucks in a sharp gasp as she takes in the winter wonderland spread out before us.

The icicles dangling from every tree branch.

An endless landscape of snow as far as the eye can see, glistening, pristine, and white, so fresh that not even the animals have moved across it yet.

A few soft flakes still flutter from the sky, which is mostly sunny for the first time in days.

This is why the mountain will always be home.

This is why people flock to Mistletoe this time of year.

It isn't just because of the cheesy decorations, the town name, or the celebrations we host.

People come because this place is still pure.

Made the way God intended it.

Relatively untouched by the hustle and bustle of modern society.

No noise and pollution.

Nothing pulling you in a hundred different directions or distracting you from the truly important things in life.

Mistletoe is from another time.

One I don't want to forget.

"It doesn't look like this in Toronto, does it?"

Even with her big parka on, I can see Noel's back stiffen, and she swallows audibly before she glances over at me. "No, it certainly doesn't."

21

NOEL

othing in Toronto is at all like Mistletoe.

We may get snow up there—lots of it sometimes, depending on how the lake is acting on any given day—but I'm constantly surrounded by pavement, skyscrapers, smog, and thousands upon thousands of people living on top of each other.

There is *nothing* like this in the city.

No real space.

And condo living for so long has made me forget how incredible it feels to not hear neighbors through the walls, cars honking on the streets, or people yelling on the sidewalks below my windows...

Being on the mountain and in Luke's cabin has reminded me how truly stunning and peaceful the north woods are—when Mother Nature isn't trying to blow you away with blustery winds and dump enough snow and ice to literally drown you.

Or make you spin off the road.

Standing out here on his porch, staring out at the beautiful landscape I still know by heart, I can't help but let my gaze drift over to where the tree that's now in the house once stood.

The full day of snow and wind yesterday has almost completely filled in the area he dug out to get down low enough to cut it, but I can still see the indentation—and the strange empty place where it used to be between a few other trees.

Last time I was up here, it had been small, only a sapling. One of many Luke planted around the cabin to give himself more privacy. But in the last eight years, it grew to be tall and strong—like the man who put it there and chopped it down.

He cut it...for me.

I fight back the tears as he presses his hand against my lower back and urges me down the bottom step. His deep footprints in the snow that must come up to at least his knees disappear around the cabin to the left.

"Luke, what are—"

He jumps off the bottom step and places his back directly in front of me, motioning with his hands. "Climb on."

I snort-laugh. "You're joking."

Having Luke Crisp give me a piggyback ride was *not* on my Christmas bingo card.

Then again, none of this was.

It was supposed to be spent with Mom. Making sure she's okay. Supporting each other through Christmas and celebrating our favorite holiday the best we can without Dad.

Instead, the last few days have ripped open old wounds and made me remember why Luke Crisp was always my person.

Shaking his head, he glances over his shoulder at me. "I only have one pair of snowshoes up here, and they aren't big enough to support both my weight and yours. Which means...the only way we're getting where we need to go is by walking the same path I already created this morning, staying in the places where the snow is pushed down, and my steps are a lot longer than yours. This will be a lot easier than you trying to keep up with me on your own."

Shit, he's right.

It's been a while since I have walked around in this type of heavy accumulation on the mountain, but I remember how easy it was to sink in too deep.

If he already created a path to where it is we're going this morning, it will be easy enough for him to stay in his own footsteps.

And impossible for me.

But it means he went to a *lot* of work before he woke me to give me a way to get to wherever he's taking me.

I narrow my eyes on him. "Where are we going?"

That tiny half grin plays at his lips. "It's a surprise."

"You know I hate surprises."

"I don't think you'll hate this one, Snowflake."

Releasing a heavy sigh, I finally relent.

I throw my arms around his neck and jump to wrap my legs at his waist. He catches me easily, grasping my legs to secure me to him. Leaning forward, I feather my lips over his ear. "At least I get to choke you."

He sputters and laughs. "I didn't know you were into that. We missed out on so many opportunities over the last two days…"

"We might still have one before I go back up to Mom's."

Luke shivers at the suggestion in a way that I can feel all the way through my body, despite both of us being bundled up.

It heats me from the inside out, though I don't really need it.

He was right about the weather. As the storm went out, warmer air came in. It's still hovering around freezing, but the bright sunlight through the wispy remaining clouds that still drop a few snowflakes warms my face.

I tip it up toward the sky as Luke sets off, stepping in footprints he created this morning.

"You're really just going to carry me wherever we're going? I thought you said it was too dangerous."

"I said it was too dangerous to take you *down* the mountain."

But we're not going down.

This way is a relatively flat area, compared to some of the steeper inclines—like the one going to the lot and road would require navigating. There's only one place we could be heading.

"Are you taking me to the lake?"

His steps falter slightly, and I know I've hit the nail on the head.

Excitement bubbles up in my chest, and I practically giggle.

The lake this time of year means one thing—skating.

In the summer, we would swim, fish, play around on the rocky shore, and threaten to throw each in fully clothed, but in the winter, the frozen-over surface serves one very important purpose: acting as Luke's own private rink.

His boots crunch through the snow. He easily maneuvers across the clearing toward the small grouping of trees we'll have to make it through to access the lake.

I wouldn't have expected anything else.

Luke was born on this mountain. He's lived here his entire life. It's a part of him.

And I expected him to leave?

That choking sadness envelops me quickly, just as it did the day I drove away from him.

Mistletoe is my home, too, and I've always loved this

mountain. But the ability to move beyond it, to spread my wings to take my dream job, trumped all that.

Plus, I always knew I would come back.

With Mom and Dad here, it wasn't like I wouldn't visit often.

Dad may be gone now—a fact I've been struggling so hard not to dwell on—but this place has stayed the same. It has welcomed me back.

So has the man whose back I'm currently clinging to.

Luke may not have been very friendly or welcoming at first, but once we made it through—or more like pushed aside and ignored—the pain of the past, he's been nothing but the same sweet, caring, and giving person I always knew him to be.

Who would *carry* me to the lake so I can skate in my favorite place.

The closer we get, finally stepping into the trees—the final barrier before we hit our destination—the more excited I become.

Luke chuckles. "You're bouncing back there."

"No, I'm not."

"Yes, you are, Snowflake." He peeks over his shoulder at me with a smirk. "I can feel it like a vibrator against my back."

My giggle carries through the woods, bouncing off the trees. "You know I can't resist the lake, Luke."

"I know, which is why I don't mind trudging through this snow, carrying you on my back to get there."

God, why does he have to be so goddamn sweet?

Why can't he just be the grumpy, grinchy Scrooge everybody thinks he is?

It would make leaving this afternoon or tonight, or whenever it finally happens, so much easier.

Instead, he's morphed back into the Luke I knew. The one I was so helplessly, overwhelmingly in love with.

Tears prick my eyes again, but I can't wipe them away without releasing my hold on him and probably falling backward to my death.

"You all right back there? You got awfully quiet…"

I lean forward and press a kiss to his temple. "Yep, I'm good."

We're almost there anyway.

I could never forget this landscape or the way to the lake, not with as many times as we went up there over the years.

Long summer nights.

Crisp fall days.

Chilly winters spent on the ice.

Those stunning springs when everything came back to life again.

We spent countless hours on the banks of this lake, and as we step through the edge of the tree line and it finally comes into view, my breath catches. Rabbit and other animal tracks mar the otherwise pristine white blanket, but instead of the mounds of snow that should be covering it, half of it has been cleared, the icy surface visible and waiting for us.

"How did you get the lake cleaned off?

He glances back at me as he approaches the shoreline and then slowly lowers me down to my feet. "I got up very early this morning."

"I would say so…"

Between trudging through the snow to reach it and then cleaning off the snow with nothing more than the shovel still propped against a bank he created, this must have taken *hours*.

A large duffel bag sits near us on the cleared shoreline. "Is that what I think it is?

He smirks. "It is, if what you think it is are ice skates."

"You have skates that will fit me?"

Clearing his throat, he glances away. "I still had *your* skates."

And he doesn't sound too happy to tell me that.

Like admitting he held on to them was somehow conceding defeat in a war we aren't fighting. At least, I don't think we are.

"But I thought..." I try to process his admission. "I thought you got rid of everything that was mine."

"I did." Luke glances at me, his eyes darkening. "Mostly." He motions to the bag. "Now go put them on. I have one more thing for you."

More?

How could there possibly be anything else?

He's already done so much for me—and *to* me—over the last few days.

Luke moves to the other side, where the bag and shovel wait, and reaches down into a snowbank for something he obviously hid there. When he pulls it back up, his gloved hand is wrapped around the last thing I expected him to have waiting for us.

I bark out a laugh. "You're serious?"

He wiggles the hockey stick back and forth, grinning deviously. "I want to see if your skills have improved at all since you've been gone. I mean, you *did* go to work for an NHL team. If you can't score on me now..."

I scowl at him. "I'm going to kill you, Crisp."

That damn grin of his only deepens as I reach down and unzip the duffel bag, then pull out the skates I spent so many hours in.

They look exactly the same.

Dirty and beat up from excessive use.

Well-loved.

Like an old baseball glove.

I lower myself onto the snowbank to use it as a bench, tug off my boots, and ditch my mittens to pull on the skates.

They still fit, still feel so familiar.

Like the man approaching me.

We still *fit*, in all the ways that should matter. But it wasn't enough then, and I don't know how it can be now.

He grabs his out of the bag and does the same, much faster than I can. As he double-knots his final lace, he glances down at my trembling fingers that are starting to go numb without the mittens, despite the warmth of the day, but I can't wear them and tie my skates at the same time.

"I got them for you, Snowflake." He pulls off his gloves with his teeth, drops them near our feet, then ties my skates and presses a kiss to my forehead. "Now, let's see if you can fulfill that promise of my death."

Smug.

But he won't be for long.

I scowl at him, and he pulls a puck out of his pocket and tosses it at me.

Busy tugging my mittens over my cold hands, I barely manage to catch it against my chest before he skates backward onto the ice, pulling his gloves on. "You don't have any goalie gear."

He barks out a laugh that echoes across the ice and the clearing. "You're not going to hit me, anyway, so I'm not worried."

I push to my feet, grab the stick, and step out onto the ice. "Pretty sure of yourself, aren't you, Crisp?"

One of his dark brows arches. "Well, I played varsity hockey, and you know I kept at it in those years after. I think those skills are going to come in *very* handy against the likes of you. You never *could* score on me."

Annoyance mixes with the warmth our banter has created in my blood, and I drop the puck, never taking my eyes off Luke as he skates back to the far side of the cleared ice, where he's drawn a rectangular goal onto the ice with something—probably a Sharpie.

"That's the goal?"

He nods, settling in front of it and crouching slightly.

"I'm going to feel bad if I hurt you, Luke."

His brow pulls down slightly, and he flinches.

Shit.

That was a really bad choice of words, considering all the damage that was done.

But it's true.

Guilt has gnawed at me since he came clean about how he felt the other night. I always felt awful for what happened, but the last few days have reopened those old wounds.

And I'm about to feel bad for what's going to happen now.

I skate over to where I tossed the puck, then nudge it forward slightly to get in a better position and line up the blade. "You're ready?"

Luke winks. "As I'll ever be, Snowflake."

That *wink* sets me off, tightening my grip on the stick. "You asked for it."

"I sure did…" He mutters it under his breath, but I still catch it.

Are we still talking about our little game of hockey or something else?

Either way, I plan on giving Luke Crisp exactly what he's asking for—at least as long as we're out on this ice.

I wind back and release the hardest slap shot I can, straight at his head.

22

LUKE

The puck comes at me like a missile…
Straight at my damn head.

"Shit!"

I barely have time to dive out of the way, into the snow-bank to the right of the cleared ice and out of the path of the projectile.

What the hell was that?

My heart thunders against my ribcage, and Noel's laughter fills my ears as the icy, wet, cold snow hits the back of my neck and sloshes down into my jacket slightly.

I stare up at the bright morning sky and thin, wispy clouds, trying to regain my breath and calm my heart rate so I don't have a damn coronary event.

The sound of her skates cutting across the ice hits me, and she leans over, a smug-as-fuck grin curling her perfect lips. She props the stick on the smooth surface under her, blade up, and leans against it casually, as if she didn't just send a wicked rocket at me. "I warned you…"

Apparently, I should have listened.

"Where the hell did you learn to shoot like that?"

We spent nearly two decades out on this lake, messing around, shooting pucks at each other, not to mention the fun pick-up games at the rink in the town square around Christmas, and she *definitely* couldn't do that when she left Mistletoe.

Not anything near it.

It's impressive.

And sexy as fuck.

But I won't tell her that.

That would only boost her ego.

Given the smug smirk directed at me, she doesn't need any help in that department right now.

The woman showed me up, and she's reveling in her victory.

She offers me a hand to help pull me up, but I grumble and wave her off, climbing from the snowbank to dust myself off. Skating backward away from me, still chuckling to herself, she watches with amusement, knowing full well that I got snow down the back of my jacket in that fall.

Noel always had a vicious side, and her competitive nature is one of the reasons I fell so hard for her.

Never backing down from anything.

Standing her ground.

She moves out into the center of the ice and does an elegant upright spin, still clutching the stick in her hands—looking like a damn ice princess, not the woman who almost beheaded me with a puck.

"I knew you could do *that*"—I motion toward her as she stops the spin—"but *that*"—I point toward where I'd been standing when she took aim and fired—"is new."

Noel grins, twirling the stick. "Not that new."

Why is this woman being so smug so fucking hot?

Because she loves a challenge.

And I gave her one that she succeeded at.

Fighting a grin, I glance back at the fake goal. "I don't think you can do it again…"

One of her blond brows rises slowly. "That wasn't proof enough for you?"

I shake my head, crossing my arms over my chest. "Beginner's luck."

I'm poking the bear.

Maybe it isn't smart.

But Noel all fired up is the only thing hotter than Noel naked.

She huffs in annoyance, clenching her jaw. "I'm not a beginner. I've been out on the ice with the team a lot."

My back stiffens slightly, imagining her receiving *private* lessons from some of the players, the type of private lessons I definitely don't want anyone else giving her.

Noel seems to sense my unease and skates away, making a loop around the portion of the ice I've cleared before she comes to a stop in front of me, spraying me with slush and ice.

"I see you learned the hockey stop, too."

A grin plays at her lips. "Perks of the job."

I don't want to know what other perks she gets.

I've seen what those players look like, and they're all billionaires…

Any one of them can offer her things I never could—and in the same fucking city.

I swallow my annoyance, not wanting to ruin my last few hours with her, but it's difficult with this new feeling hitting me.

They may call me the Grinch, but one thing I've never been is green with jealousy when it came to Noel. I never had a reason to be. She was always mine. When we were together, she never so much as *looked* at anyone else. And when she left, it wasn't because of another man.

But now, the thought that anyone else has been touching her, has been having these types of experiences with her—on the ice and in the bedroom—makes my gut twist violently.

She holds out the stick. "Do you want a turn?"

I shake my head. "No. I want you to prove you can do it again."

Nodding, she examines the make-shift, drawn goal. "Okay. How many times do you want me to do it? Two, three, four?"

She inches closer until our chests brush, and she pulls on the front of my jacket until I dip my head down low enough for her to press her lips to mine. "How about ten?"

"That's a pretty big number."

Her grip on my jacket tightens, tugging me even closer. "That's how many times you fucked me in the last day and a half."

I grin as I slowly pull my head back from her. "Is it?"

She nods, pulling her bottom lip under her teeth.

"I didn't know you were keeping track."

Her brows rise. "You weren't?"

I chuckle. "I was keeping track of orgasms, Snowflake. Not times we had sex."

Gripping the stick in her mittened hand, she leans against it, her mouth twisting as if she's trying to count in her head. "How many did you have?"

Good God, she's adorable.

I bark out a laugh, then tug her up against me again, utterly devouring her mouth and stealing her breath so that by the time I pull away, she's panting. "I was counting *your* orgasms, Snowflake. Not mine."

And there weren't nearly enough.

If I hadn't held myself back, forced myself not to touch her every single moment we were together, the number would be astronomical.

Because absolutely *nothing* compares to the beauty of Noel Jolly coming.

Anywhere.

Any way.

That bliss floating across her face.

The way her mouth falls open.

Those little gasps and strangled moans that slip from her lips.

All of it is as addictive as the woman herself.

"Oh, do you know how many?" She waggles her eyebrows playfully. "Honestly, I lost count just the first night in front of the fire."

Pride swells in my chest.

Probably far more than it should.

I dip my head and tug her ear between my teeth, biting down gently, making her twitch in my hold. "Twenty-three."

She jerks back. "No."

Nodding, I drag her back with a hand at her nape so I can keep my lips against her cheek. "I made you come twenty-three times on my cock, in my mouth, on my fingers. But you want to know what my favorite one was?"

Noel shivers, though I doubt it has anything to do with the chilly air around us.

"Yes…"

I kiss my way to her mouth, stopping with my lips hovering just over hers. "The one where I could taste both of us as you came down my throat."

Fuck.

Just saying the words is enough to make my cock strain against my jeans.

I've never done that before.

Never wanted to.

But in that moment with Noel, I needed it.

I never realized how hot it would be to know what we tasted like together. And it was perfect, just like she is.

Another brilliant memory I'm going to have to survive off once she goes home.

"Maybe we'll have time to do it again before you have to go back to your mom's."

She grins and presses a kiss to my lips. "A girl can dream."

So can I.

And I have for eight fucking years.

Every night.

Every time I close my eyes—and sometimes when I don't.

It's all been this woman.

I woke too many times to count with my hard cock in my hand, thinking about her. Had nightmares where I was screaming, chasing her down the road, begging her not to leave. Even times when I woke in tears, wishing I had said or done something else to make her stay. Each and every one of them was filled with so much regret, so much pain and remembered pleasure.

Now I've replaced some of them with the memories we've made over the last few days, but those will soon be tainted.

As soon as she leaves again, that agony of watching her drive away will hit me harder than the blizzard did Mistletoe.

But I don't want to get bogged down in that misery now.

I shake off that thought. "But first, Snowflake, I want to see you take that shot again."

She pushes away from me and skates backward. "If you insist."

The way she moves so effortlessly across the ice, looks so at home out here on the lake, it's impossible to think about her being somewhere like Toronto.

So much pavement.

So many people.

Any time she spends on ice is likely inside an arena, not like this, surrounded by rolling hills, a flawless sky, and a hawk soaring over us.

I track the massive bird, watching it float on the light breeze through the flurries. It spirals down suddenly, swooping toward the trees until I lose it in the tall pines.

Probably catching its breakfast.

Hopefully not that rabbit Noel seemed so concerned about that night.

Noel returns with the puck in hand, and I glance over to where it had disappeared into the snowbank behind where I had been standing and see a massive hole from where she stuck her hand down to get it back.

She waves it at me. "You really want to risk your pretty face?"

Grinning, I skate toward her. "You think I'm pretty?"

Snorting, she tosses it onto the ice and offers me an incredulous look. "You know what you look like, Luke."

She puck handles, moving the biscuit effortlessly back and forth on the ice.

Shit, somebody really has been teaching her.

"I'm sure part of the reason all the women in Mistletoe gossip so much about you is because they're all pissed that I was finally out of the picture and it didn't make you available since you keep yourself locked up in the cabin."

I freeze where I stand, skidding to a halt on the ice, and she looks up at me with amusement in her eyes that instantly vanishes when she realizes what she just said.

"Shit, I'm sorry, Luke. I didn't mean to suggest..." She swallows thickly. "I mean, I know you weren't single the whole time I was gone. You must have dated. You must have..."

She doesn't complete the sentence, but she doesn't have to.

I raise a brow. "Fucked?"

This was a conversation I never wanted to have with her because it brings up the inevitable question of who she's been with since we've been apart, and I don't want to know the answer to that.

But the longer she stares at me, the more I know it will be impossible to hide the truth from her.

Because I could never lie to her, and I never have.

Not in our thirty years on this planet.

And I'm not about to start now.

"There wasn't anyone else, Noel."

Her brow furrows. "What do you mean? You didn't have any serious relationships?"

Shaking my head, I take a long, deep breath. "No, there was no one. *Ever.*"

It takes a second before her eyes widen and her mouth falls open slightly. She seems to realize it and snaps it closed. "You don't mean this whole time, you didn't…"

I clench my jaw, trying not to see the pained look on her face, the way her eyes rake over me, like she's seeing me for the first time when we've been almost nothing but naked with each other for two days. "No one." I fist my hands at my sides. "I couldn't bear the thought of being with anyone else, of touching anyone else, or letting them touch me. The whole thing…"—I swallow—"the whole thing repulsed me."

"But it's been eight years, Luke, that's not—"

"What?"

"Healthy."

She snaps her mouth shut again. Her cheeks pinken, though I don't know whether it's from the chilly air or embarrassment over what I'm revealing.

I slowly skate toward her. "Does it really surprise you that much? I told you time and time again that I was always yours

—forever. Did you actually think that changed just because you went to Canada?"

Noel squeezes her eyes closed, gripping the stick so tightly I can almost hear it starting to crack. Her body trembles, and when her lids flutter open again and her gaze flicks up to me at mine, I see the truth there.

She didn't believe it.

Maybe she did at some point, when we were actually together, but after that night, she thought I had moved on. She believed I had forgotten about her and the promises I made to her.

And even after everything I've told her over the last few days, she still didn't understand what I was saying.

I reach out and tip her chin up, forcing her to look me square in the eye. "I have *always* loved you, Noel, and I still do."

It's the admission I've been holding back for the last two days, the thing I've been terrified to admit to myself and certainly to her.

When I know she is going to leave again.

When I know she's going to break my heart.

When I know I'm going to end up in exactly the same place I was eight years ago, standing at the base of my fucking driveway and watching her tear off down the road.

I watch her stare at me, the surprise and regret in her gaze.

It was a mistake to tell her.

Because now that it's out there, I can't ever take it back.

23
NOEL

Luke's confession sucks all the air from my lungs.

When I try to force myself to inhale again, the cool, crisp air is filled with that pine scent that doesn't come from the trees but from the man standing next to me, who just bared his soul and opened his heart to me again.

This entire time, he's held that in.

Somehow, he's been able to keep that shocking truth about what he's been doing—or *not* doing—the last eight years to himself, and the even more stunning declaration that has rendered me speechless has to have been eating him alive from the inside out every time we touched, every time we kissed, every time his cock slid inside me…

A shiver rolls through me at the memories, but now they're painted with the new knowledge that can't help but change the way I see them and everything that's happened.

I swallow through my suddenly dry throat. "I guess we're not pretending anymore…"

Because that's what we've been doing.

Pretending.

And we both knew it.

I just didn't realize how *hard* he was pretending, how much he was withholding.

He flinches at my words and glides back from me.

"Luke, I can't—"

Grasp any of this.

Get my mind around how any of it could be real.

Handle him standing in front of me and telling me he loves me.

"I wasn't going to lie to you, Noel. I never did. I won't start now. You asked a question, and I answered it."

I shake my head, fighting the burn of tears that hits my eyes. "You-you…God, Luke, you didn't have to tell me *that*."

Because it might be what finally breaks me.

His evergreen eyes hold mine, and the determination there sends a little shudder down my spine. "Yes, I did, Snowflake, because I've been wanting to say it for the last two days, since the moment you climbed out of that fucking car in the ditch. From the second our eyes connected and before either of us said a word. Since that moment, I've been dying to say it."

I squeeze my eyes closed and shake my head, allowing the hockey stick to clatter down to the ice. "No…"

Shaking my head, I open my eyes and start to skate back to where I left my boots.

"No *what*, Noel?"

His voice wavers, and it almost makes me stumble.

It *almost* makes me stop and turn back to him.

But I force myself to keep skating away. "You can't do this to me, Luke."

He releases a little frustrated sound that makes me wince. "I can't do *what* to you, Noel?

I turn and drop into the snowbank, tug off my mittens, and start unlacing my skates. "You can't put me in this position again."

"*What* position?"

Does he really not know?

Does he really not understand?

I tug off my first skate, toss it back into the bag, and get to work on the second one.

The sound of his skates cutting across the ice draws my eyes up, and he stands in front of me, his jaw tight, pain etched across his handsome face. "Look at me, Noel, and answer me: what position am I putting you in?"

One where I have to admit that I still love him, too.

That I always have.

That this isn't just a fling or us falling back into what we were once for a few days to try to relive good memories.

That this is more than simply being snowed in with nothing better to do than fuck.

I would have to admit that this was two people who always loved each other, despite the time and distance between them, trying to figure it the fuck out when there isn't any way to.

Somehow, even with trembling hands and tears blurring my vision, I manage to get my other skate off and tug on my boots.

I snag my mittens, pull them on, and push to my feet.

Luke's dark brows draw low over his questioning eyes. "Where are you going?"

That's a very good question.

The only answer that comes to mind is, *away from here.*

Away from you...

But I don't say it.

I release a heavy breath, one filled with all the anguish now starting to build up inside me. "My mom's."

He issues a frustrated growl. "I told you, Noel, you're not going to get down the mountain to the lot or back up the road right now."

I meet his gaze and see so much pain in it that I'm immediately taken back to the last time we had this fight, to the last time this conversation split us apart. "I can't stay here."

"Why?"

"You know why."

He has *to know why.*

Luke would have to be *blind* not to see how his confession is affecting me, how *he* has affected me over the last few days. He has to understand that this is tearing me apart again.

I take off along the bank of the lake, and he mutters a curse under his breath. But I don't let it stop me. I keep walking without looking back, trying to step in the holes he left on his way up here to avoid the deepest parts of the snow.

Tears sting my eyes, both from the chilly air and the fact that I know he's going to come after me and catch me.

He's so much stronger than me.

So much faster.

His legs are longer, and even though I got a head start, it isn't going to do me any good.

It only takes a few minutes before he's on me.

I hear the crunching of the snow before his arm loops around my waist and he tugs me back up against him, hot breath against my neck, fluttering my hair and heating that sensitive skin behind my ear.

"Don't run away from me again, Snowflake. I don't think I could survive it a second time."

Agony sears through my blood, racing to every part of my body, trying to crush my will.

I fight through it, drawing on every ounce of strength I can find not to lean into his hold or turn in his arms and do something even more stupid. "I can't have this argument again, Luke. I can't pretend anything has changed when it hasn't."

His body stiffens behind me, and his lips feather over my ear. "Everything has changed."

I wish that were true.

I wish what happened over the last few days did change things.

There were several points when I thought they might, when I believed the spark we had, the connection we still shared, might be enough, but it's not when we're both in the same position we were in eight years ago, when we're stuck worlds apart.

"Let me go."

Luke releases a little growl of frustration, but he doesn't fight my request.

He slowly slips his arm back, allowing me the freedom to push forward through the snow, but he doesn't let me *go*.

Trailing after me, close enough that I can hear his footsteps, Luke doesn't say anything else. He just lets me stalk ahead—or more like stumble through the snow—until I reach the cabin.

But I don't pause or go back inside.

Because there isn't anything in there for me.

Not anymore.

We had a great couple of days, even in the worst of circumstances, even though I wanted and needed to spend this Christmas with Mom, but now, after hearing his confession, I know that Luke has been here waiting for me all this time.

And I *can't* go back in there.

He was my first everything.

The first boy I ever held hands with. The first one I ever kissed. The first one I ever slept with. And I was his, too— and apparently his last, if what he said was true.

You know it's true.

That little voice inside my head mocks me, making acid

churn in my stomach and work its way up my throat as I stumble past the cabin toward the path that leads down to the lot and my escape.

"Noel, don't. It's too dangerous right now."

Luke's warning cuts through my downward spiral, and I look at the sharp decline in front of me through the trees and how heavy and thick the snow is despite the canopy above the ground in this area.

But I don't have a choice.

I can't stay here.

It would be far more dangerous than trying to get back down to a phone.

"I have to go, Luke." My voice cracks on the words, and I hear his sharp intake of breath, but I can't bear to look over my shoulder at him to see what he's doing or the look on his face.

Because I already know that look.

I saw it eight years ago, the last time I did this to him.

The first time I broke his heart.

He follows me quietly for a few hundred yards, well past where he apparently made an attempt to get down and turned around, abandoning the idea.

Without his footsteps to lead me down, I try to remember the way the trail veers through the trees.

I make it another couple of yards beyond his guides, take a step, and sink up to my hips in the snow.

"Goddammit." Struggling against my chilly confines, I kick out with my legs, but the pack around me doesn't budge.

And I know it won't.

There's a reason we call these "spruce traps." If you get too close to a tree out here with this much accumulation, it can suck you straight down like quicksand.

Kind of like Luke has...

He comes to stand over me, keeping well enough back that he doesn't fall into the same area. "I think you stepped off the path."

I glower at him. "No shit."

His lips twitch the tiniest bit.

Gaping at him, I point a mittened hand at him. "Don't do that."

"Do what?"

"Don't look so fucking *smug*."

He crosses his arms over his chest and leans back slightly so his full height looks even more staggering from down here. "I warned you."

The same words I used on him up at the lake come back to bite me.

Hard.

This feels a lot more serious than what I did to him, though.

If he wanted to, he could leave me like this for a while, make me suffer, prevent me from leaving or trying to, at least. He could keep me here to force me to continue our conversation without fear of me running from him.

But the Luke I knew would never do that.

He wouldn't make me suffer—at least not *this* way.

After a moment of staring me down and apparently taking gross pleasure in my failure, Luke releases a heavy sigh and squats down to slide his hands under my armpits and pull me free.

Only my UGGs stay buried in the snow.

He holds me high, my feet dangling, my red and green fuzzy socks the sole thing keeping my feet from the cold air.

Another sigh slips from his lips, and he shifts his hold on me to set my ass on the more solid ground.

"Keep your feet up and dry."

I scowl at him. "Like I didn't already know that."

"It's been a long time since you lived here. I don't know what you know or remember anymore."

The dig hurts after the last few days, after what we shared, but I can't really blame him—can I?—because I'm doing it again.

I'm fleeing.

I'm trying to get away from him before we have the same argument, and that seems to only be leading to another one.

He reaches down into the holes in the snowbank with his long arms and tugs out my boots, then tips them over and shakes them to get any snow out.

I hold out my hands, but instead of passing them over, he drops to his knees and slips them on my feet—like Prince fucking Charming and the glass slipper.

Goddammit.

Goddamn him.

And goddamn this blizzard.

None of this would have happened.

If I had just stayed home with Mom, if I had accepted the reality of Christmas without a tree, I could have had Christmas without Luke Crisp.

Is that really what you want?

To pretend it never happened.

To forget how *good* it was.

Is that what you want?

My chest tightens, remembering all the hours we spent wrapped up in each other over the last few days, and my pussy clenches, wanting it more.

He stays squatting, staring at me, waiting for me to say something or make a move.

But there isn't anything left to say.

I finally release a shaky breath and push myself up. He rises and offers me a hand, but I bat it away, brushing past him and back down what I think is the path.

Now that the trees have disappeared, it's a little harder to navigate, to remember *exactly* where to step, but I can see the barn now, and there won't be as many dangers—like possibly stepping into a well around a trunk like I just did over there —down this far on the mountain.

I could still slip and fall, maybe roll through the snow, but I don't want to think about it, nor do I need to, because I hear the crunch of the snow behind me, and he's right at my back, watching over me, protecting me, like he always did, like I always counted on him to do.

The air seems to shift before he speaks. "You're really just going to walk away after everything that happened over the last few days, after what I told you?"

I whirl to face him and find him much closer than I anticipated, close enough that I can reach out and touch him without even stretching for it.

His proximity momentarily stuns me, and I wobble slightly before regaining my balance and pushing my mittened finger into his chest. "After the last few days, after everything that happened, what you just told me was a fucking *trap*."

His brow furrows as he leans into my touch. "What exactly are you accusing me of, Noel?"

"This?" I spread my arms out wildly. "You threw me over your goddamn shoulder and locked me in your cabin. You made sure I didn't have any means of escape, which you admitted by not bringing the snowmobile up. Then you seduced me and—"

"Whoa!" He holds up a gloved hand. "I'm going to stop your tirade right there, Snowflake, because I did *not* seduce you. If I remember correctly, you were the one who came into the bathroom when I was in the shower."

My cheeks heat at the memory, and I swallow thickly, staring up at him. "*You* kissed *me*."

"You didn't stop me."

Fuck.

Having the truth thrown back at my face doesn't feel good.

And it *is* the truth.

At any time, I could have stopped him.

I could have said no, and he would have let me be, continued to take care of me during the storm, but never touched me once the entire time we were trapped together.

Luke is nothing if not a gentleman—outside of sex, that is —so really, it isn't fair for me to pin that on him.

But I can't admit my own role in what happened between us this Christmas because it would be admitting how much I hurt him.

After hearing his words up on that ice, I now comprehend that it's far worse than I ever knew.

And that will be my ultimate undoing.

2 4

LUKE

Noel stands speechless, somehow stunned by the fact that she was a *very* willing participant in everything that went down in my cabin.

Being reminded of that seems to suck the fight right out of her.

Her shoulders sag slightly, and she stares up at me with her big blue eyes, as violently stormy as the one that trapped us together. Tears trickle out of the corners and down her cheeks, but she doesn't even seem to notice. "I-I have to go."

Not again...

Her blond hair whips out behind her as she spins away from me, and she trudges through the snow the last few yards to the barn—where she will probably try to convince Mom and Dad to lend her the snowmobile so she can try to get up the road to her house…

And away from me.

As if putting physical distance between us will make this any easier.

It fucking won't.

Fighting the desire to catch up, wrap my arms around her

again, and *force* her to finish this conversation, I follow her, scanning the property for any signs of damage from the storm like I normally would.

But everything looks perfect.

No broken portions of fence.

No missing signage.

Nothing but untouched, pristine snow as far as I can see.

Including on the lot and the walkway up to Mom and Dad's house.

My footsteps falter slightly as I narrow my gaze on what should have been cleared a long time ago.

They would have known I was snowed in.

They would have come by now to at least *start* clearing the snow and to get up to me.

Ignoring Noel stomping toward the office—since the door is locked and she's not getting in no matter how pissed and determined she might be—I move in the other direction toward the path that will take me up to the house.

I hear her jiggle the door, a few muttered, unintelligible curses, and her footsteps behind me through the crunching snow.

"Luke"—she sounds out of breath trying to keep up with me—"where are you going?"

Unease curls around the base of my spine, tightening the closer I get to the house. "To check on my parents."

Noel inhales sharply, then jogs to try to catch up with me, but my long strides are too much for her. "Luke, wait. Is something wrong?"

I finally glance back at her to see the true concern in her gaze. "I don't know. They're usually up and working on snow removal by six in the morning with me, and since I was up at the cabin without the snowmobile, they would have seen it in the barn and known they would need to bring it up to try to help clear the path so I could get out easier." I scan the property again, worry now gnawing at my stomach. "And they haven't touched anything."

Her eyes widen slightly as she reaches me. "Shit…"

I climb the porch and try the door, but it's locked. "I'm going around the back."

"Luke—"

Whatever she has to say can wait.

Panic threatens to overwhelm me as I work my way through the deep snow and drifts the wind left against the house, trying to peek in the windows, but they're mostly frosted over. As is the kitchen door that they always leave unlocked.

I turn the handle and push it in. "Mom, Dad?"

The eerie silence of the house doesn't help ease my worry. I scan the kitchen.

A pot sits on the stove, lid halfway off.

Two dirty bowls stand on the counter with what appear to have the remnants of soup in them.

The TV drones on in the living room to my right.

Mom would never leave dirty dishes out or the TV on if she or Dad weren't in there watching it.

My chest aches, like iron bands are tightening around it more and more the longer I see the state of the house. I don't bother taking off my boots; I just rush through the kitchen to the staircase. "Mom, Dad, are you here?"

There's no way they left.

They couldn't have.

When I checked on them after I threw Noel into the cabin, they were fine. Mom said Dad seemed to be doing better. She said she was planning her usual Christmas spread for the two of them and they were going to watch movies and ride out the storm.

They were fine…

"Mom! Dad!" I keep calling for them as I take the steps

243

two at a time to the second floor, then scramble the few feet it takes to get to their door, which stands wide open, allowing me to see in.

Their inert forms lie on the bed, both of them on their sides.

Unmoving.

Mom has her back to me, but Dad faces the door, his skin a sickly pallor I don't think I've ever seen on the man.

"Shit…" I rush in and drop to my knees on his side of the bed. "Dad!"

I shake his shoulder and press a hand to his forehead.

It isn't just warm; it's *hot*.

Fuck.

He releases a little moan from between dry, cracked lips.

"Shit, shit, shit, shit."

I rush around the bed to the other side to find Mom in much the same condition—her lashes fluttering but not responding, skin hot, looking pale and dehydrated.

"Luke?" Noel's voice carries in from the stairs, and a second later, she appears in the doorway with wide eyes. "Oh, God, are they—"

"Call an ambulance." I incline my head toward the phone on the dresser, and she rushes in, tugging off her mittens and shoving them into her pockets. "What's wrong with them?"

"I don't know." I return my focus to the bed. "Mom." I shake her gently, and her eyes flutter open. "Ma, can you hear me?"

Her cracked lips part slightly, and she releases a shuddering cough filled with unhealthy fluid sounds. "Luke, what are you doing here?"

"The storm's over, Ma. I came to check on you." I push sweat-dampened hair from her forehead. "You're sick."

She hacks again and tries to push herself up into a sitting

position with the hand not pressed over her mouth. "Just caught whatever your father has. We'll be fine."

"You don't look fine, Ma, and neither does Dad."

Noel's hand shakes as she dials the number on the cordless, and she tosses me a look filled with all the same fear flooding me right now.

Mom glances at Dad, then up at Noel. "What are you doing here, dear?"

"It's a long story, Mom." I press my palm flat to try to better gauge her temperature. But only one description comes to mind—*burning the fuck up.* "When did your fever start?"

She shakes her head and coughs. "I don't know." More rattling. "Yesterday sometime? Your father's broke—"

"No, it didn't, Ma." I glance at him, but he hasn't moved and doesn't even seem to realize there's anyone else in the room or hear the conversation happening right next to him. "Or it did, and it's back." *With a vengeance.* "He doesn't sound like he's breathing very well."

The rattling and wheezing every time he draws a breath makes my own chest feel so tight that each one becomes agony.

Maybe that's the anxiety sneaking up again.

But I have to keep it at bay.

If I let it overwhelm me, I won't think clearly. I might miss something or make a mistake that could be costly—and not just to me.

Noel's eyes widen slightly as something inaudible leaks around where her ear is pressed to the phone. "Hi, yes. Bonnie, it's Noel." She meets my gaze. "Belated Merry Christmas to you, too. I'm out at the Crisp farm. We need an ambulance right away. Luke's parents aren't doing well."

She examines them, looking more frantic each moment while I try to remain calm so I don't panic them even more.

"I'm not sure. The flu, maybe?" Her blue eyes dart up to me in question. "How long have they been sick, Luke?"

They both start coughing so loudly I can barely hear myself think. Dad winces, like it's acutely painful. Mom reaches over and pats his shoulder, offering support in any way she can.

I wrack my brain, trying to remember specifics through the static everything that's happened has created in my head. "I think my dad started not feeling well the day you arrived in town. They've been cooped up in the house together since then." Which was how I ended up in town on Christmas Eve day under that tree with Noel. "Mom was taking care of him. She seemed fine when I checked on them Christmas Eve, early evening when you got here."

Noel nods and relays all the information as I climb to my feet and rush into the bathroom to fill two glasses with water for them.

By the looks of it, they haven't left this room in a while.

They're probably incredibly dehydrated, which will not help them fight off whatever is ravaging their systems right now.

When I come back in, Noel is chewing on her bottom lip, phone still pressed to her ear, none of her panic relieved. If anything, she looks more tense, more worried than when I left the room.

"What is it?"

Her brow furrows. "The road isn't plowed."

"Fuck."

Something I would have already realized if I'd actually been paying attention to that as I came down the mountain instead of having my laser focus on Noel.

I hand Mom a glass of water. "When can they get some-body up here?"

Noel releases a little rushed breath, filled with her anxiety. "I just asked. Bonnie's going to radio the maintenance department to check."

Watching Mom struggle to even lift the glass to her lips to take a sip, and seeing how weak Dad is, barely able to lift his head and unable to fully sit up, her news doesn't give me any confidence in where this is heading.

I kneel next to Dad and help lift his head to take a drink. "We're going to have to take them."

"What?" Noel's mouth gapes. "But you said the road isn't passable."

"It isn't, but by the time they actually get a plow up here…"

I don't finish the thought.

Because I don't want Mom and Dad to hear, nor do I want to admit it's a real possibility.

But Noel knows what I'm saying without the words ever leaving my mouth.

Mom and Dad have always been incredibly healthy, far more active and youthful than some people half their age, but they're still almost seventy years old, and whatever this is that's attacking them, it moved quickly.

Mom was fine only a day and a half ago.

Just like I was before Noel showed back up.

Noel releases a long breath, returning her focus to the phone. "Okay. Yes, I'm still here." Her worried gaze meets mine again. "Bonnie said potentially two hours…"

Far too long.

We have no idea how long they've been this bad, and we can't risk that it might take them even longer to get through all the snow to us.

I shake my head, glancing between Mom and Dad again, assessing them the best I can. "We have to try in the truck. Give me the phone."

She hands it off to me with a trembling hand.

"Hey, Bonnie, it's Luke."

"Luke"—Bonnie's worried voice cuts through the line —"I'm so sorry, but the plows are way out on County Highway 23, and by the time they come all the way back to your side of town and try to get up the mountain—"

"I know. It's not your fault, but…" I turn away and try to lower my voice, putting my back to the three people I care about the most in the world. "I don't think they're going to last long enough for us to get them to the clinic if we wait."

That bile threatens to finally show, and I have to struggle to keep it down and prevent myself from heaving on the damn carpet.

She sucks in a sharp breath. "Can you get them out?"

It's the same question that now sits heavy on my shoulders and in my heart.

"I don't know, but I'm going to try."

If I have to get out of the damn truck and carry them to the clinic, I will.

"Okay"—Bonnie clicks something on a keyboard—"Frank is in one of the trucks. I've already sent him your way. I'm going to tell him you're heading to the emergency clinic. If he can help, he's going to try."

"I appreciate that."

It's all I can ask.

And it's one of the best things about Mistletoe—anyone here will do *anything* for a friend or neighbor.

Which means for anyone, since we're *all* friends and neighbors.

"Can you call Doc Woodson and let him know we're coming?"

Her typing comes again. "Of course, as soon as we're off the line."

"Thanks."

The fact that Doc lives close enough to town that his

access to meet us at the clinic won't be blocked the way we are on the mountain gives me a modicum of hope.

I end the call and drop the phone back into the cradle. When I turn back, Noel's concern-and-tear-soaked eyes meet mine in question. "You need to help me get them into the truck."

"Of course."

She glances toward the phone, and without saying a word, I know what she's thinking.

"Call your mom quickly. Tell her what's going on, but we can't waste any time."

Noel's head bobs emphatically, then she snags the phone and dials as I start tugging open dresser drawers and pulling out heavy, warm clothes for Mom and Dad.

I don't even know if they're strong enough to walk.

Dad probably isn't.

And they can't go out in this cold and the deep snow and all the way over to the barn in just their pajamas.

Plus, if we get stuck, it's going to get really fucking chilly out there waiting for someone to get us out.

Mom coughs and watches me scramble to find what I'm looking for. "I really think we'll be fine, dear." Another hacking fit. "You're overreacting."

"I'm not, Ma, and even if I am, I'm not going to risk that I might be right."

The mere thought of how this might go…

Bile climbs my throat, and I choke it back as I bring Mom a heavy sweater and a pair of fleece leggings. She accepts them with a trembling hand, and I grab Dad a pair of jeans and his favorite UW-Madison Bucky Badger sweatshirt.

"Hi, Mom." Noel turns to watch me as I start helping Dad out of his pajamas and into the clothes. "Yes, I'm fine, but Luke and I need to take his parents into town to the clinic." She releases a little hiccup that borders on a sob. "Yes, I know

249

the road isn't plowed yet." Her blue eyes bore into mine. "They're really sick, Mom. I don't know how long I'll be, but I'm okay. All right. I love you, too. I'll call you as soon as I can."

She ends the call and quickly races to the other side of the bed to Mom, dropping to her knees with a kind smile. "Hi, Mrs. Crisp."

Mom reaches out to pat her cheek like she has a million times, then seems to think better of it and tucks it back against her chest. "You're such a beautiful girl."

Noel's smile grows, but it can't wipe away the trepidation in her gaze. "Thank you." She pats Mom's leg. "Let's get you dressed."

I manage to get the pants on Dad, and Noel starts by helping Mom with her leggings.

Mom blinks a few times, watching her, then glances over at me before refocusing on Noel. "What are you doing here? Were you and Luke together?"

Shit.

For a split second, the tiniest smile curls Noel's lips before it disappears just as quickly. "I'm surprised he didn't tell you."

For Christ's sake...

This is not the time.

Mom looks over at me. "Tell me what?"

Noel clears her throat awkwardly. "Um, that I came on Christmas Eve."

Coughing again, Mom presses her hand over her mouth to cover it before turning back to Noel. "You did?"

I offer Noel a little warning glare as I get off Dad's pajama top.

There was a *reason* I didn't tell my mother that Noel was going to be riding out the storm in my cabin.

The last thing I wanted to do was to have Mom and Dad

wondering what Noel and I would be up to trapped together for two days.

Which is exactly what Mom is likely doing right now.

And she's a smart woman.

Which means she's probably right in her speculation.

Dad seems so out of it that I'm not even sure if he recognizes me. I help him sit up and tug the sweatshirt over his head, then immediately lay him back down because he can't seem to hold himself upright.

Watching Noel finish getting Mom dressed, I push to my feet. "I'm going take him down first, then come back for her."

Her lips quiver, those tears barely contained. "What should I do?

At this point, there's only one thing we *can* do.

"Pray."

25

NOEL

By the time Frank finally meets up with us on the road with his plow, my hand already aches from clutching the door handle so tightly.

I release a heavy breath of relief as his blade easily cuts through the snow in front of us, clearing a path the rest of the way down the mountain through drifts we could very well have been stuck in otherwise.

The first two miles, I barely breathed, my throat so tight I couldn't swallow. Even in Luke's massive truck, and with all his sheer will and determination, we got stalled six times in just that short distance.

Only Luke's winch tied to trees along the road freed us.

And that took valuable time we don't have.

Every time I glance into the back seat at his parents, I have to fight the choking sob that threatens to crawl at my throat.

Luke was right.

We couldn't have waited.

As it stands now, even with Frank freeing up our path,

I'm not so sure when we get them to the clinic that things *are* going to be okay.

Not with their rattling coughs.

The heavy, wet sound of their lungs.

Oh, God, please keep them safe.

I glance over at Luke and his death grip on the wheel, alternating his focus between Frank on the road in front of us and the rearview mirror to check the two most important people in his life. "How are you doing?"

He flinches at my question and then peeks my way before refocusing ahead. "I'll be a lot better once Doc sees them."

We all will.

Bonnie has probably already gotten word across Mistletoe of our frantic drive down the mountain to get them help.

And with Bambi spreading news like an STD, that means everyone will be worrying and praying, waiting for news.

I just keep holding my breath, hoping nothing else interferes, while worrying that the stress and anxiety may make Luke actually snap.

My hands itch to reach out to him, to rest my hand on his arm and squeeze to comfort him, to say or do something that might make him feel even remotely better about the situation, but after the argument we just had, I'm not so sure he'd want me to touch him right now.

It might only make things worse, and that's the last thing I want to do.

I've done enough to ruin his life as it is.

Something I've become abundantly aware of over the last few days.

He spent eight years alone, eight years loving me and hoping I would come back. Secluding himself from the things and people he once loved.

And it turned him into a monster.

It turned him in to the type of man no one in town liked, that no one wanted to talk to.

No one even bothered to try.

Swiping the tears from my eyes, I turn back and twist as far as I can in the seat, but I still can't reach Mrs. Crisp behind me. I unbuckle my seat belt, climb onto my knees, and lean back.

Luke's strong hand hits my back. "What are you doing?"

"I'm checking on your parents."

I glance at him and his tight jaw. A muscle tics, concern flashing in his green eyes before they move to the road.

"I don't like this without your seat belt on."

Muttering a curse under my breath, I twist back toward him more so I can see his eyes when he peeks over at me again. "Do you want me to check on them or not?"

The truck rocks slightly, drawing his attention back to the road.

Hell.

I could cut the tension with a knife.

And this isn't the good kind of tension we shared in the cabin, the type that simmered and bubbled until it boiled over in the most delicious way.

Not at all.

A lot of it has to do with the fact that neither of his parents look good, resting with their heads against the doors in the back seat, growing paler and paler and coughing more every minute that ticks by as we descend the mountain.

The rest is likely due to how we left things when I tried to run from the lake.

Regardless of Luke's objections, I manage to scramble back enough to get my hand to Mrs. Crisp's cheek. "Hey, Mrs. Crisp."

She lifts her head slightly, her eyes fluttering but not fully opening.

"Can you hear me?"

The tiny bob of her head almost tips her over.

"How are you feeling?"

It has to be shitty.

The woman is burning up.

I twist to look at Luke. "She's warm, really warm. Feels worse than at the house."

He glances back at me. "Shit."

"I'm okay, dear."

She isn't okay, and she knows it, too. But the woman never lets anyone worry about her. Like my own mother, she's constantly taking care of everyone else, and when Luke and I were together, she always treated me like the daughter they never had.

Tears threaten to spill over from my eyes, and I swipe them away with the back of my hand and stretch to the seat behind Luke to try to reach his dad.

The truck slips, sending us sliding slightly to one side.

"Shit." I shift sideways and slam into Luke's headrest, but a strong arm slides up under and around me, securing my waist and holding me steady.

He regains control and then looks back at me. "You all right?"

Definitely not.

None of this is all right.

Not the situation with Luke and me.

Not the things that were said.

And certainly not the current rush to try to save the life of the people who were like second parents to me since the day I was born.

Flashes of that call from Mom, telling me Dad was gone, echo through my head, threatening to take me to the place I haven't allowed myself to go since stepping into the Crisps' bedroom—a place where I lose them, too.

I choke back the sob sliding up my throat. "I'm fine..."

Luke probably knows I'm lying.

The man reads me far too well. With his strong, warm arm wrapped around me, holding me steady, I almost wish he would press me, that he would do or say something to make it better.

But he can't take care of me right now when we're trying to take care of his parents.

That's my job.

I push through my worry and pain and stretch to reach his dad. "His fever seems...I don't know. The same? Maybe worse?"

"Fuck..."

Luke's arm tightens around me with the low, almost-growled curse.

God, it feels too good.

It shouldn't.

Not under these circumstances.

I TAP his hand to tell him to release his grip on me, and I settle back in my seat, buckling my belt again without daring to look at him. Instead, I focus on the plow, on the snow flying out to the right, along the bank, creating massive drifts. "We're still, what, five miles out?"

He nods. "But with Frank in front of us, at least now, we're going at a decent clip. We'll be there within half an hour, tops."

The steel in his voice belies how close he is to the edge of completely losing it.

But he has to keep it together.

And I'll be damned.

I don't give a shit if he doesn't want me here, doesn't want my touch right now. His cemented me, held me steady. And I have to do the same.

Or at least try.

Even if he hates me for it.

That certainly wouldn't be a new feeling for him...

I reach out and curl my hand over his on the wheel, tightening my fingers across his. "They'll be okay."

The look he gives me tells me everything I need to know.

He doesn't believe me.

I wasn't here when Dad died—never could have made it in time after he had the heart attack so unexpectedly. So, I can't imagine what Luke is feeling right now, wondering if he was too late to save them. But I can sympathize with the pain.

It fills the truck cab.

Growing with each slowly passing mile behind the plow.

I eventually pull my hand back, returning to my seat to watch the road pass by agonizingly slowly.

By the time we hit the four-way stop at Main and Mason Street, my knee is bouncing so wildly I can't control it, and Luke has been clenching his jaw so tightly for so long that I wouldn't be surprised if he's cracked some teeth.

We pull through, not bothering to even pause, since the roads are still empty.

Frank pulls to a stop a few doors down from the clinic and climbs from his plow, racing back toward us. Luke is out the door before I can even get my seatbelt off.

Once I manage to, I slide out, slam my door, and move to the back as Frank and Luke work to get his father out. I open the door, carefully sliding my hand in to catch her as his mom falls toward me, unable to hold herself upright.

Her eyes open halfway, enough that they seem to focus on me slightly. "Noel?"

I give her a tight smile, then reach over and unbuckle her belt. "We're going to get you in to see the doctor."

"Oh, did he come to the house?"

She doesn't even know where we are?

That can't be a good sign.

"No, we're at the clinic."

Her eyes close again as renewed panic sets in. I turn and watch Luke and Frank carry his dad in as I wait for someone to come help me. Because there isn't any way Mrs. Crisp is walking in on her own power, and I can't lift her.

She drops her head against my shoulder and releases a little sigh. "I'm so glad you two are back together."

It's as if Luke's axe has been driven straight into my heart.

I open my mouth to reply when the door to the clinic flies back open and the man himself storms out, barreling straight for me.

His hard, determined gaze meets mine as he reaches the truck. "I got her."

He urges me out of the way and slips into place, scooping her up easily and carrying the woman who gave birth to him like she's a child.

I take a long, deep breath, trying to stop the breakdown I'm teetering on the edge of, then go around, climb into the cab, turn off the truck, and close all the doors before running into the clinic.

Frank stands near the reception desk, eyes wide, looking as panicked as I feel. "Are they going to be all right?"

I give him a tense look. "I don't know…they didn't look good."

"No"—he shakes his head—"they didn't. I've known the Crisps my entire life, and I've never seen them look like that." He inclines his head toward the back. "Doc had us take them back there right away."

He runs a hand through his hair, glancing out the front windows toward his truck.

"Go." I motion toward it. "You have more work to do."

His lips twist down. "I don't want to leave them."

Dammit...

A knife twists in my heart.

He has no idea how hard his words hit.

Or how painfully.

I grab his shoulders and squeeze. "You did what you could. Thank you. I don't know if we would have made it without your help."

He gives me a tight smile, pulls me into his arms for a quick hug, then heads to the door but stops with it halfway open. "Will you make sure to call me and let me know?"

I nod, and as soon as he makes it to his truck, I take another cleansing breath, trying to ready myself for what might happen.

You weren't here when Dad died, but you can be here for this.

For Luke.

My eyes drop to the phone on the receptionist's desk, and I slide around and drop into her chair, dialing Mom's number quickly.

She answers on the first ring, as if she's been waiting for it. "Hello?"

"Hi, Mom. We made it to the clinic."

"Oh, thank God. Are they okay?"

I squeeze my eyes closed, pinching the bridge of my nose, trying to rid my brain of the image of them looking half-dead in the back of the truck. "I don't know. I'll let you know as soon as I have an update."

"Is Luke all right?"

Her question almost hurts more than the one about his parents because when it comes to him, I always seem to be the one causing him the most pain.

Even if his parents pull through, his heart will still be broken.

"He will be." The words burn like acid as I speak them. "I think...as long as they are."

Mom releases a frustrated sigh. "If I could get down there to be with you guys, I would."

The thought of having her here, to hold me, to stand by Luke's side and hold one of her best friend's hands through this makes me slap my hand over my mouth to prevent a sob from slipping out.

I force myself to swallow it, clearing my throat. "I know, Mom. Just stay safe. I'll be home when I can, and I'll call you with an update. I promise."

Luke's raised voice reaches me from the back of the clinic as I set the phone back into the cradle.

That doesn't sound good.

I push out of the chair and jog back toward the exam rooms at the rear that stand open, light spilling out into the hallway from both.

Luke stands just inside the one on the left, hands propped on his hips, chest heaving as he glares at the doctor standing over the exam table his father lies on.

Doc Woodson offers him a hard look. "Luke, there's nothing else I can tell you right now."

Pacing now, Luke throws up his hands. "How can you not know what's wrong with them?"

"Because it's been less than five minutes, and it could be a hundred different viruses." He works on Mr. Crisp's arm, cleaning it and searching for a vein. "It could be the flu. It could be just a really wicked bronchial infection. I'm going to run flu tests. I'm going to run blood tests...but I'm not going to have any answers immediately."

Luke's eyes dart over to meet mine, then move to where his mother is spread out on an exam table across the hall from us. "In the meantime, I'll get IVs into both of them and start antibiotics and antivirals."

"Jesus." Luke shoves his hands back through his hair. "How did they get so sick so fast?"

Doc glances up. "You said your dad started feeling ill three days ago?"

Luke nods.

"And your mom seemed fine when you saw her on Christmas Eve? What time was that?"

His eyes cut to me, and I clear my throat.

"I got to the farm around five, and you were back at your cabin by six."

He nods again. "So, maybe twenty minutes before that, 530-ish, I saw her, and she seemed okay. She said she was making soup for them, that Dad was being a terrible patient, as always."

Doc's lips twitch into a half grin. "Sounds about right."

"Are they going to be okay?"

Luke's voice cracks on the last word, and all I want to do is go to him and pull him into my arms to assure him that it will be all right, but I know I shouldn't say anything when I don't really know.

"The IVs will definitely help." Doc fiddles with the IV bag on the stand, ensuring the proper flow. "They're severely dehydrated, and between the antivirals and antibiotics, hope- fully, one will start attacking whatever this is before we even get the results of the tests back."

Luke releases a long, heavy breath, then scrubs his hands over his face before he turns and brushes past me to go into the other exam room with his mother.

He drops into the chair beside her, reaching out to rest his hand on top of hers that doesn't hold the IV.

Doc glances up at me. "He appreciates your help and you being here, even if he doesn't say it."

Why does he feel the need to tell me that?

Is the tension that obvious?

While everyone in town is privy to my history with Luke, he has no idea what's gone on between us, what's been said over the last few days.

He can't possibly understand the situation when I don't.

All I do know is that I'm drawn across the hall toward Luke, pausing at the doorjamb to watch him gently stroking his mother's hand, whispering something to her that I can't hear.

Sensing me, he looks up, his eyes brimming with tears. "You don't have to stay. See if Frank can get you up the mountain to your mom."

I scowl at him. "Do you really think I'd leave you right now, even if Frank wasn't already gone? Do you think I would?"

His jaw hardens, and the hand resting on the top of the arm of the chair clenches around its edge. "I don't know anything when it comes to you anymore, Noel. I really fucking don't."

26

LUKE

The steady beep of the machines that has filled the hospital room for the past day and a half continues incessantly.

It would drive me to the brink of madness if it didn't mean that Mom's and Dad's heartbeats were both steady at this point.

Finally.

Evening out after several dangerous drops of blood pressure and heart rate during that first twelve hours before the antivirals started kicking in and attacking the mystery virus that almost killed them.

I blink open my eyes, brain still slightly foggy, and lift my head from the back of the chair to scan the now-familiar hospital room that has been our home since the roads were clear enough to get them here from Mistletoe.

That storm did its damnedest to prevent it, but we got them out.

And I don't ever want to relive anything the wind and snow brought to my door and into my life.

None of it.

I shift more upright and blink away the last vestiges of sleep.

Dad snores peacefully in his bed to my left, and I turn to my right to find Mom watching me intently, like she's been *waiting* for me.

That's never a good sign...

Yawning, I run a hand through my hair. "I fell asleep?"

She nods. "And now, you need to get out of here, go home, take a shower, clean up, eat some real food, and sleep in your own *bed*."

The last time I was in that, it was with Noel...

Before I took her up to the lake.

Before it all fell apart.

Again.

I shake my head. "Nah, I'm fine."

Staying here has been as much about not wanting to leave Mom and Dad as it has about not wanting to be *there*.

Where it will still smell like her.

Where I'll still taste her on my tongue with each breath I take.

But Mom levels her glare at me, clearly feeling better. "It wasn't a request, Luke, you smell."

I scowl at her, but her lips curve the tiniest bit at the sides.

At least her sense of humor hasn't been affected by all this.

"We're okay, hon. You know the doctor said we'll probably go home tomorrow—"

"Then I'll leave tomorrow."

She purses her lips and reaches out to slide her hand over mine, where it rests beside her on the bed. "I know you're worried, but we're fine now."

No matter how many times she says that to me, no matter

how many times the doctors assure me that they're both going to make a full recovery, I can't get the way they looked lying in that bed out of my head. I can't get past that drive and thinking that by the time we got to the clinic, it would be too late.

Even now, seeing the life returning to her eyes and the color back in her skin, the thought of leaving them makes my stomach turn.

She interlocks her fingers with mine and squeezes tightly. "What do I need to say to snap you out of it?"

"Nothing."

"What if I asked you what was happening with you and Noel?"

I wince at her question and avoid eye contact, watching the heart monitor next to Dad's bed.

The man always could sleep through anything, but I could really use a rescue here, an interruption of *any* kind...

Mom squeezes my hand. "Are you just going to ignore me?"

I tug mine out from under hers and push out of the chair. "I think it's better if I do."

"Why is that?"

Because if I open my mouth and start discussing anything having to do with Noel, that thin thread of control I've managed to maintain over my emotions that is already so badly frayed will finally give way.

And I'm afraid I'll drown in the tsunami it releases.

I turn to face her, wanting to walk out, but I can't, not until she and Dad are released. "Nothing's happening with Noel and me."

Not anymore.

Mom watches me pace, following me back and forth at the end of both beds. "I heard a lot of what you said to Doc

267

Woodson, and to each other in that car. I may have been feverish, possibly hallucinating, but it sure sounded like something happened between you two. She was at your cabin for two days…"

I chew on the inside of my cheek, wrapping my hands around the edges of the stupid tray that sits at the foot of her bed to use when her meals are delivered.

Mom always did love Noel.

She had prayed we would work things out.

Acted as my biggest cheerleader when I got on that plane and flew to Toronto to try to convince Noel to return to Mistletoe.

I don't want to give her any false hope, not like the false hope I let myself develop with every kiss and every touch and every moment we were entwined with each other this Christmas.

"Things are complicated, Mom."

Her graying brows rise. "Aren't they always? That's what relationships are."

I release a heavy sigh. "Noel and I don't have a relationship."

She laughs loud enough that Dad shifts in his bed, glancing over his shoulder at us, blinking awake.

"What's going on? Everything all right?"

I scowl at her for waking him, and she holds up her hands innocently, but she's not sorry, not one bit.

"I was just questioning your son about Noel…"

Dad nods slowly as he pushes himself up to a fully seated position, yawning and rubbing at his gray hair that's already disheveled. "Then I better stay awake because I'm interested in this, too."

"For the love of God, you two, my love life, or lack thereof, is off the table for conversation."

They exchange a look that tells me my objection is going

to go unheeded, but before they can say anything else, one of the nurses flutters in with a happy smile and a tablet in hand.

"Mr. And Mrs. Crisp, you're both awake." She gives me a pointed look. "And you're still here."

Mom laughs. "I told him to go home."

The nurse sets her tablet next to Mom's bed and fiddles with some of her machines, checking different stats. "I've been telling him the same thing for a day and a half." She glances back at me. "He doesn't listen very well, does he?"

Mom fights a laugh, shaking her head. "He doesn't. Didn't as a child, either."

I throw up my hands. "I'm standing right here, you know?"

As happy as I should be that Mom and Dad are back to trying to insert themselves where they don't belong, we certainly don't need the interjection from a random nurse.

She rolls her eyes and mutters something I can't quite make out—though the word "Grinch" is loud enough for me to hear.

We aren't even in Mistletoe, and this woman already knows my fucking nickname.

Great.

I look away from them to find Dad staring at me intently. He motions me over to him while Mom and the nurse gossip about something I don't want to be involved with. He pats the side of his bed, urging me to sit.

With an annoyed sigh, I comply.

The old man almost died.

I really can't say "no."

"Your mom can be pushy."

"So can you."

He smirks. "That's what I love about her, and that's what you always loved about Noel."

Locking gazes with him, staring back into the same shade

of green I see in the mirror, I can't keep up the pretense. "You don't need to remind me why I love Noel."

He offers me a tight smile. "Why did she come to the lot on Christmas?"

To break my fucking heart.

To crush the shards she left behind eight years ago further into dust.

I release a long sigh, lowering my head back to stare at the drop ceiling above us. "She drove down in the storm to get a fucking tree."

Dad chuckles, coughing lightly as the infection still tries to work its way out of his body and his lungs. The doctor said it could take weeks before that cough is finally gone, but it will go away—eventually. "She's so much like her father."

That draws a genuine smile across my lips.

"She really is. Apparently, Mrs. J never got a tree this year, and it bothered her far more than it bothered her mother."

"I can see why."

I return my gaze to him. "Did you know she wasn't aware that her dad picked the town tree every year?"

Dad's eyebrows rise. "Really?"

I shake my head, rubbing at the tension in my neck from spending so many hours dozing in that chair. "I told her earlier that day when I was in town getting you the medicine from the pharmacy. I ran into her and said some things I probably shouldn't have…"

"So, she was probably really happy with you when she showed up to get the tree."

"Shit." I snort. "Definitely not happy with me. And to be fair, I wasn't very happy to see her, either. The storm wasn't at full force yet, but it was bad enough that she shouldn't have been driving."

Mom and the nurse finish whatever they're gabbing

about, and the woman in the blue scrubs moves over to Dad's bedside, absently flipping her hand toward me.

"Oh, keep going. I'm very interested in the story."

Mom raises her brows. "Well…go on."

I cast an annoyed glare at the eavesdropping woman changing out Dad's IV bag, but with both him and Mom staring at me, waiting expectantly, I can't put it off any longer.

It's time to come clean.

Mostly.

"Well"—I rise from the bed and pace again, unable to sit still as the memories that are still so fresh come racing back —"I wouldn't let her leave."

Dad chuckles low. "How did you manage that? Noel isn't really someone you tell what to do."

"No, she isn't." I glance at the nurse who eyes me as intently as a grandmother waiting for the big reveal on her favorite soap opera, then from Mom to Dad, preparing myself for their reactions. "I threw her over my shoulder, and I took her to the cabin."

Mom gasps, and the nurse's jaw drops.

Dad coughs and then clears his throat. "You *idiot*."

I snort. "Thanks."

"I bet she wasn't too happy with that." Mom scowls at me. "I wouldn't have been in her position."

Unhappy.

That feels like an incredibly tame description of how she reacted.

And for the way she tore into me the second I walked back into the cabin.

"No, she wasn't, but she was stupid enough to drive in a storm that was only going to get worse, and she expected me to strap a tree to the top of her car and let her drive back up the mountain with it. What the hell was I supposed to do?"

Mom offers a slight shrug, the hospital gown shifting over her slender shoulders. "Reason with her."

"Oh, yeah." I snort. "Because reasoning with Noel Jolly always goes so well."

Dad laughs slightly. "Okay, that's fair, but there had to be a better way to handle the situation than that."

I run a hand through my hair, glancing at the nurse, who seems to have stopped whatever she was doing. "If you're just here for the story, you can go."

She narrows her gaze on me, then glances over at Mom. "You'll fill me in later?"

Is this a fucking joke right now?

Mom nods her agreement, and the nurse flutters out of the room with a wink at me.

Jesus Christ...

I turn to face both of their beds. "Look. I took Noel to the cabin. We stayed in the cabin. We came down from the cabin. We found you. End of story."

Dad snorts, and Mom laughs again.

She rolls her eyes, adjusting the blanket over her lap. "Yeah, you're definitely acting like that's the end of the story."

I clench my hands at my sides, opening and closing them as I try desperately to control what's building up inside me— the anger over letting myself get back in the same position I was in eight years ago, feeling the same pain, allowing the same agony to overwhelm me.

"It doesn't matter what happened." I shake my head. "She's leaving in a few days…"

Mom's brows rise slowly. "What do you mean 'in a few days?' Today's the 28th, right?"

I nod. "Yeah, and she usually goes home right after New Year's."

"Oh, honey." Mom's face falls. "She isn't staying that long this time."

Her words register slowly.

"What-what do you mean?"

Mom's lips twist. "I talked to her mom, and she said the Leafs have a big home game this year on New Year's Day, so she needs to be there a few days early to help with some PR stuff, getting things ready. In previous years, they've either been off or had away games, so she wasn't required to be back…"

It shouldn't matter.

She's leaving.

When that happens is irrelevant now.

"Good riddance."

Dad coughs. "Why don't you just say what you mean?"

I glare at him. "I just *did.*"

"No, you didn't." He raises a hand that no longer shakes and points at me. "I can see it in your eyes. If there's something you want to say to that girl or something you want to do before she leaves, I suggest you do it quickly."

Something about the way he says it makes panic well up inside me, heavy and thick like molasses.

"When is she leaving?"

Mom and Dad share a look, and Mom offers a sympathetic smile. It's one I've seen far too many times not to recognize as one she only gives me when she feels like she's telling me something I won't want to hear.

"I believe later today, hon."

Shit.

I force myself to take another breath. "It's fine." Another one burns my lungs. "I don't have anything to say to her."

Dad presses his lips together in a firm line, his jaw tightening. "That's bullshit, son. We've been begging you for eight years to have a conversation with that woman, and if you didn't have it and things that you needed to say weren't said in that cabin over Christmas, then you should do it now before she leaves again."

Beyond frustrated now, bordering on rage, I throw my hands up. "But that's just it, Dad. She *will* leave. She always *does*."

The corner of Mom's lips curl slightly. "Maybe this year, you'll get a Christmas miracle."

27

NOEL

Mom stands at the kitchen counter, a mug in hand—likely hot cocoa, given the giant marshmallows floating above the rim. "Are you all packed and ready?"

Thinking about my suitcase waiting near the front door and her question, I give her a tight smile. "I'm packed, but I don't know that I'm ready to go."

She nudges another mug sitting on the counter toward me. "I made you some cocoa."

"Ooh!"

I reach over and pick it up, the rich chocolate scent invading every breath I take as I hold it up.

That familiar smell brings with it a flood of childhood memories. Sitting by the fire with Mom and Dad with him reading to us. Snowball fights that led to frozen fingers that needed a warm mug—and sometimes tears. Ice-skating and tumbling into Luke's house, where his mom always had some waiting for us on the stove.

Shit.

The last one hurts more than the first, somehow.

Maybe because it's fresher.

Because I've spent the last two days, since I left the clinic after the gut punch from Luke, feeling even worse than I did eight years ago.

Because even after his confession on the ice, *nothing* has changed.

I still can't stay; he still won't leave.

It's a vicious cycle that has repeated itself.

Like some gut-wrenching déjà vu...

I sip at the hot liquid to try to clear the emotion from my throat, intentionally pulling one of the floating marshmallows into my mouth for that extra dash of sweetness.

It coats my tongue and warms my stomach. "Thanks, Mom. I needed this."

She releases a tense little laugh. "I bet. This has been a pretty unusual Christmas."

That's a pretty big understatement.

I rest my hip against the counter, staring down at the bobbing marshmallows.

Even though two whole days have passed, I still haven't been able to get that look on Luke's face out of my head. His rejection of my concern at the clinic stung more than I care to admit, and the fact that he hasn't called since suggests he still feels exactly the same as he did in that moment.

That this has all been pointless.

Just another way to hurt ourselves and each other.

"I spoke to his mom, you know."

I glance up at her again.

She takes a sip of her cocoa, wrapping her hands around the mug like it's a pot of gold. "A couple of hours ago."

"I'm going to swing by there when I leave town, on my way back to Green Bay for my flight so I can say goodbye."

Mom nods slowly. "Good idea. It sounds like they're going to be released tomorrow."

"Oh"—some of that tension in my chest releases slightly—"that's good news."

Considering how sick they were, it was very touch and go for that first twenty-four hours, until they started seeing some improvement with the antivirals.

"It is." Mom watches me over the mug rim as she drinks. "And hopefully, that virus they had doesn't affect anyone else in town."

I hope not.

No one knows how they were exposed, since the rest of Mistletoe seems to have escaped its wrath.

Probably something a tourist brought up with them that infected Mr. Crisp while interacting on the lot.

Which hopefully means it died when it stopped being contagious in them.

I drink my cocoa and scan the living room, my eyes drawn to the corner that still remains empty of a tree, then over to Nutsack on the mantle. "This certainly was a strange Christmas, but at least you had Nutsack to keep you company while I was gone."

She laughs, the sound so light that it instantly lifts some of the tension that has threatened to suffocate me over the last couple of days—but not all. "Oh, he and I had a hell of a time, let me tell you…"

"I bet you did." I clear my throat at the emotion starting to clog it. "I just feel so awful that I wasn't here with you."

"Noel, we've talked about this." She slides her hand over mine on the counter and squeezes. "You did what you had to do. You needed that tree to cope with not having Dad here, and that's fine. We all cope in our different ways." A little sigh falls from her lips. "Maybe I should have physically tried to stop you."

"I don't know how you would have done that?"

Her laughter becomes almost hysterical. "Hey, I can body slam."

I roll my eyes, chuckling at the absurdity of her suggesting it. "Yeah, right, Mom…"

She grins. "But honestly"—she peeks at me like she's about to say something and she isn't sure how I'm going to take it—"I was better than I thought I would be."

"What do you mean?"

We've discussed what happened over Christmas—at least, *some* of it—over the last few days, but she never mentioned anything like this to me. And the saintly woman never asked what happened between Luke and me, almost like she could tell that if she did, I would break completely.

"You know I miss your dad more than I can put into words. Every day is"—she draws in a long, slow breath—"a struggle, and I really thought Christmas was going to be the worst, for obvious reasons. But being here, in the house by myself, with the fire roaring, the wind outside howling, and the blanket of snow coming down, it felt like, I don't know, the world was washing away all the pain and the anguish and giving me a clean start." A tear drips from her eye. "Your dad is always here. He always will be. It isn't without him; it's just with him in a different form."

A half-sob, half-laugh slips from me. "Christ, how can you be so *wise* and calm about this?"

She laughs, swiping away her tears. "I don't think I'm being very *wise* or calm. Believe me, I've cried plenty and raged and fell apart hundreds of times over the last six months. But the last few days with him gone and you not here have shown me that I can do it." Pride fills her words. "I can be by myself, if I need to, if you have to work and can't make it home for Christmas."

Even if she says she's okay with it, the thought of her being alone again makes my lips twist. "Or, you know, you could always go to Luke's. The Crisps would love to have you."

"Oh, I know, sweetheart." She pats my hand. "They invited me this year, if you weren't coming home."

"They did?"

She nods.

That reminds me of another thing Luke revealed that surprised me, though maybe it shouldn't have.

"Did you know that Luke doesn't eat with them anymore? Won't even set foot in their house at Christmas."

She chews on her bottom lip. "I did know that."

"Do you know why?"

Her shoulders rise and fall slightly. "I can speculate."

The anguish on his face when he told me the truth ripples back through my entire body, like being punched in the gut.

"He said it was because I love Christmas, and he could never separate me from it. That every time he heard or saw anything Christmas related, it made him think of me and that was too painful."

She nods slowly and takes another drink of her cocoa, swirling it around in the mug. "I kind of suspected as much. You don't go from having that kind of holiday cheer your entire life to randomly becoming the town grinch practically overnight. And it did coincide with you leaving."

It's going to get worse because of what happened while you were in that cabin...

"Shit." I squeeze my eyes closed, tightening my grip on the mug to attempt to ground myself in some way. "I let something happen that I shouldn't have."

A momentary silence hangs between us before Mom finally speaks. "What makes you think it shouldn't have happened?"

I will myself to open my eyes and meet hers. A humorless laugh falls from my lips. "Because now I feel even shittier than I did when I left eight years ago. Luke is furious with me, and he probably has every right to be. It wouldn't surprise me if no one ever sees him again after this."

"I don't think his parents will let that happen. I'm sure they'll try to convince him to come back to the land of the living."

"I doubt it's possible."

Her brows rise. "Could you do that?"

"What? Get him to come back to the land of the living?"

She nods with a little half-smile playing at her lips. "Or is his heart just three sizes too small?"

I have to grin at that reference.

How much do I tell her?

There are things that went down—literally—that I definitely don't want to be discussing with my mother.

But she's the only person who might actually understand.

It spills out before I can stop it.

"I broke his heart. I didn't realize how badly. I thought he made his choice and moved on. I thought he was living how he wanted to, but the truth is, he was just waiting for me to come back and to *stay*." A little hiccupped sob fills the kitchen before I realize it's come from me. "His heart...I saw it over the last few days, and it is definitely not three sizes too small. It's far too big, and I don't deserve it."

"Why would you say that, Noel?"

"Because I was selfish, and I took the job." I meet her gaze, and she's blurry now, distorted by my tears. "I left."

"Oh, no." Mom sets her mug on the counter, walks around it, and pulls me into her arms. "This isn't your fault. People break up, Noel. People die. Relationships end for a hundred different reasons. And everyone has to figure out their own way to go on after that." She pulls back, taking my face between her palms like she used to when I was a child and she was *really* trying to get through to me. "You have a beautiful life in Toronto. A job you *love*. Friends you *love*. He chose how he reacted to it, not you. You didn't force him to become that grumpy, reclusive, angry man. He let that fester. He let himself become the Grinch, not you." She brushes away my tears. "And if he gets worse, then that's on him, too, not on you. No matter what happened down there… You are consenting adults, and I know whatever it was meant something to both of you, and that can be *enough*."

I release a shaky breath, trying to control my heart seizing in my chest so violently. "You really are a wise woman."

She smiles. "I always was. You were just a stubborn kid and didn't want to believe that I knew what I was talking about."

"You think I believe you now?"

Her features soften, the concern melting into something else. "I hope you do…"

I sigh as I glance at the clock, the darkness now outside the windows and sliding glass kitchen doors a sign that I need to hit the road. "I need to get going if I'm going to stop at the hospital on my way."

Mom nods slowly. "You do. Just know that he's not there."

Her words make my spine bristle. "I'm surprised. I figured he would have stayed with them until they got discharged."

She returns to her cocoa. "Nancy said he tried, and that was his plan. But…" Offering a slight shrug, she takes a sip and then sets the mug down. "Apparently, his plans changed."

"Apparently…"

Or he went back to hide in his cabin.

I guess it shouldn't surprise me if that's precisely what he did.

If he returned to lock himself inside now that his parents are out of the woods.

Being around all the people and the hustle and bustle of the hospital after living the way he has for so long had to be a lot for him.

He undoubtedly needed the serenity of the mountain.

Where he can go back to being the Grinch.

I skirt the edge of the counter to hug Mom one more time. "I'll see you in a few months."

She nods against my shoulder, squeezing me tightly. "I love you, kiddo. Remember, you have to do what's right for you, not what's right for someone else."

Such a wise woman.

Just like Dad, she always encouraged me to reach for my dreams, to try to grasp them and cling to them tightly. And she doesn't want me to wallow in guilt even though that's probably precisely what I'll end up doing, in spite of anything she says.

She follows me down the front hallway, and I pull on my jacket while she tugs open the door.

"Drive safely. We don't need you sliding off the road. Again."

I scowl at her. "Not funny, Mom."

"It was kind of funny."

Maybe I could laugh about it.

What that damn rabbit caused.

But knowing what it ultimately led to, I can't bring myself to.

Not ever.

I lift my suitcase, give her a final hug, then head down the stairs and make my way over to the rental car.

This piece of shit is the entire reason I ended up in that ditch in the first place.

I could have gone another Christmas without seeing Luke, without confronting the Grinch of Mistletoe and all the love and pain that comes with him, but instead, I ended up in his arms, in his bed, and let him work his way back into my heart.

Stupid.

It was so *stupid*.

All of it.

Letting him rattle me when I slid into the ditch.

Allowing him to get under my skin even more when we stood under the town square tree.

Giving in to my need by practically begging him to touch me the way he did.

Permitting my desire to override my common sense and self-preservation instinct.

Because I knew this would happen.

That we'd be back here again.

To a place where both our hearts are broken in a way that can't be fixed.

I toss my bag into the back seat, climb in, fire up the engine, and turn in the driveway to head back to the road.

"He's not there."

Mom's warning echoes in my head, almost as if she knew what I had been thinking, that stopping to say goodbye to the Crisps would also give me an opportunity to say goodbye to Luke, even if he didn't want me to.

Even when it wouldn't change anything.

It's probably better that I don't.

He made it abundantly clear how he feels. Even though his words said he didn't know, his actions spoke incredibly loudly.

Luke didn't want me there for the same reason I won't stop at the farm and make my way up to the cabin to see him. Because sometimes it's easier not to say goodbye when you don't want to leave. When there's a part of you that wants to stay so badly when you can't, and I'd be lying if I said there wasn't.

But my life is in Toronto now.

My future is there.

No matter how much I may love Mistletoe or the people in it.

Sometimes, a bird has to fly the nest.

That's what Dad always used to say.

And it's time for me to fly home.

I turn onto the road and flip on my Christmas playlist to random, immediately cringing, as "Baby, it's Cold Outside" floats through the speakers.

The damn song that played as Luke fucked me in front of the fire, wearing that damn ugly sweater...

I quickly reach over and turn it off.

Silence is better than the memories.

Definitely.

And silence is better than saying goodbye and breaking his heart all over again.

It's better than having the *same* argument with the *same* outcome.

It's better to just slip out of town and pretend the last few days didn't even happen.

2 8

LUKE

Darkness envelops me as I lean against the barn, staring out at the almost pitch-black road. Out here, the only light comes from the winter moon, and the trees growing on either side block it from reaching most of Jolly Lane.

My eyes still somehow find the spot where Noel spun out into the ditch.

Despite how calm it is tonight, how beautiful the moonlight is spilling across the glistening snow on the property, the longer I wait, the tighter my chest becomes, threatening to suffocate me if it doesn't give my lungs some room to move.

What are you doing, Luke?

This could go badly, so very badly.

It did the last time, and really, nothing's different now.

We might have shared two glorious days together, pretending that the rest of it didn't affect us, that it wasn't all going to lead to this moment again, but we can't ignore it anymore. And if I let her drive away again without making this last-ditch effort, I'll never be able to forgive myself.

This is your only chance.

The phone in the office rings, and I push off the barn and make my way down the driveway to the road.

My hands tighten on the small box cradled in them.

Noel's headlights come down the mountain, bright in the utter dark and still night.

I step out into the middle of the road...and wait.

This is so stupid.

This is so stupid.

This is so stupid.

She could hit the gas instead of the brake, and given the way I snapped at her at the clinic, she might be well within her rights to want to.

I had reached the end of my ability to process anything.

The argument I had just had with her at the lake.

What was happening with Mom and Dad.

Our race into town to the clinic.

Still not knowing what was wrong with them or if they would recover.

All of it had overwhelmed me.

It made me bite her head off when she was trying to offer me the comfort I needed.

I just didn't want it from her when I knew she was going to be the one hurting me by leaving again.

Tonight, all I need her to do is stop.

All I need is a minute—sixty seconds to try to convince her of the thing I couldn't years ago or even during our argument that night in the cabin or at the lake.

I just need a *chance.*

The headlights grow closer and closer as she moves toward the farm.

Too close.

She isn't slowing down.

Shit.

The car passes the tree line where it opens up to the

property, where the moonlight should help allow her to see in front of her better, but she still doesn't slow.

Shit.

Bad idea.

REALLY bad idea.

I prepare to dive out of the way if necessary, but Noel slams on the brakes. The car skids slightly, careening toward me, bright headlights blinding me before it comes to a stop, only a few feet from running me straight over.

My heart thunders against my rib cage, blood rushing in my ears.

Shit, that was too close.

The driver's side door flies open, and Noel launches herself out, blond hair swirling around her like a golden halo —on one very pissed-off angel. "Luke, what the hell are you doing?"

I lift my hand to block the headlights so I can see her wild blue eyes. "Waiting for you."

She spreads out her hands wide, her jaw dropping open. "In the middle of the fucking road?"

Her reaction shouldn't be funny.

Because she really *could* have killed me.

But I can't fight the smirk.

"Where else would I wait for you?"

"I don't know. Maybe someplace *not in the middle of the road*!" She huffs, her breath crystallizing in the cold air. "Why are you waiting for me, anyway?"

Apparently, because I'm an idiot.

And insane.

Isn't that what they say insanity is?

Repeating the same thing, expecting a different result…

This is now the fourth time I'm going to have this conversation with her, that I'm going to try to get her to stay, and none of those have gone particularly well for me.

But this time, I have a secret weapon—or two—in my arsenal.

I approach her tentatively, holding out the box in front of me like a peace offering. "To give you this. I couldn't let you leave without it."

Her gaze softens slightly. "And you couldn't have brought it up to the house?"

"I was busy."

Once I left the hospital, I had barely had enough time to launch my Hail Mary, last-ditch effort and get back to the farm before she started coming down the mountain.

She shifts nervously in her UGGs. "I hear your parents are doing better."

"Much."

God, she's so adorable when she's nervous.

Fiery, feisty Noel is addictive, but *this* Noel is a heady seductress.

I want to go to her, but I force myself to remain where I am, not wanting to spook her.

Biting her lip, she vaguely motions in the direction of the highway. "I was about to stop and say goodbye to them on my way out of town."

"They'll like that." I motion toward her with the box. "Take it."

Her gaze narrows on it skeptically, like it might contain a bomb or something.

"Please, Noel..."

She approaches slowly and accepts it, flipping open the top to look inside. Her eyes widen slowly, and she reaches in and pulls out the contents, rushing to the front of the car to examine it in the headlights.

The beam reflects off the green globe ornament—the one that bears the same design as the one she broke, the one I gave her when we were sixteen.

"Where did you find this?" She peers up at me, still turning it in the light. "I looked in town. Bethany didn't recognize it."

I shake my head, watching her wonder and awe. "She wouldn't have."

Soft blond brows draw low. "Why not?"

"Because I made it."

She pushes to her feet suddenly. "You what?"

"I mean…" I rub at the back of my neck. "I didn't do the glass blowing. I bought the plain glass ornament from Rose, but I painted it. This one and the original I gave you."

Her mouth opens and closes, but she can't seem to manage any words.

"I know you didn't break it on purpose, and I know how upset you were. I could see it that day at the town square tree, so…I…made you a new one."

Lips quivering, she carefully slides it back into the box like it's the most precious thing she owns. "When? When did you paint it for me?"

I run a hand back through my hair, glancing away and up toward the cabin.

She follows my gaze. "When we were up there?"

I nod.

Her eyes widen. "Is that why you kept disappearing?"

All those times I had to tear myself away from her…

Leave her alone and usually naked in my bed or shower…

"Yeah…" Now I shift in my boots, suddenly uncomfortable under her scrutiny. "All my painting supplies are in the shed. I converted it into a little studio, has a space heater and everything. I didn't want you to know what I was doing." I swallow past the lump forming in my throat. "I had planned to give it to you when we came back from the lake."

"Oh, my God." Noel presses her hand over her chest and leans back against the car, apparently not caring how dirty she's getting the back of her jacket and her jeans. "I had no idea you could do this, that you had this much talent. How did I never know that?"

I offer a half shrug. "How did I never know you wanted to leave Mistletoe so badly that you actually would do it without me?"

She flinches and squeezes her eyes closed, releasing a long, heavy sigh.

This is it.

My last chance.

"You love it here, Noel. You always have." It's hard to keep the waver out of my voice when I so badly want her to *hear* me. "Don't tell me it doesn't feel like home."

She glances up at me, her eyes suddenly shimmering. "Of course, it feels like home. It *is* home."

I fist my hands at my sides. "Then why have you spent the last eight years in Toronto instead of here with me, with your parents, with everyone who loves you?"

"People love me in Toronto."

This time, I flinch.

All those nightmares I had imagining her "private lessons" with the players flash through my head.

"Shit. Not like that, Luke. I don't have a…boyfriend or anything. But I have friends, a life there."

"And your dream job, right?"

She nods. "And my dream job."

Here goes the Hail Mary.

"What is it you love so much about that?"

I clench and unclench my fists, wanting so badly to go to her, to pull her up against me, to feel her as we have this conversation.

Noel's slender shoulders rise and fall. "You know how much I've always loved hockey, and doing PR for the team is like…I don't know how to describe it."

"It's nothing you could ever do here…"

Her brow furrows again. "No. It's not."

For all the benefits a small town like Mistletoe offers—the untouched beauty, the friendly people, the safety, and the community—there aren't a lot of opportunities for anyone who doesn't want to work at Town Hall or one of the small shops that line Main Street.

Or on their parents' farm.

And I didn't see it until it was too late.

She always felt like her talents were wasted here, that she couldn't grow or use her skills for anything that *meant* something when she was stifled by the size of Mistletoe.

That's what she gets now working for the team.

Acid churns in my stomach as I take a step toward her. "What if it was?"

Her eyes widen slightly. "What do you mean?"

I approach her tentatively, afraid she might bolt and climb right back into the car. "What if your dream job was here in Mistletoe?"

A tear trickles down her cheek, and she pulls her lip under her teeth and shakes her head. "But it's not, Luke."

"Not *that* job, Noel." I give her a tight smile. "Unless the NHL decides Mistletoe is the *perfect* location for an expansion team. They could play up at the lake."

That earns me a tiny smile.

"What's the *one* thing you love more than hockey, more than just about anything?"

The corners of her mouth twitch slightly. "Christmas."

"Christmas." I inch closer. "You know your dad did, too, and he cherished his role as the head of the decoration committee."

She nods slowly. "Yes, he did."

"No one has taken his place."

Her brow furrows. "Really? Then who did everything this

year?"

I offer a shrug. "Half the town. Everybody did a little piece here, a little piece there, kind of haphazardly thrown together. I think you could see that result in the rush and scramble to get the ceremony ready in time."

She snorts. "It did seem a little mismanaged. The tree was the only thing that seemed to be done right."

Damn.

The compliment melts away the chill of the frigid night air, and I take another step closer.

"You know how important tourism is to Mistletoe…"

"Of course."

Here goes nothing.

"Think about what you could do for this town if you headed that committee"—I swallow back any lingering nerves about laying this out on the table—"and if you were head of the entire PR department for Mistletoe."

Her back stiffens. "That position doesn't exist."

"What if it did?"

She stares at me for far too long, until I don't think she's going to respond.

"Noel? Would it be enough to make you stay?"

"Don't-don't"—her body trembles, and she shakes her head—"do this to me again, Luke."

I can't stop myself from going to her this time and taking her face in my palms to tilt it up. "Don't do what?"

"Don't try to convince me to stay when you know I can't."

"Not even for a job like that? Where you can promote Christmas year-round. Where you can help every single person you love, everyone you grew up with, and their businesses succeed. When you can be the one picking the tree and in control of the decorations for the whole town." I release a little laugh. "God, Noel, do you have any idea what you could do for Mistletoe?"

Her eyes flutter open to meet mine.

"We need someone like you who understands modern social media marketing, how to reach new customers, how to draw people here—and *not* just in November and December. There are so many things we could be doing that we're not, so many steps we could take that would bolster the economy, that would help us grow, that would ensure everyone here has what they need to survive"—I take a fortifying breath —"to ensure that *I* have what I need to survive."

"What's that?"

Her question is so soft I barely hear it over the engine running.

"I need you, Noel. I always have." Pain and soul-eating anxiety sear through me. "The last two days that we spent together have proven that to me because I felt alive again for the first time in eight years. And as soon as my mom told me you were leaving again, I felt like I had died inside. I was terrified I wouldn't catch you in time."

"How did you?" She glances back toward the farm. "Have you been standing out here, waiting for me all night?"

I shake my head. "Your mom called when you left your house."

Her eyes widen, and her gaze drifts up the mountain toward where her mom probably waits to see the results of our mothers' matchmaking work. "She knew?"

I chuckle. "Noel, look at me."

Her eyes flick over to meet mine.

"I'm serious, Snowflake. I talked to Mayor Nielsen about all this."

"You what?"

"As painful as it is to admit, I understand why you need a challenge. That having a job you love, where you feel needed and like what you're doing matters." I brush my thumb across her cheek through the damp track her tears have left.

"But I also know you love Mistletoe, these people, and Christmas more than anybody else. This job is literally being created for *you*. This is *your* job. If you want it."

New tears fall as she stares up at me. "And what if I don't?"

I swallow. "Then…I'll come with you."

Disbelief flashes in her gaze. "You don't mean that."

Eight years ago, I wouldn't have.

Even a week ago, I would have said the thought of leaving home and Mistletoe was crazy.

Yesterday, sitting in that hospital room, I would have said it was completely out of the question.

And I didn't *plan* to make the declaration when I stopped this car.

But there isn't a single thing I'm more sure of now.

"Yes, I do, Snowflake. It's what I should have said eight years ago when we were standing in almost exactly the same spot."

"No." She shakes her head, swallowing a sob. "No, no, no, you can't leave the farm. You can't leave your parents. God, look what just happened."

I take her face in my palms and tilt it up, forcing her to meet my gaze. "I will hire someone to come help them. Your mom will check in on them every day. They won't be alone, just like your mom isn't."

"But what would you do in Toronto?"

It's the same question I asked her only a few days ago, the one that kept me from going to her and staying all those years ago.

"Well…" I glance down at the ornament in the box. "I'm not bad with a paintbrush."

She follows my gaze and then looks back up at me. "You would sell painted ornaments to people?"

I offer a half shrug. "To start, I guess. I always loved art class, and I wasn't terrible at it. I had a lot of free time over the last eight years to mess around with it. I've been painting a lot. I don't know if I can turn it into anything, a career or a job, or a way to make any sort of money, but I could try."

"You would try?"

That disbelief I saw in her eyes leaches into her voice, and the fact that she could *ever* doubt me claws against my chest.

"I would for you, Snowflake. For us. For this. For what we had in the cabin for that day and a half to be what we have every day for the rest of our lives."

Her sob slips out now, and she slaps her hand over her mouth to fight it.

Brushing away her rapidly falling tears, I press a kiss on her forehead. "Please don't cry like that. It makes me think you're going to say something I'm not going to want to hear."

I tug her against my chest and let her cry, and she wraps her arms around my neck, burying her face against my skin.

"What am I supposed to do, Luke?"

"Whatever you need to, Snowflake. Whatever makes you happy."

She pulls back and kisses me softly. "You, you're what makes me happy."

"That doesn't tell me what you're going to do, Noel."

Squeezing me tightly, she drags me down, hovering her lips over mine. "There's only one possible thing I can do."

"What's that?"

"I can't take you from your parents. I can't take you from this place. I love it too much. You love it too much. You'd be fucking miserable in Toronto, even if we were together, and eventually, you'd resent me."

I jerk back, tipping her chin up. "I could never resent you, Snowflake."

"Yes"—she laughs, but there's no humor in it—"you could, and I won't allow that to happen, not when you've created the perfect solution. And this opportunity for me in Mistletoe, it didn't exist eight years ago…" Her whole body trembles. "You *created* a dream job for me."

"I'd do *anything* to make you stay." I kiss her gently, letting my lips linger on hers. "I can't watch you drive away again."

She smiles. "You'll never have to again."

"Good." I slip away from her, duck into the car, turn off the engine, flip on the flashers, and return to her with keys in hand. "You won't need these, then."

"What are you doing?" She glances at the car. "You can't leave it in the middle of the road."

"Yes, I can. Your mom is already at home, and my parents won't be released from the hospital until tomorrow. No one is coming up here."

I tug her away from the hood and up against me again.

She offers a confused look. "Where are we going?"

To relive one of my favorite memories.

I motion behind her toward the lot. "To the barn. I have unspeakable things that baby Jesus definitely won't like that I want to do to you in there. *Again.*"

Throwing her over my shoulder, her yelp echoes through the night, and motion along the side of the road draws my eyes in that direction.

A rabbit hops slowly to the middle of the road and pauses, its ears perked up, eyes locked on us.

Noel shifts on my shoulder, pushing herself up slightly. "Is that—"

I nod, tightening my grip on her. "Yep."

It may look like an innocent animal simply trying to cross the road, but I can see it for what it is now.

Something—or *someone*—intervening and ensuring *this* happened.

Our own Christmas miracle.

EPILOGUE

NOEL

ONE YEAR LATER

The light flurries fluttering down from the night sky float over and through the massive crowd gathered in the town square.

Locals.

Visitors.

Families.

Every single person laughing and enjoying themselves on the ice rinks, at the various food stands, and exploring vendors selling ornaments and other holiday knickknacks.

The annual Christmas Eve ceremony has gone off without a hitch, and I fight back tears as I mark off the last thing on my checklist, watching the mayor thank everyone for coming.

A round of applause goes up as he works his way off the stage, and I scan the crowd, looking for Luke.

Just like always, my breath catches when my eyes collide with his evergreen ones. And I find him exactly where I somehow knew they would be, directly under the enormous tree we picked, laughing at something someone said to him.

Luke grins at me, then winks before he leans down and kisses my mom on the cheek. He then does the same to his mother, whispering something to his dad before he backs away and disappears into the crowd.

Where the hell is he going?

I try to follow him, pushing up on my tiptoes, but there are way too many people—five times the normal crowd we get on Christmas Eve.

Living, breathing proof that what I've been doing over the last year in Mistletoe is working, and hopefully, it will only continue to increase as more tourists are drawn to our cozy, Christmas-obsessed small town.

That will become a year-round destination—if I do my job right.

But tonight, as soon as the crowd disperses, I am officially "off duty" for the next week.

A very, very, very needed break after the rush of the last two months.

And I only want to spend my vacation one way...

Wrapped up in Luke.

If I can find him.

I make my way down the spot near the tree where I last spotted them and find Mom still chatting with the Crisps, each holding a steaming bright-red cup of hot cocoa.

Mom opens her arms as she sees me coming. "Hello, dear, everything looks perfect." She embraces me, careful to keep her hot drink held out. "Dad would be so proud of you. I sure am."

Unlike last year, when standing here brought so much pain and longing with joy, now, my tears are only happy ones.

I know Dad helped me so much.

I felt his presence in every decision I made, drawing me in the right direction.

Like I'm confident he played a role in bringing me back to Mistletoe and Luke—permanently.

"Where's Luke?" I check over their shoulders, looking each way. "I saw him earlier, but…"

His mom and dad exchange a look.

Mrs. Crisp pats me on the shoulder. "He had to go back to the cabin to take care of something."

"Oh." Unease crawls across my skin. "Is he all right?"

She leans in and kisses my cheek. "He's fine, sweetheart. He just said he'll meet you back up there whenever you're done."

"Oh, okay…"

We took separate cars, since I had to be here all day and he had things to do back home. I guess it makes sense if he had something else to finish up.

But still, something niggles at the back of my mind, a feeling I can't shake.

It follows me the rest of the evening as I bustle around, ensuring everyone is where they're supposed to be, things like maps stay stocked, and our first real major event since I took over goes off without a hitch.

A permanent smile curls my lips until the final person wanders away from the town square, but by the time I finally pull into the Crisp farm, it's been replaced by a grimace of pain and exhaustion.

I release a groan as I stare at the now-paved, narrow path that will take me up to the cabin. It's far better than what used to be here, just earth and snow packed down by Luke's heavy footsteps and constant use, but if we're going to live here permanently, I really need to talk him into an escalator or something.

They can do those outdoors, right?

Wracking my brain, trying to remember if I've ever seen one outside a mall or the airport, I sigh and start to make my way up slowly.

At least Luke has plowed and salted it, ensuring I won't slip off into a tree well when he isn't right by my side to rescue me—or laugh at me and *then* rescue me.

By the time I reach the top, I'm ready for nothing more than to collapse into bed with the man who has given me everything I've ever wanted.

Except an easy way to get to the cabin.

Light starts to filter through the trees, only it looks slightly different.

What the hell is going on?

I reach the edge of the small clearing and find path lights sticking out of the snow, leading around the side of the cabin along the narrow path to our little rear deck.

Convenient in the summer, when we sit out almost every night and enjoy the mountain and how it comes alive once the sun goes down, we haven't been back there in months.

But it's cleared of the snow that fell yesterday, and the lights definitely weren't there when I left.

Nor were the rose petals scattered across the path.

My mouth goes dry as I take my first step onto the red, my legs trembling in anticipation. "Luke?"

He doesn't respond, but another noise hits my ears—bubbling water.

No!

He didn't!

I race around the corner, and my breath catches when I find Luke sitting in the hot tub that has *never* worked since we put it in several months ago due to some electrical issue.

He leans back in one of the corners, watching. A grin spreads across his lips, and he holds up the bottle of champagne. "I've been waiting for you."

And now I understand why he left early.

It's Christmas Eve, and he couldn't have done this alone.

"Apparently, you have…and I see you got the hot tub working."

He smirks. "I had Barry come up and connect the hard line to the solar panels earlier today. While you were gone, I came back from the ceremony early to make sure everything was working properly."

I approach him and stare down at the water. The bright-blue lights inside make it sparkle as much as Luke's smile does.

A dark brown rises slowly. "Are you going to join me, Snowflake, or just stand there and ogle me? Since you know I'm naked…"

Tossing a smirk his way, I adjust my focus in the water, right at his crotch—that is definitely not concealing every-thing waiting for me. My body heats, my pussy clenching as I pull my lip between my teeth. "So…we're doing this naked, then?"

He pops the top off the champagne, the sound making me jump. "We sure are. Toss your clothes onto the porch and get in here, Snowflake."

I practically giggle as I strip, not caring that another one of Mom's ugly sweaters is getting tossed onto the snow-covered porch with the rest of my clothes. "Naked hot tubbing on Christmas Eve…what would sweet, innocent baby Jesus think?"

Luke barks out a laugh that carries through the still night air, his laser-focused gaze on my every move as I climb up and sink down into the hot, bubbling water.

"Oh, God, this feels good."

Better than good.

Fucking incredible.

Especially against the sharp bite of the cold air this

Christmas Eve.

It's exactly what I needed.

Luke watches me move toward him. "I figured you were going to be sore. You spent the last two months going non-stop and were on your feet all day today."

I float over to him and wrap my legs around his waist, looping my arms around his neck and running my hands through his wet hair that's already starting to freeze slightly. "You'd be right. My back is killing me."

His hands slide down to that area, and he starts rubbing it in long, hard strokes that make my pussy throb. I release a groan, my eyes closing as I drop my head against his neck. "God, that feels good."

His hard cock presses up against the apex of my thighs. "I can do something else that will make you feel even better."

I twitch in his lap, and he chuckles, nipping at my ear.

"Do you like the sound of that, Snowflake?"

This man does not *need to ask that.*

"You know I do."

He keeps rubbing my back, and I shift in his lap, gliding my pussy along his length slowly, well aware of what it does to him when he feels how slick I am before he takes me.

By the time I lift my head again, his eyes have gone almost black save for the fiery heat of lust burning across the surface. He captures my mouth before I can say another word, delving his tongue inside, tasting, exploring, and seeking as if he doesn't have all of it memorized already so completely. As if he doesn't *own* me in *every* way.

Fuck...

I moan and tighten my grip on his neck, shifting my hips to allow the head of his cock to slip inside me.

His chest rumbles against mine, and his hands slide from my lower back to my hips, pushing me down and fully impaling me on him.

"Fucking hell, Snowflake." He wraps one hand around my wet hair and tugs my head back slightly. "This water is 103 degrees, but your cunt is still the hottest thing here."

I squeeze around him just to watch that muscle in his jaw tic, just to see his control weaken that slightest bit.

The only thing hotter than seeing Luke Crisp lose his tightly held control is watching him decimate a tree and bring it to the ground.

Every swing of his axe might as well be his thick cock driving into me.

Lumberjack porn fantasies in the flesh.

He releases his grip on my hip and grabs the bottles of champagne, bringing it to his lips to take a long swig. But he doesn't swallow it, just leans forward and kisses me, opening his mouth and letting the cool, bubbly, sweet liquid glide across our tongues.

I moan, shifting in his lap, taking him that half inch deeper until my clit rubs against his pelvis in the most delicious way.

Luke moans, and I swallow the champagne greedily and pull my head back.

A gasp tumbles from my lips as he returns his hands to my hips and helps lift me, only for me to slam down on him again. "Is this what we're going to do every night?"

That grin that utterly destroys my ability to speak makes an appearance, along with his dimple. "If you want, but I'm kind of partial to the bearskin rug."

He thrusts up into me again, stealing my breath.

"Fuck…me-me, too."

I lean back and glance up at the stars above us, partially hidden by the wispy clouds that also try to conceal the moon and offer the flurries floating through the air.

Each one that hits my skin melts instantly.

A minuscule bite of icy coolness as a fire rages through me.

Luke lifts my hips, making my whole body shudder before he drives up into me again, pushing me down at the same time to fully impale himself. I gasp, my eyes rolling up and my vision short-circuiting to a blinding white.

His lips find my collarbone and then my neck, and he kisses and licks and sucks his way up that spot behind my ear. I tip my head to the side, giving him better access. He rumbles his approval, pulsing his hips up as I roll down, and we find a languid rhythm.

Our bodies move as fluidly as the water around us.

My back arches, hips thrust and grind, nails score down his neck.

And he's right.

The bubbles around us might be hot, but it's nothing compared to the scald of his calloused hands against my skin or his hot breath against all the parts of me above the water, or the way his cock filling me ignites a fire deep in my soul.

"I have another surprise for you, Snowflake."

I groan at his low, gravelly tone, trying to concentrate on his words around the spinning in my head and the pulsing between my legs. "What's that?"

He nips at my ear, and I jerk upright, my eyes flying open as I continue to ride him, and he keeps pumping up into me.

"Not only can we do this every night if you want—or I can fuck you in front of the fire, or on the bed, or the kitchen counter, or in the shower, or against a tree in the woods, or out at the lake—"

I gasp as he rolls his hips, catching the head of his cock in exactly the right spot. "You don't have to tell me all the places you've fucked me, Luke. Believe me, I remember every single one of them."

He issues a low growl and tugs on my hair again. "You

have no idea how much I love that, Snowflake. Or you."

"Oh, I think I do."

And his cock throbs inside me, letting me know how much and close he is coming.

Just like I am.

"Well, not only can I fuck you in all those places, but I can also fuck you in the new addition."

I freeze, my rhythm faltering. "What?"

"I'm putting an addition on the cabin, Noel, and I already talked to my parents about putting a fully paved road up here so we can drive up instead of having to park at the barn and walk."

"You did?"

He nods, taking my lips again in a long, slow, sweet kiss. "I know this place is small, and especially in the winter, isn't exactly fun to try to get to, but this is our place, your place. I don't ever want to be anywhere else with you. So, we're going to make it our home however we can."

My heart stutters in my chest. "Fuck, Luke, that's romantic."

His brows wing up. "Are you saying I'm not normally romantic?"

I laugh and squeeze around his cock in a way that makes him grumble.

"You keep doing that and we're going to have to drain and clean this thing tomorrow…"

He has a point.

"What do you suggest, then?"

A devious grin spreads across his lips. "Oh, I have ideas, Snowflake."

"I bet you do…"

He lifts me from his cock so fast I barely know what's happening, then spins me around. "Grab the edge of the tub behind you."

I reach back and do it, my shoulders pressed against the ledge, arms spread out wide, and he lifts my hips above the waterline, tossing my thighs over his shoulders.

He buries his face between my legs as he slides his fingers where his cock just was and settles his mouth over my clit.

The flash of ecstasy that sears through me elicits a sharp, gasping cry.

Without even looking, he reaches out with his other hand and grabs the bottle of champagne, pouring it across my stomach. The already icy-cold liquid hits my cool skin, sharp enough to make me twitch in his hold, but then he licks it clean, tilting my hips so that it pours down my cunt and into his mouth.

Just like he did Christmas Eve with the bourbon, he laps up every drop.

A sensual assault designed to drive me mindless until I finally come hard against his mouth.

My legs tighten around his neck, body twisting and contorting at the pleasure drowning me before I gasp again and sag back.

His hand slides along my hips to hold me steady as he lowers me back into the water, then rises up out of it like Triton, his rock-hard abs directly in front of my face, his cock bobbing just above the waterline.

Oh, God, yes!

The icy air doesn't seem to bother him at all as I take his cock into my mouth all the way back.

I hum around him and swallow, and his hands move into my wet hair, tightening painfully in his attempt to control his own release longer.

I pull back until only the head is in my mouth, flicking my tongue across the most sensitive spot, then take him deep again.

Over and over.

Until his hips are moving.

Until he's fucking my mouth.

Cold air bites at my exposed skin, but all I can feel is his hot, hard body in front of mine. I slide my hand down under the water, fingering my throbbing clit, and when he comes, his roar envelops me completely, dragging me with him for another orgasm.

When his body stops twitching, he pulls his cock free and sags back into the water, tugging me up and into his lap again as we both drop our heads to the edge and turn them toward each other.

This grin is slow and lazy. The one he reserves for only these moments. "I hope this Christmas Eve is the best you've ever had, Snowflake."

I giggle. "I don't know, Luke. Last year was pretty damn good."

Something sparks in his eyes that always makes my heart skip a beat. "But this year, we know it's forever."

A single tear trickles out of my eye, and I nod. "Forever and always. All I want for Christmas is you."

I HOPE you enjoyed Luke and Noel's holiday romance story! If you love broody, grumpy lumberjacks, check out the Lumberjacks in Love Series, available now at all retailers, starting with *Billionaire Lumberjack*!

Billionaire Lumberjack: books2read.com/ BillionaireLumberjack

To stay up to date on news, releases, and sales from Gwyn, sign up for her newsletter here: www.gwynmcnamee. com/newsletter

ABOUT THE AUTHOR

Gwyn McNamee is an attorney, writer, wife, and mother (to one human baby and two fur babies). Originally from the Midwest, Gwyn relocated to her husband's home town of Las Vegas in 2015 and is enjoying her respite from the cold and snow. Gwyn has been writing down her crazy stories and ideas for years and finally decided to share them with the world. She loves to write stories with a bit of suspense and action mingled with romance and heat.

When she isn't either writing or voraciously devouring any books she can get her hands on, Gwyn is busy adding to her tattoo collection, golfing, and stirring up trouble with her perfect mix of sweetness and sarcasm (usually while wearing heels).

Gwyn loves to hear from her readers. Here is where you can find her:

FB Reader Group: https://www.facebook.com/groups/1667380963540655/

Facebook: https://www.facebook.com/AuthorGwynMcNamee/

Newsletter: www.gwynmcnamee.com/newsletter

Website: http://www.gwynmcnamee.com/Twitter: https://twitter.com/GwynMcNamee

Instagram: https://www.instagram.com/gwynmcnamee

Bookbub: https://www.bookbub.com/authors/gwynmcnamee

ACKNOWLEDGMENTS

Thank you to everyone who helped me create Mistletoe, Wisconsin and who loved Luke and Noel enough to want to see their story come to life.

OTHER WORKS BY GWYN MCNAMEE

If you loved Luke and Noel's story, meet Gwyn's other reclusive, damaged lumberjacks in the Lumberjacks in Love Series! Each book is a complete standalone!

LUMBERJACKS IN LOVE

Billionaire Lumberjack

Lost.

Alone.

Freezing on the side of a desolate mountain in a massive snowstorm.

Until a rugged man with an ax saves me.

AVAILABLE AT ALL RETAILERS:

Books2read.com/BillionaireLumberjack

Billionaire Lumberjack's Baby

A wounded billionaire in hiding.

A surprise baby.

One woman trapped on the mountain with them…

AVAILABLE AT ALL RETAILERS:

Books2read.com/BillionaireLumberjacksBaby

Billionaire Lumberjack's Bride

A reclusive billionaire who needs a wife.

A woman with no other options.

Two lost souls forced together on the mountain…

AVAILABLE AT ALL RETAILERS:

books2read.com/BillionaireLumberjacksBride

Billionaire Lumberjack's Beauty

A wounded billionaire known as The Beast.

A young woman forced onto the mountain with him…

AVAILABLE AT ALL RETAILERS:

books2read.com/BillionaireLumberjacksBeauty

Billionaire Lumberjack's Bargain

A widowed single mother lost and alone.

A young man intent on defending his family's legacy.

An attraction neither of them saw coming on the mountain…

AVAILABLE AT ALL RETAILERS:

Books2read.com/BillionaireLumberjacksBargain

You can find information on the rest of Gwyn's books on her website:

www.gwynmcnamee.com

www.ingramcontent.com/pod-product-compliance
Lightning Source LLC
Chambersburg PA
CBHW071535260626
47170CB00002B/638